MRS. MILLIONAIRE

Short Story Book Series
Volume 1
by
Marissa Marchan

MRS. MILLIONAIRE

Short Story Book Series Volume 1
Copyright © 2020 by Marissa Marchan

First Edition: Mrs. Millionaire Short Story Book Series Volume 1
ISBN-10: 1697400426
ISBN-13: 978-1697400427
Second Edition: Mrs. Millionaire Short Story Book Series Volume 1
ISBN-13: 978-1-953577-05-4 (eBook)
ISBN-13: 978-1-953577-10-8 (Print)
Third Edition: Mrs. Millionaire Short Story Book Series Volume 1
ISBN: 978-1-953577-16-0 (eBook)
ISBN: 978-1-953577-17-7 (Print)
Published by 3 Ways Publishing

https://marissamarchan.com[1]
https://3wayspublishing.wordpress.com[2]

---

1.   https://marissamarchan.com/

2.   https://3wayspublishing.wordpress.com/

Dear friends,

∞

A dream I had about my mother inspired Mrs. Millionaire. I wrote every detail as soon as I woke up. I developed my characters using the emotions I felt in the dream. It was amazing to see how the story came together. This is how Mrs. Millionaire series was born.

The story revolves around a wealthy young woman who, after experiencing a tragic event, undergoes remarkable personal growth. She recognizes that money, when used responsibly, spreads kindness and generosity. She believes that by giving a million dollars to someone who deserves it, she can make a significant impact on their lives. This book takes its readers on a journey that instills hope and encouragement. It highlights the concept that even when faced with adversity, there is always that one person who can bring about positive change in your life.

Tilly's character is based on my mom, Matilde. Using my father's real name, Vedasto, I modeled Dusty after him. I hope readers can learn valuable lessons from the story and find the courage to pursue their passions. I have enjoyed writing about Tilly's adventure, which has fostered a profound sense of connection with my parents, who have passed away.

∞

All the best,
Marissa

THANK YOU

For the love and support

Leo
Ray-Angelo
Haley-Alexis
Kayla Marie
Lesley-Anne and Hardy
Matt-Derek and Maria

INTRODUCTION

Many of us have encountered individuals who have made significant life changes and overcome adversity. However, only a small number have experienced such a remarkable transformation. In Mrs. Millionaire and the Homeless Woman, the first book in the Mrs. Millionaire series, a single act of kindness triggers a chain reaction that leads to many positive actions. The book encourages people to help others and embrace a purposeful life, changing many lives along the way.

Wild child. Reckless youth. Unruly. Obstinate.

Matilde Jane Parker, or Tilly to her friends and family, is best known for her rebellious personality and reputation as a party girl. An heiress and socialite from an upper-class family, she is the daughter of a wealthy industrialist. Tilly, despite being intelligent and headstrong, despises school and everything it represents, even though she excels effortlessly. She enjoys making mischief, and as she grows, her out-of-control behavior worsens.

Tilly meets Dusty, the man of her dreams. She learns for the first time when to give in and walk away from a relationship. This experience has made her appreciate her parents more than ever before. Tilly recognizes the value of having a loving family and considers herself fortunate. She is determined to make the most of every moment with them, live each day to the fullest, and prioritize the people she loves.

Sadly, it was too late. It turned Tilly's entire world upside down in the blink of an eye. An automobile accident claimed her parents' lives. It left her feeling helpless and isolated. Thanks to Dusty, she found solace in his unwavering support and unconditional love. He helped her heal and regain self-confidence.

Another traumatic event altered Tilly's self-perception. Someone attacked her in her building's underground parking lot. Tilly changed her outlook on life after being saved by a homeless woman and given a second chance at life. Rather than living as a victim, Tilly uses her wealth and power to help those who cannot defend themselves. She finds herself in various situations and sometimes works as an amateur detective, helping people in need solve their problems.

This story is about Tilly's transformation from a troubled adolescent to a philanthropist. She is an example of hope and resilience. Tilly reminds us we can all make a difference, and one person's action can have a major impact on others, even in the darkest of times. There are no magical powers or amazing abilities in her, only an extraordinary heart and a determination to change people's lives one day at a time.

MRS. MILLIONAIRE AND THE HOMELESS WOMAN

CHAPTER ONE

"**D**ance, dance, dance... Keep on dancing."

The music blasts from the speakers. The lights were dim, and the disco ball above the dance floor spun. Sparkling lights filled the room like fireflies. Tilly and her best friend, Angie, danced happily, bumped into each other, and laughed. They had the time of their lives. As they swayed to the beat, they felt the crowd's energy.

Tilly and her college friends were in Cabo San Lucas, a well-known place for spring breakers and other travelers to party. Everyone enjoyed themselves and laughed a lot. Loud music and high energy filled the room. They let go of their worries and enjoyed the moment. It was a night of celebration and togetherness.

Tilly needed some fresh air, so she wiggled her way through the crowded bar with her friends and headed to the pool, where Latin music wafted. There was a sense of infectious music that everyone got into, regardless of their dancing ability. Tilly and her friends joined the party, and soon everyone was doing their versions of salsa, bachata, and merengue. Tilly felt free and alive, and the music spoke to her soul. It was as if she was a part of the rhythm, and the song beat was her heart.

Tilly ordered vodka on the rocks for the guys and tequila shots for the girls as the group returned to the bar. One shot led to another. Alcohol flowed freely, and everyone had a blast. As the night wore on, the group got louder and more rambunctious. They were so drunk that the hotel staff had to help them back to their rooms. They collapsed on their beds and woke up nauseated the next morning. It was just another day in Tilly's life, who was just 21 years old.

Angie's boyfriend broke up with her via text message a few days later. She couldn't believe he had ended their relationship so coldly and impersonally. Although Angie did not genuinely care for him, she was upset, as she wanted to be the one to end the relationship first. She felt blindsided and disrespected.

Despite Tilly's efforts to talk to her friend, Angie felt overwhelmed by her emotions and declined to discuss the matter. Tilly was unaware of Angie's shame and confusion. It was embarrassing for Angie to be dumped by her boyfriend, and she didn't know how to talk about it. She didn't want to burden Tilly with her problems, so she handled it on her own.

Tilly thought Angie was hurting after the breakup. She felt helpless and frustrated, not knowing what to do to help her friend. The best thing she could do for Angie was to support her without making her feel uncomfortable.

Tilly realized Angie needed time away to heal. She planned a vacation for just the two of them. There were major Asian cities to visit, but she picked Monte Carlo in Europe this time. It was the perfect place for Angie to focus on herself, forget about her ex-boyfriend, and get some much-needed rest.

MONTE CARLO WAS THE ideal location for a quick getaway. Magnificent landscapes, breathtaking views, an enthralling culture, and the playground of choice for the rich and famous. When Tilly and Angie arrived, the heat surged. It irritated Tilly that their trip had begun so disastrously. She had to replace her wardrobe with shorts and shirts as the temperature reached triple digits. Tilly despised it, but Angie did not. Angie traveled to Monte Carlo to escape everyday life. The thought of spending a few days at a luxurious destination sounded like the perfect solution. She was ready to embrace this adventure and take the first step towards healing her broken heart. Angie was there to have fun, and that's what she planned to do. Meeting someone would be a blessing, but if that was not possible, that was fine, too. Angie wanted her trip to run smoothly. She adored touring the town, and getting lost was her favorite part. Tilly trailed behind her. Even though she hated the long walk, she promised her friend she would support her.

They shopped at the Grimaldi Forum and Metropole. Their journey even included a detour to Saint Paul's Anglican Church, which featured incredible interior and exterior drawings. The picturesque landscape, trees and bushes, ponds full of koi carp, a waterfall, a teahouse, lanterns, and bridges in the Japanese Garden impressed them.

Following a two-hour street shopping spree, Tilly was exhausted. She claimed her legs were stiff from all the walking they had done. A nearby outdoor dining cafe provided them with a relaxing environment where Tilly ordered a seafood platter and a bottle of Merlot for lunch. Angie remained cheerful despite being tired, too. A smile spread across her face as she walked to the restroom to refresh herself. Tilly frowned. She couldn't help but wonder if her friend was okay or just pretending.

The server poured Tilly's glass for tasting when the wine arrived. Tilly took a small sip and expressed her satisfaction, prompting the server to refill her glass.

"Bring another bottle of this with our meal," she instructed the server, who bowed before leaving.

It soon filled the cafe with street sounds. Tilly looked around, trying to see where it came from. A street performer who sang and played accordion was on the scene. His voice and music captivated Tilly. It reminded her of a trip she took with her parents five years ago to celebrate the Rio de Janeiro Carnival. She was only sixteen then, but she remembered the celebration's vibrant energy, colorful costumes, and infectious music. Tilly felt the same joy and connection she had experienced back then. She closed her eyes and smiled as she remembered that magical time.

Tilly saw Angie approaching a few moments later but frowned when she saw her arm in arm with a handsome Italian guy. Tilly noticed her friend's smile, suggesting she was in delight. Angie and the man clicked instantly. They both laughed and chatted as they walked to her table. It appeared Angie had moved on from her heartbreak so quickly.

Angie sat the man down after a quick introduction. Tilly watched them chat. The two appeared to enjoy themselves. It pleased Tilly to see her friend's smile return. She invited them to share a glass of wine with her.

"Don't mind if I do," the young man, who introduced himself as Luke, said.

Tilly glanced at him. She couldn't help but notice Luke's gorgeous looks. He had dark hair and dark eyes that glistened. He was tall and slim, with a muscular build. His skin was fair, and he had a charming smile.

Angie pushed her chair closer to Luke.

"Luke has invited us to spend the weekend at their villa in Tuscany for a wine tasting tomorrow. Are you up for it, Tilly?" With a cute pout, Angie pleaded, "Say yes, please say yes."

"Angie, you just met him." Tilly murmured, "We know nothing about him."

Luke heard their conversation.

"Please come to my villa. I promise you'll have the best shrimp linguine in town, in Scout's honor," he said. He spoke fluent English with a lovely Italian accent while holding up the scout's gesture with his right hand. Luke appeared to have spent some time in America.

"Tilly, you always tell me to enjoy myself and not take life too seriously, so now is the time. May we go?" Angie asked, her voice pleading. Her face shined with excitement.

Tilly, however, shook her head. "I don't know," she said.

Angie's face fell. Her shoulders slumped in disappointment. Tilly felt terrible, but they needed to protect themselves. They couldn't be too trusting.

"Why not?" Angie asked.

Tilly shook her head again. "We don't know him."

"But he might be interesting," Angie argued. "We might pass up on an opportunity."

Tilly sighed. "I'll say it again. We know nothing about him."

"Tilly, we are here for an adventure, and this is it," Angie said. "Please, can we come?"

Tilly hesitated for a moment before nodding. "All right, we'll go, but only because I want to end your begging. But we have to be careful."

Angie smiled. "Thank you, Tilly."

"I guarantee you'll have fun. You are staying for the weekend, right?" Luke asked. "I'm leaving for Tuscany tonight, but I'll arrange for a car to pick you up at your hotel in the morning. Is seven all right?"

"Seven is perfect. Thank you, Luke," Angie said, settling in a bit. "How will we recognize your car?"

"The driver will know. Don't worry," he assured her.

TILLY AND ANGIE WERE standing in front of the hotel early in the morning when a black Mercedes-Benz EQE SUV pulled up. A driver got out and opened the door for them.

"Are you here for us?" Angie asked.

"Yes, ma'am," he replied, taking both their bags and placing them in the trunk. "Luke sent me a picture of you and asked me to pick you up."

The girls grinned.

"Impressive," Tilly said.

"Isn't it?" Angie laughed.

They sat down and enjoyed the ride. The wild and romantic view through which they passed enchanted Tilly and Angie. Italy's dramatic landscape includes mountains, rolling hills, vineyards, and sea views. They couldn't believe they hadn't appreciated it before. The scenery was breathtaking, with views from every hilltop. It was an enjoyable drive through some of Italy's most picturesque areas. The girls were in awe of the country's beauty and grateful for the unique opportunity to explore it. The driver drove through town before arriving at the winery.

It was after two o'clock when they entered a private driveway, where an iron gate opened. The villa was built on a hilltop surrounded by natural vegetation, such as vineyards, olive groves, and meadows. There was a stunning view of the valley that stretched for miles. A fountain sat in the middle of a large garden. There were two pools, a tennis court, and flowers hanging from a pergola around the house. Angie and Tilly knew Luke was wealthy, but they didn't know he lived lavishly.

"What did I tell you?" Angie asked with a smile.

Tilly sighed. "Just calm down, okay?"

"You said I should trust my instincts," Angie said.

Tilly nodded. "As much as I hate to admit it, you were right."

The friends laughed.

Luke stood outside the house when the car stopped in front of it. He opened the car door and held Angie's hand as she stepped out. She smiled and kissed Luke on the cheek. The driver helped Tilly get out of the car. Angie and Luke walked hand in hand up the steps to the front door. Tilly followed them. Luke opened the door, and they stepped inside. The servants carried their belongings to their respective rooms.

"Welcome," Luke said, smiling.

He led them inside the villa and into the living room. Angie's jaw dropped open in disbelief. Artwork adorned the house interior, furnished with antique furniture. The villa was an architectural masterpiece, with marble floors and large windows offering stunning views of the surrounding countryside.

"Luke told me his cousin was much better looking than he is," Angie teased, nudging Tilly's arm.

Tilly rolled her eyes at the prospect of Angie matchmaking again. She tried it once before, but the man was married. During a conversation, he brought up his wife, Gretchen, and their two children. He realized his mistake and looked away, embarrassed, and changed the subject. Tilly hit him with her purse and poured water on him. She was furious, and she stormed out of the restaurant.

"Angie, you know I don't like you setting me up again. We've discussed this before. I'm not ready to start a relationship."

"I'm just saying," Angie laughed. "Luke thinks his cousin is attractive. It won't hurt to check him out."

Tilly laughed and said, "Luke's cousin? I don't think so. For all we know, he is fat and bald." She smirked and laughed, implying she didn't believe Luke's cousin was as attractive as Luke.

Angie rolled her eyes and said, "I'm just saying it's worth a look."

Tilly shook her head and said, "No, thanks. I'm not interested."

Angie smiled and said, "We shall see."

"You must be Angie. Luke keeps talking about you."

Tilly and Angie turned their heads when a voice interrupted their conversation. The sight of the handsome man behind them choked them. Tilly thought he was the most beautiful creature she had ever seen. He stood six feet tall, with sensual lips, thick brown hair, and brown eyes. Luke introduced the man as Vedasto, his cousin, best friend, and the vineyard's owner.

"Nice to meet you, Vedasto," Tilly stammered as she extended her hand to him.

Vedasto held Tilly's hand, getting closer. "Call me Dusty." He never looked away from her. "Luke is correct. You're stunning."

Tilly blushed with embarrassment. She glanced at Luke. "I'm afraid to hear what else he says about me."

"Don't worry, it's all good," Dusty said, smiling. "I'm sure you'll enjoy your stay here. I'll show you around the villa myself. Wait until you taste our wine. We only use the finest grapes when making Bonaventura wines."

"That's helpful to know," Tilly said, smiling at him.

Dusty returned her smile. His grin was genuine. Tilly's heart raced, and she became agitated.

Angie sensed a connection between her friend and Dusty. She nudged Tilly and whispered in her ear, "Are you sure you are not interested?"

"Shh," Tilly responded. "He might hear you."

Angie gave Tilly a serious look and said, "Well, you better get ready soon!"

Dusty and Tilly stood silently, gazing at each other. Dusty smiled, and Tilly looked away, blushing. Angie didn't want to ruin their awkward but magical moment, but she couldn't wait to explore the vineyard and taste the wine. She cleared her throat.

"By the way, my name is Angie. Nice to meet you, Dusty," she said.

The young man turned to look at Angie. He still had Tilly's hand in his, but in a flash of nervousness, Tilly took it away.

Dusty responded, "Hello, Angie. Luke can't stop talking about you."

"Yes, I know. You already said that," Angie responded with a chuckle. "Are we about to explore the vineyard now?"

Dusty looked at his watch. It was four in the afternoon. "It's late, Angie. I presume that both you and Tilly must be weary after the trip. We'll get an early start tomorrow morning."

A young man dressed as a servant entered the room and poured wine glasses for everyone.

Luke raised his glass to toast. "To new friends," he said.

Everyone raised their glasses and said, "To new friends!"

A young girl approached and said something in Italian a few moments later.

"It appears our dinner is ready," Luke said as he took Angie's elbow and led her to the dining room.

He pulled out her chair and helped her sit down. His charming manners endeared him to Angie. In every way, he was a true gentleman. He was nothing like her ex-boyfriend. What was his name?

After accepting Dusty's hand, Tilly felt his warmth. Their eyes met. A giddy smile spread across her face. Tilly could feel her heart flutter as they walked into the room. Just like Luke, Dusty was a true gentleman, pulling out her chair and helping her into her seat. He sat down next to her and smiled, and Tilly knew this was going to be a good night. She felt like she knew him forever.

The food was delicious—a mixed chef's salad topped with crabmeat, followed by shrimp linguine with white wine. The chef also served hot Italian bread and the finest wine from the Bonaventura collection, followed by gelato and tiramisu for dessert.

After dinner, they spent hours laughing, talking, playing cards, and sharing their hopes and dreams. Angie spoke about her struggle with her ex-boyfriend and the relief she felt when they parted ways, which surprised Tilly. Her friend's words made Tilly frown. Angie wasn't heartbroken at all. Luke complained about his bad luck in love, while Dusty said he had no time for love. Tilly refused to talk about her experiences, fearing Dusty would lose interest in her wild ways. Still, Dusty encouraged her to be open about her feelings, and Tilly soon poured out her heart. She appreciated Dusty's support and his non-judgmental nature. They shared stories about their successes and failures in love, and Tilly soon realized that Dusty accepted her for who she was. They spent the night laughing and talking until the sun rose.

CHAPTER TWO

The next day, Luke and Dusty hosted a private wine tasting for Tilly and Angie. They poured themselves glasses of a rich red Cabernet, the finest vintage from the Bonaventura wine collection. Dusty explained that winemaking decantation improved flavor. Tilly inhaled the wine's aroma. She swirled it, observing its color and clinging to the glass. Tilly savored a sip of the wine, allowing it to coat her mouth and throat, and found its exceptional quality to be impressive. It surprised her at how smooth and full the flavor was.

Tilly's father taught her to appreciate fine wines, and she developed a taste for them at a young age. After turning 21, she celebrated with friends at a local bar. While she enjoyed a few drinks, wine was her favorite. It became her passion, and she appreciated the subtle nuances of different wines.

Tilly took another sip, relishing the flavor, then finished her glass and proclaimed it the most exquisite wine she had ever tasted. Angie, too, enjoyed the wine. Luke and Dusty were relieved that their wine impressed their guests. The group then drank Chardonnay and Merlot, closing their eyes in pleasure. Dusty was an excellent host, and he seemed thrilled that Tilly shared that moment with him. He and

Luke toasted Tilly and Angie, and everyone enjoyed the moment.

Dusty wanted some time alone with Tilly after the tasting, while Luke and Angie went for a swim.

"Would you like to join me for a walk?" he asked.

Tilly nodded with a tense expression on her face. "Sure," she said.

She took a deep breath and followed him out the door. Dusty took her hand and led her outside to another breathtaking vineyard view. They enjoyed gazing out at the mountains in the distance and smelling the fresh air. The vineyards stretched as far as the eye could see. Dusty plucked fresh grapes from the vine and handed them to Tilly.

"Isn't it beautiful here?" he asked.

"Yes, it is. If I lived here, I would never leave," Tilly stated. Dusty stared at her. She questioned him with a raised brow.

"What?" she asked. "Is there something on my face?"

"You are so beautiful, Tilly," he exclaimed.

There was an undeniable chemistry between Dusty and Tilly. It was like a bond between two people that transcended time and space.

Tilly's face flushed as she sensed warmth emanating from all directions. Dusty found himself drawn to her that he couldn't explain. He wanted to be around her, no matter the circumstances. Dusty reached down, wrapped his arms around her waist, and kissed her. Tilly kissed him back without hesitation, caressing his face with her fingers as if memorizing it. Dusty pulled away, and their eyes met. He brushed her hair away from her face and looked into her eyes. Tilly felt her heart swell with emotion and joy. Their connection was like nothing she had experienced before. They knew it was love at first sight.

Dusty dated many girls over the years but had never experienced such an attraction before. When he thought about Tilly, he felt every symptom of love and an overwhelming desire to be near her. Tilly felt it, too. Dusty was such a gentleman. His words and the way he said them drew her to him. The sweet Italian accent made her heart race. Tilly didn't know where things were heading, but one thing was certain—she had never been happier in her life. Tilly and Dusty sensed a strong connection, even though they had only met.

Someone disrupted their magical moment when they heard loud voices. Dusty and Tilly broke their passionate kiss, blushing.

"Oh, my gosh, get a room, guys," Luke and Angie exclaimed, laughing.

Angie couldn't stop laughing at Tilly as they walked back to the house, nudging each other by the elbow. Tilly remained silent and blushed as she became embarrassed. What was it about that kiss that had such an impact on her? It couldn't have happened, could it? Would it be possible for her to fall in love with someone she had just met?

Tilly learned a lot about Vedasto Bonaventura, the man who won her heart so quickly, as the day progressed. After lunch, they spent the rest of the day talking and strolling around the vineyard. Dusty, 23, had business interests in Asia, Europe, and the United States, besides owning the vineyard. He inherited it from his grandparents and made it flourish. Dusty worked hard to make it a success. He managed the vineyard with dedication and skill, nurturing the grapes to produce some of the finest wines in the region. The result was an incredibly successful winery.

The more Tilly listened to him, the stronger her attraction to Dusty grew. Tilly and Dusty became close enough that Tilly extended her vacation. They traveled everywhere together and talked about everything: their lives, their hopes, their dreams, and even marriage. The similarities they shared surprised them. The more time they spent together, the stronger their bond became.

Two weeks had passed. Dusty knew Tilly was leaving soon, and the thought shattered his heart to pieces. He couldn't lie anymore. Dusty was smitten with her. He planned a romantic evening with candles and flowers tomorrow night. Dusty would ask her to be his girlfriend. He had already chosen the restaurant and the menu. Dusty was nervous and excited at the same time. He wanted to make sure this was a night Tilly would remember forever.

Meanwhile, Tilly knew she had fallen in love with Dusty, but there was one problem: his family. Dusty grew up Catholic. His parents traveled extensively to aid people in underdeveloped parts of the world. They gave millions of dollars to charities and participated in charity fundraising. Tilly can't remember caring about anything or anyone before. The last time a beggar asked her for money, she told him to get a job. What could she offer Dusty and her family when she couldn't even make her parents proud of her? The only thing she gave them was heartache. She admitted her actions were shameful. Tilly didn't want to embarrass Dusty in front of his family. There was no way she could do that to him.

Tilly realized she had to choose. Either she continued the relationship and accepted Dusty's family's lifestyle, or she ended it and walked away before making a fool of herself. Was she willing to change her wild ways for Dusty? She was used to her free-spirited lifestyle and could not give it up. It was up to her to decide which was more important to her. She needed time to think it over. The last thing she wanted to do was rush into things. Tilly admitted she cared about Dusty, but things moved quickly between them. She was at a loss for what to do, but after much thought, Tilly felt it was better to walk away. It was a tough decision, but she was adamant that it was the right one. It was better to end things now than to regret them later. Tilly felt she needed to work on herself and her parents' relationship before focusing on someone else.

Tilly made sure Dusty was on the field before leaving the villa, fearing she would collapse in front of him. She left a note in his room. Tilly hoped Dusty would understand her decision and forgive her. She made the toughest decision of her life and flew back to the United States. Dusty might be upset with her, but she knew it was better this way. Angie stayed behind to spend time with Luke. She admitted she liked him very much and hoped their relationship would blossom. Despite the risk, Angie took a chance. She was certain Luke shared her sentiments.

This time, the ride to the airport was different. Tilly knew she would miss Dusty and remembered all the memories they shared. She couldn't help but feel emotional.

Tilly closed her eyes and took a deep breath. Her time with Dusty was unforgettable. She hoped to find someone else who could make her as happy as he did.

Tilly returned home with a broken heart. One thing she learned from her failed romance was that it was now time to mature and take her responsibilities seriously. Tilly decided that the only way to find happiness was to focus on her studies. If another love came along, she would be ready to fight for it.

IT'S A BEAUTIFUL DAY in New York. Flowers and trees were in full bloom everywhere she looked. Having just returned from Italy, Tilly yearned for a compassionate listener. It saddened her to see that her parents had gone to the country club for a fundraising event. They invited Tilly to join them, but she did not want to attend. Her mother's voice sounded disappointed when she told her she was not up to it. Tilly felt guilty for not joining them. She knew they needed her support, but she needed time to adjust to being at home and processing her emotions. Tilly retired to her room to rest. She curled up in her bed and cried. Taking out her phone, she scrolled through the photos on her camera. Tilly found an old picture of her and her parents together. She felt at peace and knew everything would be alright.

Tilly awoke a few hours later to pouring rain. She heard footsteps outside her bedroom door and a light tap on the door a minute later. Tilly struggled to get out of bed. When she looked out the window, she saw raindrops illuminated by distant lightning, and she heard thunder a few seconds later.

Tilly realized it was late at night. She didn't know how long she slept.

"Just a minute, I'm coming," she yelled as she flung open the door. "Uncle Roger," she said, surprised. Roger was her father's older brother. She threw her arms around him in delight. "How are you?"

Roger gave her a look. "I'm sorry to wake you up, Tilly."

"Uncle Roger, what's with the long face? Is there a problem?"

"Tilly, I'm not sure how to tell you this. Your parents..."

"What about my parents?" Tilly asked. When he didn't respond, her heart rate increased. "Uncle Roger, please tell me. What's going on?"

Roger stood there, tears streaming down his cheeks.

"I'm sorry, Tilly. There was an accident, and..." He began but couldn't finish.

Her uncle didn't have to say anything else. Tilly understood what it meant.

"No!" she screamed. She fainted as the room spun.

A car accident killed Tilly's parents, leaving her with immense guilt. It was a single-car accident, and his father lost control of the vehicle due to slick road conditions. She blamed herself for the accident, thinking she should have been there to protect them. Tilly felt a deep sense of sorrow and confusion as she realized she had lost her parents forever.

Tilly looked around the house. It didn't feel like home anymore. She blamed herself for taking her parents for granted. If she had agreed to accompany them to the club when they asked, they might still be alive. A car accident wouldn't have happened to them. They would have stayed at the hotel after the event, as they do. Instead, they drove home so she wouldn't be alone. Tilly would have done things differently if she could travel back in time. She would have come home more frequently and spent more time with her mother and father. No matter how much Tilly cried or begged for their forgiveness, she could not tell them how much she loved them. They couldn't hear her anymore.

Tilly had to mature quickly following her parents' deaths. She met with lawyers, board members, accountants, human resources officers, and department heads to learn more about her parents' business and financial history. Her uncle Roger helped her until she graduated from college, but it was a significant change. There was so much to do and an empire to manage. Many people rely on her. Tilly wanted to cry, but no tears came out. She tried to scream but ran out of voices. There was no way out or anywhere else to escape, except she didn't expect Dusty to find her.

Tilly was in the living room, a picture of her parents covering her heart. She always blamed herself for their untimely deaths. Tilly partied with her friends when she should have been with them. She regretted all the moments and opportunities she wasted. It filled her with guilt and remorse. She felt guilty for not giving them the attention they deserved. Tilly missed them so much and wished they had witnessed her graduation. How she worked hard to finish school, the late nights studying, and the hours spent in the library. Her eyes welled up with tears, despite her efforts to hold them back. Tilly whispered a prayer, hoping her parents would look down on her with pride. Despite being alone, she felt their spiritual presence alongside her. Tilly wept. How many times did she wish she could turn back the clock to be with them?

The doorbell rang, startling Tilly. She opened the door, and there he was, standing in front of her in jeans and a denim shirt, so handsome. Her heart raced faster. She felt like she was dreaming.

"D-Dusty," she mumbled.

"I'm sorry about what happened to your parents," Dusty said.

He fixed his gaze on her. Tilly appeared pale and frail, but she was always beautiful—more beautiful than anything he had ever seen. He placed his hand on her cheek. Oh, how he missed her.

Tilly felt his warm touch. She couldn't stop the rush of feelings for him. Her eyes welled up with tears as if a wave of joy washed over her. Dusty was the rock she needed to lean on. She approached him and fell into his arms. She missed him. They kissed and hugged each other with passion and love. Tilly didn't care what happened tomorrow. She didn't care if Dusty's parents liked her or not. All she wanted was to be in the arms of this gorgeous man, her one true love.

"How did you find me?"

"When I heard about your parents' passing last year, I wanted to be there for you. However, I knew you needed to focus on your studies. You didn't need a distraction. I didn't want to add pressure or stress to your already difficult situation. That's why I waited until the moment was right to see you. I wanted to make sure you knew I was here for you, no matter what."

"How did you know?"

"Angie told me."

"How is she?"

"Luke proposed to her, and they're engaged. She will call you to give you all the details."

"I feel so fortunate to have you with me, Dusty. Thank you," Tilly said.

"I'm always here for you, sweetheart. You can always count on me."

They kissed for a long time, struggling to let go of each other. They pulled away and looked at each other, their eyes filled with emotion. Tilly gave him a gentle hug and whispered in his ear, "I love you." He returned the embrace and whispered back, "I love you too." There would be no more roadblocks. They both knew their love was strong, and they were in it for the long haul. Today, they picked up where they left off.

TILLY AND DUSTY MARRIED a few months later. A 6,000-square-foot penthouse with six bedrooms, walk-in closets, six bathrooms, a large living/dining area, and an eat-in kitchen was Dusty's wedding gift to his wife. Located in Greenwich Village, New York, the apartment provided a splendid view of the city. The large windows allowed plenty of natural light to enter the room. The layout was spacious and airy, with an open kitchen and plenty of storage, and the bathroom was luxurious and comfortably sized. It was just the right place for the couple to start their life together. The sunset view each night was the icing on the cake.

Tilly got along fine with Dusty's parents, and she worried about nothing. She enjoyed spending time with them, and they treated her like their own daughter. Tilly felt comfortable and safe in their company, and she loved spending time with them.

Dusty kept his Italian citizenship but split his time between Italy and the United States. Tilly often traveled with him, and they visited different parts of the world together. They enjoyed exploring various cultures, experiencing unknown places, and meeting interesting people along the way. Dusty and Tilly also shared a passion for photography, often taking hundreds of pictures of their travels.

With Dusty's parents' encouragement, Tilly continued her mother's charitable work. Her involvement raised millions for orphanages and shelters. She even organized a Christmas event for the homeless. Tilly's work touched many lives and inspired others to follow. Her work helped create a more compassionate and accepting society. She exemplified genuine kindness and generosity. Dusty's parents were so proud of her, but despite all their efforts, Tilly never understood what giving meant. Her only motivation was to make her parents proud. She felt she owed them and wanted to repay them in this way.

CHAPTER THREE

The rain clouded the sky and distorted the view of the buildings on the other side of the road. Tilly watched lightning streaks as rain fell outside her window. She wore a depressed expression. Tears filled her eyes. Storms reminded her of her parents' tragic deaths. Her life felt lost, and she thought she could not move forward. Thanks to her uncle Roger, who helped run the family business, she gained respect in the business world at age 23. Roger remained the company's vice president, in charge of day-to-day operations, while she served as president.

Tilly carried on her mother's charitable work and donated millions of dollars to various charities and organizations bearing their names through her foundation. She also provided scholarships for students from low-income households and funding for various community initiatives.

Outside, lightning struck the sky repeatedly. Thunderclaps rang out, and rain poured down in torrents. Tilly stood in the lobby, hesitant to leave in the pouring rain. She should have left for home three hours ago, but her meeting took longer than expected. Tilly walked down the stairs to the ground-floor parking area, her heels echoing through the empty garage. She noticed a man in filthy clothes and an old, tattered coat behind her. Tilly's heart raced as she walked faster, determined to reach her car and get out as fast as she could. She heard the man's footsteps grow closer until she was sure he was following her.

Tilly became terrified. She looked around. There were several large utility vans in the designated building maintenance area, although no individuals were present. Tilly gathered herself and hurried, but she parked her car in a reserved area that seemed further away than when she arrived. She reached her car but couldn't get the key in because her hand trembled. As the man caught up to her, he grabbed her arm and pulled her away.

"Give me your money, and I will not hurt you," he shouted near her ear.

Tilly reached into her purse for her wallet. The man grabbed it from her grasp before she could open it. Tilly looked at him. Despite his grimy face and disheveled hair, the man did not seem homeless. He appeared to be accustomed to society. The man knew the garage structure, where the three surveillance cameras were located, and when to duck out of sight. The man planned it. She was the intended victim all along. Tilly was sure of it.

"Take them all. Just don't hurt me," Tilly pleaded.

The man examined her face as he stared at her. He smirked and grabbed Tilly's arm. He pulled her closer, and Tilly felt her heart race as he spoke. The man seemed familiar to her as if she had seen him before.

"It is my pleasure to make you happy, lady, since you say so. Get in your car and take me to your house. It's raining outside, and I need a warm place to stay," the man said.

This scared Tilly to death. She knew he would kill her if she got into the car with him. And how about her husband? She would risk his life, too. Tilly would fight the man if she had to. She would not let him take her. Tilly clutched her purse. It wasn't a weapon, but she thought she could use it as a getaway device. Her arm shot wildly in desperation, but she missed. The man pushed her down, knocking her to the floor. Tilly was helpless as the man advanced toward her. He raised his fist, and Tilly closed her eyes, bracing herself for his punch.

Startled by the sound of an eerie whistle, followed by a loud hiss and approaching footsteps, the man fled. As he ran away, he dropped Tilly's wallet. A homeless woman appeared, pushing a squeaking cart with all her worldly possessions. The woman helped Tilly stand up. She picked up the wallet and handed it to her. Tilly thanked the woman for her timely intervention, expressed gratitude for the woman's act of kindness, and hugged her.

"Are you okay?" the woman asked.

Tilly wrapped her in a tight hug again. "Thank you for saving me," she mumbled.

"I ran to the garage for shelter as the rain poured down. When I saw that man watching you, I knew he was up to no good. I'm glad I stuck around and scared him off. You would have encountered trouble if I had not stepped in. I'm glad you're safe now. Let's just hope he doesn't return."

This scared Tilly. She interrupted the woman mid-sentence and told her to wait a minute. Tilly pulled her phone from her bag, dialed 9-1-1, and reported the incident. She hung up the phone and took money from her wallet. When she turned around, the woman disappeared. Her call to the police must have scared her.

Fearing the man would return, Tilly jumped into her car, slammed the door, and locked it. Soon after, a security patrol car pulled up beside her. A report of an incident in the parking lot prompted him to investigate. He stepped out of his vehicle and tapped on her car window. Tilly rolled down the window, and the security guard recognized her. He asked if she was okay. Tilly said she was fine.

"What happened?" the guard asked.

She told him someone had mugged her. Tilly asked the guard to look for the woman who had saved her.

"Was she pushing a cart?" he asked.

"Yes, how did you know?"

"We saw a homeless woman pushing a cart and waving a note in front of the lobby entrance. She left it on the sidewalk. The message intrigued us, so we read it. The note was about a mugging in the parking area. I'm here for that reason. I'm investigating it. It's unfortunate, Mrs. Bonaventura, that you were the victim."

Tilly's recount of the events shocked the guard. He reported the incident and called for help on his walkie-talkie. The other members of the team responded and arrived on the scene. They checked the area but found no one. A few moments later, several police cars surrounded the building. Tilly spoke to the detective when he arrived.

"I'm guessing this wasn't a mugging. I was a target," Tilly said. "The man knew that the hidden cameras were in the parking lot, and he couldn't see them unless he knew where they were."

Detective Spencer, who led the investigation, dismissed Tilly's claims. His return was unlikely, he said. The detective's arrogance irritated Tilly. She felt he was not taking her voice seriously or giving it enough importance. How he spoke to her was offensive and insulting.

The police chief was on his way home. As he drove up the road and saw the blue flashing lights ahead, he pulled over and got out. It surprised him to learn that Tilly was the victim. Their friendship dates back to high school. She told him all the things she had told Detective Spencer, including the woman who saved her life. The story touched the police chief and led to a thorough investigation into the case. He promised to find the woman who saved Tilly and investigate further. Detective Spencer listened, without protest. It was a complete shock to him to learn Tilly was friends with the police chief.

"Don't worry, Tilly. I'll take care of it," the chief said. He had a hunch that the woman and the suspect may have fled into hiding. The chief issued an order to the officers to conduct searches in alleys, streets, local businesses, apartments, and other nearby locations. The search turned up nothing. He instructed the police officers to keep looking and check any CCTV footage in the area. The chief vowed to take every measure necessary to bring the culprit to justice. He was determined to find the woman and ensure she was safe.

The chief's instincts were correct. The police discovered a man hiding in a dumpster who matched Tilly's description. They took him into custody and questioned him. The team also apprehended another accomplice sitting in a van a block away. As soon as they confronted him with the crime, he confessed to its commission without hesitation. He was remorseful and expressed sincere regret. The man agreed to cooperate with the authorities.

The culprit turned out to be the building's newly hired security guard. Knowing Tilly was wealthy and owned the property, he stalked her. The plan had been in the works for months. The man even worked as a security guard in the building to understand their security system. There was much more to the crime than just a robbery. They planned to kidnap Tilly and demand a huge ransom for her release. The officer handcuffed the man and took him into custody. The investigation continued to uncover more details about their plan.

Dusty rushed to the police station after learning what had happened to his wife. He was relieved to find her safe and unharmed, but furious at the men who tried to take her.

"Are you alright? Did they hurt you?" Dusty asked, concerned.

"Don't worry, sweetheart. I'm fine. I'm just a bit rattled."

Dusty thanked the officers before taking his wife home. He kissed and hugged Tilly, keeping her safe. This event caused Dusty anxiety. He told his wife he would feel at ease if he was sure Tilly could protect herself. Dusty wanted her to feel safe and secure, so he taught her self-defense moves.

He also showed her how to use pepper spray and to trust her instincts.

His wife's safety was still a concern for Dusty, so he insisted Tilly take a self-defense class to address his concerns. Tilly refused, but Dusty would not budge, regardless of how hard she tried. Tilly gave in and started self-defense, martial arts, and aerobics. It ended up being a lot of fun for her, and she even earned a few belts. Dusty was proud of her accomplishments and encouraged her to continue training. Tilly felt better about herself and developed a sense of pride and empowerment. She was now more skilled at handling difficult situations, and Dusty couldn't be happier.

IT WAS A PLEASANT, sunny day in September. Tilly found a spot to enjoy her lunch—an outdoor patio shaded by large red umbrellas. She watched the kids play while sipping iced tea. She felt a tug at her heartstrings, remembering her carefree childhood.

A homeless woman with a shopping cart approached restaurant patrons, asking for spare change. Everyone turned away. Tilly felt a twinge of guilt as she watched the woman walk away empty-handed. She left after being pushed out by the server. Tilly stared at the woman. She recognized her. Tilly had been searching for her for a long time. Her gaze followed her. She took her wallet, pulled out a few dollars, placed them under the plate, and left. Tilly saw the woman turn the corner, and she ran as fast as she could to catch up with her. By the time she arrived, the woman had vanished into the alley. Tilly realized she had lost her chance to find the woman. She strolled back to the cafe, her heart heavy with disappointment. Tilly realized she had missed her chance to find her, and now all hope was lost.

It rained just as Tilly left the cafe's parking lot. Her eyes widened when she saw the same woman pushing her cart on Lincoln Street. She followed her, careful not to scare her. The few drops multiplied into torrential rain, and the wind blew hard.

The woman struggled to push her cart while shielding her face from the pouring rain. She spotted a large tree and took refuge in its branches. The woman sat there, huddled against the tree, her clothes soaked and her face dripping with rain. She pulled the hood of her jacket over her head and closed her eyes, trying to forget about the rain. Suddenly, something fell and hit her in the head, causing her to pass out. Tilly witnessed everything. She jumped out of the car and dialed 9-1-1 in panic.

The woman awoke in a hospital bed. She opened her eyes and noticed the air was cold. She could smell the antiseptics but did not know where she was. The woman tried to get out of bed, but her head hurt. She looked around and saw bouquets of colorful and beautiful flowers filling the room.

The woman blinks, perplexed. "Where am I?" she asked, groggy, as if she'd been sleeping for a week.

"You are still not well enough," an unknown voice reassured her.

After her eyes adjusted to the glare, the woman noticed Tilly but did not recognize her.

"Where am I? What happened? How did I get here?" she asked.

Before Tilly could respond, a nurse entered the room to check the woman's vital signs.

"Oh, I see you're awake. How do you feel?" she asked.

"My head hurts. Could you please let me know where I am?"

"You are in the hospital," the nurse responded while checking her pulse, temperature, and blood pressure. "You were in an unfortunate accident. Can you remember what happened to you?"

After a moment of confusion, the woman looked back at the nurse, trying to remember what had happened.

"Everything is blurry," she replied.

"You should thank Mrs. Bonaventura. She called 9-1-1, and the ambulance brought you in. You have a nasty cut on your head from a falling tree branch."

"Cut? What kind of cut?" The woman attempted to stand, but dizziness overcame her. "Ouch!" she exclaimed, feeling a large bandage wrapped around her head.

"Take it easy. You lost a lot of blood, but don't worry. We're working on it. The good news is that there is no sign of internal bleeding." The nurse said this as she fixed her pillow before leaving the room to call the doctor.

A brief pause followed before the woman spoke to Tilly.

"Thank you for saving my life."

Tilly smiled. "It's a good thing I was there."

"I owe you for saving me, even though I feel it would have been better if you had left me. I don't deserve to live."

"What are you talking about? You have your entire life ahead of you. There is still a chance to start over."

"I know who you are. I saw your picture in the newspaper. You look the same, only older," she added.

"You know me?" Tilly asked.

"I was at the ribbon-cutting ceremony when your mother opened the Brooklyn shelter. The grocery store where I worked was next door. I am sorry to hear of her passing. She was a very kind lady."

"That was a long time ago. I can't believe you remember that. It was one of those rare occasions I attended my parents' charity events," Tilly lamented. "Please don't fear me. I'm a friend. I know you're feeling unwell right now. We can talk in the morning."

"Are you for real?" the woman asked. "There is nothing free in this world. So, lady, what do you want from me?"

"I want nothing from you. I just want to make sure you are okay. Trust me and leave everything to me. In the meantime, get better," Tilly said as she walked away, leaving the woman in confusion.

CHAPTER FOUR

Tilly and Dusty returned to the hospital the next morning. Dusty carried a fruit basket, and Tilly held fresh roses. It relieved Tilly to see that the woman looked better than the day before.

According to the doctor, there were complications, and he recommended the woman remain in the hospital under observation. The woman thanked the doctor but insisted she was fine and ready to leave. Tilly looked at her and noticed she had a worried expression on her face. She felt sorry for her and knew staying in the hospital wasn't pleasant. Tilly assured her that the doctor was cautious and would discharge her as soon as she was fine.

"If this is about your bill, it's settled," Tilly said.

The woman smiled. "Thank you, ma'am. But, if you don't mind me asking, why are you doing this to me? Why would someone of your stature help someone like me? You don't even know me."

Tilly took her hand in hers and said, "You may not remember me, but I was the woman you saved from being mugged that night in the garage."

The woman needed a second look to recognize Tilly. She could not believe she was the same person she remembered from the ribbon cutting at the shelter.

"Was that you?"

"Yes, it was me. You left in such a hurry. I never thanked you for saving my life."

The woman apologized for leaving her that night. "There's just something about cops that scares me," she laughed. "Sorry for leaving you. I should have waited until you were safe, but I didn't. I hope you understand."

"You don't have to apologize. I get it," Tilly said. She thanked her for reporting the incident to building security.

"I was worried the mugger would return. So I alerted security the way I knew how."

Tilly and Dusty learned the woman's name was Mary. She was thirty years old.

"What brought you to the street, Mary?" Tilly asked. "You seem like a smart lady."

Mary told her story with tears in her eyes. She detailed her account of being abandoned by her family and left with no financial support. Mary looked for work but found nothing. She had no choice but to turn to the streets. Tilly and Dusty listened without speaking.

"After I returned a customer's wallet that fell on the floor at the grocery store where I worked, Mr. Madison, a wealthy business executive, hired me as a live-in housemaid. Given my experience working part-time at minimum wage, I accepted his job offer without hesitation. Soon after, he promoted me with a bonus and a sales associate position at one of his jewelry stores. I completed a two-week training session. Mr. Madison told me it was his plan for me from the beginning. He wanted to repay me for my kindness. He said he needed someone to work in his newly opened store."

Mary paused for a moment.

"My job at his store was a blessing. I worked hard to earn Mr. Madison's trust and respect. He treated me well. While waiting for my replacement as a maid, I juggled working in the store during the day and being a housemaid at night. One day, Mrs. Madison cornered me in the store and told me she didn't like me. I was told not to get comfortable because I would not stay there long. That night, while Mr. Madison was out on a business trip, Mrs. Madison informed me she had found a studio apartment for me. After giving me the key, she asked me to leave the house immediately. So I did."

Taking a deep breath, Mary finished the story. "Believe me, there is no relationship between me and Mr. Madison. I admire both of them," Mary said. "Anyway, I showed up for work the next day, and Mrs. Madison accused me of stealing jewelry from the store. The police took me for questioning but cleared me of any wrongdoing. A few days later, Mrs. Madison accused me of stealing her jewelry from her home. Although I denied it, she was very convincing. Everyone believed her, including Mr. Madison. It was Mrs. Madison's word against mine. The police arrested me. The court found me guilty and imposed a one-year prison term. Unfortunately, the stigma of being a thief has been with me ever since. I have been trying to rebuild my life after my release, but it has been difficult. My family and friends turned against me just when I needed them the most. I don't blame them, though. Who would admit to knowing an ex-con, anyway? I could not find work because of my criminal record. My job prospects weren't even good enough to clean toilets. I found myself in desperation, searching for food behind restaurants. The time I spent in shelters and abandoned buildings remains unknown. I don't even remember the last time I saw my family. Don't you see? I didn't have a choice," Mary sobbed.

Tilly sat for a while, looking into Mary's eyes with sadness. Mary broke the silence.

"Ma'am, why do you waste your time on me? You should distance yourself from someone like me. I bring bad luck."

"Mary, you saved my life. I'm not sure what would have happened if you hadn't helped me. Your random act of kindness to help a stranger has given me a second chance at life. It's my turn to help you. I want to repay you for what you have done. I will do anything to support you in any way I can. My only concern is your recovery. I want you to rest and not worry about anything. Leave everything to me. Can you do that?"

Mary nodded, tears streaming down her face. Tilly had saved her, so the least she could do was listen to her. Mary squeezed Tilly's hand. "Yes," she said, her voice barely above a whisper. "Who am I to complain about that?" Mary laughed.

Tilly laughed along with her. "Get some rest. I promise everything will be okay."

"My story was something I had never shared with anyone. Thank you, Tilly, for listening to me," Mary said as she closed her eyes and fell asleep. It was the best night's sleep she'd had in a long time.

Meanwhile, Tilly believed Mary had told the truth. She saw it in her eyes. Tilly felt compelled to assist Mary. She showed complete dedication to helping her attain justice. Tilly was determined to find the truth, clear Mary's name, and help her reunite with her family. Mary saved her life, after all. She deserved a happy ending.

Dusty contacted Garrett, his private investigator, to assist Tilly in her investigation of Mary's case. He asked Garrett to look into Mary's background and get back to him as soon as possible. Tilly hoped Garrett could get to the bottom of the mystery. Mary's story intrigued her, specifically what she stole during the robbery. They started their investigation.

Tilly learned from a reliable source that Mr. and Mrs. Madison would host a fundraiser on Saturday. She thought this would be an excellent place to find a lead in their investigation. Tilly planned to get close to Mrs. Madison, her number one suspect. She hoped being close to the suspect would provide more information, as she suspected jealousy was the motive for the crime. Her intuition had never let her down before.

Getting Tilly to the party was easy. She received an invitation to Madison's fundraiser dinner because of her social standing. Tilly was excited to attend the party and snoop around. She was prepared to find something that would lead to a breakthrough in their case. Tilly was confident that her detective skills would pay off. She watched *Inspector Mom* and *Murder, She Wrote* at least a hundred times. Tilly thought she would make a brilliant detective. It was her mission to crack the case and solve the mystery of stolen jewelry.

Tilly looked stunning in an elegant Givenchy lace gown. She completed her ensemble with simple diamond drop earrings and a princess-cut diamond tennis bracelet. She wore her hair in a sophisticated bun, and her minimal makeup emphasized her natural beauty.

"Wow!" Dusty kissed his wife and said, "You're gorgeous." Dressed in a black Armani suit, Dusty showcased rounded collar lapels, straight-cuffed pants, and a bespoke white shirt.

Tilly blushed and thanked her husband for his kind words. She adjusted her earrings and smiled as they walked out together.

"Are you sure you want to do this? It's not too late to back out." Dusty asked, concerned.

"I'm certain. More than ever before. Keep in mind this is for Mary."

"I understand," Dusty replied. "I'm here for you." He squeezed her shoulder and smiled.

THE MADISON PARK AVENUE apartment features five bedrooms, a fitness center, a landscaped garden, and an outdoor entertaining area of over 2,000 square feet. Tilly and Dusty arrived to find a large crowd. The men wore their finest suits, and the women were dressed to impress. The atmosphere was electric with excitement as everyone awaited the start of the grand event. Tilly and Dusty were the cutest couple in the room. They fixed their eyes on the Madison's as they greeted their guests.

"Thank you for inviting us," Tilly said, reaching out her hands to them.

Mr. and Mrs. Madison responded in unison, "Thank you for coming."

Tilly complimented Mrs. Madison's evening gown. That sort of thing appeals to women. She wanted to be as close to her as possible. She clung to her like glue, and it worked. Tilly gained Mrs. Madison's trust and spent the evening laughing and talking. By the end of the evening, they had become close friends. The two ladies mingled with the guests all night. When Mrs. Madison needed a break, Tilly knew it was time to put her plan into action. She invited Mrs. Madison to join her on the patio for a drink.

"I have to hand it to you, Jennifer. You know how to throw a big party," Tilly said. "Everyone had a good time."

"I'm pretty good at it, if I may say so myself," Mrs. Madison said. She looked around the room with a cheerful expression on her face.

"Jennifer, I hope you don't mind me asking, but I overheard a few guests discussing a theft at your jewelry store. Is that true?"

"Oh, yes, you are correct. It happened a couple of years ago."

"It must have been terrifying for you!"

"I'm still stunned. It's unbelievable to imagine that one of our employees would steal from us."

"What do you mean by a staff member? What happened?"

"My foolish husband allowed a stranger to clean our house," Mrs. Madison explained. "It surprised me that he hired her as a sales associate in one of our stores. How could he trust someone he didn't know well enough to work with high-end jewelry? It proved to be an expensive lesson for him, but one that imparted valuable insights. He now checks potential employees' backgrounds before hiring them. He also asks for references and interviews to ensure the person he selects is trustworthy."

"What happened to the employee?"

"We fired her, of course. The court sentenced her to one year in prison."

Tilly thought the police had cleared Mary of the theft, but Mrs. Madison talked as if Mary had committed it.

"How do you know she stole those jewels?" Tilly asked.

"It had to be her. Only she, my personal secretary, the store manager, the security guard, and myself were in the store that day. My secretary could not have been responsible. The entire time I was at the store, she was with me. She had always been a trustworthy and loyal employee."

Tilly nodded. "How about the security guard?"

"An object fell over his head early in the morning, knocking him unconscious. It's unlikely that he was the thief since an ambulance took him to the hospital. The police searched his clothing for anything but found none there."

"And the manager?"

"Roy? He couldn't have done it. For five years, he has been one of our most reliable employees."

"So, where was he at the time?"

"I don't remember. I'm sure the incident rattled him."

Tilly frowned. She felt something wasn't right about Roy.

"Is he still employed at the store?"

"Yes, he is. Until recently, Roy took an indefinite leave of absence because of personal issues at home."

"Leave of absence?"

"That's what he said," Mrs. Madison replied. "He left two weeks ago. He mentioned his plans to fly to Los Angeles for a family emergency. However, I thought I saw him in downtown Manhattan last week during a business meeting, but it couldn't have been him. I'm sure it was someone else."

Tilly became suspicious of the manager's unexpected leave of absence, but the robbery occurred two years ago. If Mrs. Madison saw him in Manhattan, what was his reason for lying about being in Los Angeles when he was actually in New York? What's the connection? Tilly had no major leads, and it could have been a dead end, but she had to concentrate on her only suspect, the manager. She had an uneasy feeling about him.

"Can you tell me the manager's name?"

"Roy Chavez."

"Roy Chavez," Tilly repeated, nodding.

"Why are you asking all these questions?" Mrs. Madison asked.

Tilly shrugged and smiled. "I'm just wondering what happened." She paused for a moment, then said, "I'm just curious."

"It was a long time ago, and it's best left in the past. It doesn't matter anymore."

"You are right, Jennifer. I apologize."

Tilly looked for her husband after Mrs. Madison left to speak with an old friend. He was talking to Mr. Madison when she found him.

"May I borrow my husband for a minute?" Tilly asked.

Mr. Madison replied, "Of course. The governor signals for me to come. Dusty, I'm glad I spoke with you. We'll meet up soon, okay?"

"That sounds fantastic," Dusty said as he watched him walk away.

"Sweetheart, we can go home now. I have the information we need," Tilly said in a hushed tone.

"It's about time. I'm tired of listening to these arrogant, snobbish people."

Tilly kissed her husband on the lips. "You need to calm down. I hope you won't tire of hearing me tell you what I've gathered."

"I never tire of listening to you, darling, no matter what time it is."

Her husband's corniness made Tilly laugh. "It's cute, honey, really cute."

CHAPTER FIVE

Garrett was sipping Irish coffee in the living room when Tilly and Dusty walked in. He brought photos of stolen jewelry from the Madison store. A brilliantly crafted diamond necklace in platinum and gold, a sapphire ring and bracelet, and an emerald tiara. The police estimated the stolen jewels at a million dollars, which they never recovered.

"A million dollars?" Tilly exclaimed. "I'm shocked. I'm curious why Mary received only a lighter sentence."

"Because there was no evidence," Garrett explained.

"Excuse me?"

"The police took her into custody for questioning after Mrs. Madison accused Mary of theft at the store. They searched her, the store, the surrounding area, and her apartment, but found nothing."

"Are you saying they arrested and sentenced Mary with no evidence?"

"They didn't charge Mary with the crime because there was no evidence she stole anything from the store. Surveillance footage revealed no unusual behavior on her part. It was a robbery that no one could solve. The police investigated but found no leads. The jewels disappeared without a trace."

"How did Mary get convicted?"

"From what I've gathered," Garrett added. "Mrs. Madison also accused Mary of stealing jewelry from her home just days after the theft. When the police searched Mary's apartment for the second time, they discovered them in her purse."

"Wait, what? I'm confused?" Tilly asked. "I thought the police searched Mary's apartment the day of the store theft and found nothing," Tilly asked.

"Indeed," Garrett said. "Mary claimed she didn't know how the jewelry got there. The studio apartment she moved into was still empty, except for the personal items she brought with her. She had been staying at her mother's house since the store incident. The cops found nothing when they searched Mary's apartment on the day of the store robbery. They discovered Mrs. Madison's jewelry in Mary's apartment days later. Even though Mary had never set foot in her apartment since the store theft, the court still ruled she was guilty. She received a one-year jail sentence. It makes no sense, but I don't have all the details. I'm sure I missed something here. There are many unanswered questions, but just give me a couple of days and I'll figure it out."

"It's fine, Garrett," Tilly said. "We have two tasks at hand: to prove Mary's innocence and clear her name. Second, we need to find the actual thief."

"How do we do that?" Garrett asked. "The police have been without leads for two years. Why would you think we can solve not one but two cases?"

"Let's review, shall we?" Tilly said.

Dusty and Garrett were all ears.

"It's obvious Mrs. Madison set Mary up for the second crime. Seeing that the police were not charging Mary for the theft, she accused her of another crime, or should I say, framed her?"

"How do you know that?" Garrett asked.

"Mrs. Madison told me at the party that she disliked Mary. In her words, I could tell she harbored jealous feelings toward Mary. When Dusty and I visited Mary in the hospital, she told us that Mrs. Madison had found her an apartment and given her the key. So it begs the question: Whose name was on the lease? I'm sure if we dig deeper, we will find that Mrs. Madison has a key to Mary's apartment. Framing Mary was easy for her."

"I see what you mean. So, what now?" Garrett asked.

"We have solved the second crime. We know what needs to be done to clear Mary's name, but for now, let's just work on the first crime: the theft at the store. I have a strange feeling about the store manager, Roy Chavez," Tilly said. "Based on what Mrs. Madison told me, she did not know where he was when they discovered the theft. The store manager was the most likely suspect. He didn't have an alibi. No one knew where he was. My question is why the police ruled him out as a suspect. We need evidence to back up my suspicions. I believe we should concentrate our efforts on him. Let us see if he has any skeletons in his closet."

"Okay, I'll do it when I return to the office," Garrett said. "Meanwhile, I have a lead about the stolen jewelry. A private collector purchased a similar set just a week ago."

"A week ago?" Tilly's eyes widened as she inquired. "Don't tell me, Manhattan."

"How did you know?"

"Mrs. Madison informed me that the store manager requested a leave of absence two weeks ago. He said he was flying to Los Angeles, but Mrs. Madison thought she saw him last week in Manhattan. If the manager was involved in the theft, considering the crime occurred two years ago, why is he selling the jewelry now? Why wait two years to sell it?"

"I believe it is time to investigate his activities. Who knows? We might get lucky," Garrett speculated.

Dusty watched Tilly and Garrett engage in verbal combat with fascination. He couldn't help but laugh at the idea of his wife becoming like Columbo. Their witty banter and her always being one step ahead of him amused him. Dusty admired Tilly's sharp wit and ability to solve mysteries using her gut instincts.

Garrett had an uncanny ability to connect with people when no one else could. He began his investigation by asking about Roy Chavez and discovering he frequented a bar on the outskirts of town. Garrett checked it out, and the cocktail waitress remembered Roy.

"Does he come here often?" he asked.

"He's one of our regulars."

"When did you last see him?"

"He was here every night. He bought drinks for everyone but got into fights with them when he drank too much."

Garrett nodded. Tilly was right. Roy Chavez did not travel to Los Angeles. He never left New York.

"I'm sure he'll show up tonight. I hope you get him," she said.

"You don't like him at all, do you?"

"He treats me and the other servers here as if we were lower life forms. He deserves what's coming to him."

Garrett lingered and sat in the bar's darkest corner, ordering a beer to unwind. He finished his drink and was about to order another when Detective Spencer entered. Garrett wasn't expecting to see him. Detective Spencer was his partner before leaving the force and starting his detective agency. The two shook hands.

"What are you doing here, detective?" Garrett asked.

"I'm meeting a friend," Detective Spencer replied, scanning the tables as he spoke. "I guess I'm early."

"Why don't you take a seat and join me for a while?" Garrett said as he motioned for the cocktail waitress to approach.

Moments later, Roy Chavez walked in. He sat down at the bar. Garrett smiled when he saw him. He approached Roy and tapped on his shoulder. Roy turned around and nearly passed out when he saw Detective Spencer behind Garrett. He recognized him. Detective Spencer questioned him about the jewelry store theft two years ago. In a state of panic, he punched Garrett in the face, knocking him to the ground. Roy tried to flee, but the waitress hit him over the head with a beer bottle. He cried like a baby when Detective Spencer handcuffed him and took him to the police station.

Roy Chavez proposed a full confession of his role in the jewelry store robbery for clemency. This surprised Garrett and Detective Spencer. His admission of guilt was unexpected. Roy Chavez claimed he had fenced the jewels and waited two years to sell them. Garrett and the detective were skeptical, but Roy Chavez insisted it was true.

Detective Spencer shook his head in disbelief. He thought he had arrested Roy on assault and battery charges. It turned out to be much more than that. Garrett asked Roy Chavez to explain why he had waited so long to sell the jewels. Roy said he was waiting for the right time and buyer. He thought he was in the clear. Roy wondered how they knew he was involved. Garret said an anonymous source informed them. The authorities arrested Roy after he admitted to his guilt.

"I must admit, Garrett. This is one of my most unusual arrests in years. For two years, I investigated this case but found no leads. I'm glad it's over. I think I might even get a commendation. Do you mind if I take credit for solving this case?" Detective Spencer asked.

"I get no points for doing it, so it might as well be you," Garrett said. "If you hadn't asked, I would have suggested it."

"Thank you, Garrett, but I'm curious. How did you know the manager committed the robbery?"

"I didn't," Garrett admitted. "I got some help from my friends."

"Some friends you have. I miss working with you, Garrett."

"Me too, buddy," Garrett replied.

Garrett kept Detective Spencer informed of all the details. During a search of Roy's home, police found several stolen items in the freezer's icebox. Roy concealed the items by wrapping them in paper. After the investigation ended,

Detective Spencer expressed satisfaction with the outcome and thanked Garrett for letting him enjoy his five minutes of fame.

MARY HAD BEEN STAYING in the hospital for a few days, and the doctors would soon release her. She was relieved and thanked the staff for their care. Despite her eagerness to return to normal life, Mary was concerned about being thrown back on the streets. It surprised her to receive an unexpected visit to her room.

"Mr. Madison, what are you doing here?"

"Mary, I'm glad to see you. I apologize for accusing you of stealing. I should have known better. You returned my wallet with a large sum of money in it, so I should have believed you when you said you didn't steal the jewels. Can you forgive me?" Mr. Madison asked, his voice trembling.

Mary did not respond, but she broke the silence a few moments later.

"How did you know I was here?"

"Dusty told me."

"I don't understand."

"Tilly and her husband conducted their own investigation. Roy has stolen from me for years. He replicated some jewels and replaced them with forgeries. Roy sold them to unsuspecting buyers and pocketed the money. I trusted him and suspected nothing was wrong."

"Mr. Madison, I still don't understand."

"I met Tilly and Dusty at the police station. We talked, and they told me what had happened to you. I'm not sure how they did it. They saved my business from bankruptcy. The police recovered the stolen items from my store. They returned them undamaged, and I resumed normal operations. I was relieved that the store avoided further losses."

"I'm happy for you, Mr. Madison."

Silence fell between them.

Mary broke the silence. "Where is Mrs. Madison?"

"Mary, we are not together anymore," Mr. Madison said. "In response to a tip, the police questioned Jennifer about why she did not mention having a key to your apartment. Jennifer admitted she put jewelry in your bag, intending to get you arrested. A police officer took her into custody."

"We cannot change what has already been done. How can you give back two years of my life?" Mary asked.

"My mistake was not listening to you when you told me you didn't do it. I hope you forgive me. They cleared your name, and you can now resume normal life."

Mary wept with joy. She didn't expect that. Mary didn't know what to say.

"I am sorry to have taken your life away from you. Tilly told me about your family abandoning you and becoming homeless. If you allow me, I'd like to make it up to you. As soon as you are well enough to return to work, there is a job waiting for you in the store. It comes with a promotion and a raise. You don't have to decide right now, Mary. Please get better, and I hope I can visit you again. We have a lot to discuss."

"Yes, Mr. Madison. I like that very much."

Mr. Madison smiled before saying goodbye. He kissed Mary on the cheek and promised to return. Mary could feel her cheeks flushing and her mind racing with thoughts and questions. She felt lost in the moment, unable to understand her feelings. Mary could only watch Mr. Madison walk away. She was not sure what to think or feel. It would be interesting to see what the future holds for her and Mr. Madison.

Mary was looking forward to Tilly's visit. A lot had happened, and she wanted to know every detail. Tilly cleared her name and regained Mr. Madison's trust. It was an overwhelming feeling of joy for her. Suddenly, the door swung open wide. Mary turned her head, expecting to see Tilly. Instead, she saw her mother and twin sisters standing there. They ran towards her, sobbing as they hugged one another. Tears flowed again, but this time, they were tears of joy. They hugged again, trying to make up for all the missed hugs over the last two years. The door opened, and the nurse entered, interrupting their reunion.

"Mary, Mrs. Bonaventura left this for you," the nurse said, handing her a white envelope.

"What is it?"

"She was here a while ago, but you were sleeping. She said to give you that envelope when you woke up, but when I returned, I saw you had a male visitor. I didn't want to interrupt. I hope you don't mind me coming in. My shift ends in ten minutes. I just wanted to make sure you received it before I left."

"Thank you. I appreciate that very much," Mary said, taking the envelope in her hand.

After the nurse left her room, Mary opened the envelope to find a check and a letter inside. Without looking at it, she set the check down. She read the letter.

It's okay to believe the world is against you. It's all part of the learning process. I hope this check will help you start over with your mother and sisters. Use it wisely. P.S. I found and contacted your family. They realized their mistake when they sent you away, and they've been looking for you for a long time. It's time to forgive and forget. I wish you well. Thank you for saving my life. I'm eternally grateful. Always, Tilly.

"Oh, my God," Mary sobbed. Tilly gave her the best present she could ask for—her family. Mary felt overwhelming happiness, and she knew her life would never be the same. She was ready to face the world with her family by her side. Mary was determined to make the most of this second chance. She read the letter repeatedly and felt grateful for everything Tilly had done for her. She gave her life back and even gave her money to start over. Mary picked up the check and stared at it. Her eyes widened as she realized how much it was. Mary clutched at her stomach. She couldn't breathe. Her mother snatched it from her grip. It also shocked her. Her eyes widened. Confused by how they looked, the twins removed the check from their mother's hand and looked at it. It was a million-dollar check made out to Mary.

"Oh my God! Who gave it to you?"

Mary replied, "Someone who saved my life—a friend with a beautiful heart."

"Who?" the twins asked.

"Mrs. Millionaire," Mary responded, her gaze fixed on the million-dollar check in her hand.

"You're rich, Mary," they exclaimed, jumping up and down with delight.

"You mean, we're rich!" Mary corrected them, laughing as she threw her arms around them.

They screamed loud enough that everyone could hear them. Tilly, who stood outside the door, heard everything they said and smiled.

Mrs. Millionaire, what a noble name! She couldn't help but chuckle to herself.

Mary had given Tilly another chance in life, and she didn't want to squander it. Tilly wanted to make the most of her second chance. Now, she understood it. She realized that her parents' charitable work was out of love and not an obligation. Tilly learned a lot from this experience. It was about recognizing the significance of helping others and creating positive change in their lives. It inspired Tilly to continue her charitable work, not just to make her parents proud, but because it was the right thing to do.

Mary believed Tilly helped her, but in reality, Mary taught Tilly the value of giving and sharing. Tilly's life took on new meaning, and she embarked on a mission to assist those in need. It appeared simple, yet powerful. Tilly felt ecstatic, so she desired it even more. She devoted most of her time and energy to social work, particularly with the underprivileged children at the orphanage. She donated a theme park area for children to play in. Her scholarship program encouraged students to pursue their studies and careers. Tilly turned her life into serious philanthropy.

Tilly founded Mrs. Millionaire, a secret foundation for assisting people in challenging circumstances. She chose this name in honor of the person who saved and inspired her. Tilly used the inheritance money from her grandparents to fund the institution. Through a million-dollar gift, she supported deserving individuals and allowed them to transform their lives for the better. Mary was the first recipient.

In her opinion, Mrs. Millionaire was her greatest legacy. Tilly believed that providing opportunities to those in need would help them and their families achieve a better future. Tilly's aspiration was to improve the lives of the less fortunate, one day at a time.

MRS. MILLIONAIRE AND THE BAD FATHER

CHAPTER ONE

T he scent of fresh pine, roasted chestnuts on an open fire, and an ornate Christmas tree wafted through the air. Christmas lights twinkled, and Christmas carols played in the stores. It filled the streets with anticipation and joy. The city was bustling with excitement as people rushed to finish their shopping. The first snow of Christmas marked the beginning of the holiday season.

Matt Calderon was a devoted husband and caring father to his two children. Everyone loved him—his family, friends, coworkers, and the community. He was a hardworking man who worked two jobs to support his family. His routine included delivering newspapers early in the morning in temperatures below zero. He then proceeded straight to his next job at the Finnegan Toy Store, Lake Placid's largest toy factory.

The Finnegan Toy Store sells toys, bikes, board games, video games, dolls, miniatures, and other items. Matt worked in production. He hand-assembled the toys. Matt started his job as a part-time seasonal worker a few years ago because jobs were scarce in a small town like Lake Placid. He knew it was a great way to expand his experience and skills. Matt worked hard and was eventually offered a full-time job. Their busiest days were around Christmas when large corporations placed orders with them.

Matt and his wife, Maria, had a tough year. Their children had been begging for Christmas presents since June, and they struggled to save money. With Christmas just around the corner, they ran out of options. They wanted to give their children something for Christmas, but they did not know how to make it happen.

To make matters worse, Maria developed asthma and visited the doctor's office whenever she had an attack. Despite having no allergies, the wheezing occurred suddenly and without apparent cause. Doctors could not help her. They prescribed medication, but it had no effect. Maria's health made it difficult to find work. She applied for assistance but did not receive benefits. Even though Matt worked two jobs, money was still tight. Maria and Matt's financial situation was stressful, and with the holidays approaching, they worried about how they would afford their children's presents.

Matt arrived home that night exhausted. Upon entering the house, he tossed his coat, scarf, gloves, and a Finnegan Christmas catalog onto the chair. His heart broke when he saw his wife and children adorning their eight-year-old artificial Christmas tree. The branches were so old that they lost their plastic needles.

Matt walked into the living room and saw his kids staring up at him, their hopeful faces making him feel even more guilty. With a heavy heart, he sat down beside them. At the table, stockings were waiting to be hung. He knew his wife had either made them or bought them secondhand.

She filled them with small matchboxes, knit socks, scarves, or candy bars. Matt expected this year to be special for his children. He counted on Mr. Carlton's Christmas bonus, but he had not yet distributed it. His hopes of getting it faded. Mr. Carlton was a stingy spender.

Matt was so preoccupied with his thoughts that he failed to realize his six-year-old son, Ray, held the catalog he had brought home. Ray smiled as he looked at each toy. He wanted a brand-new bicycle. One of his friends, Jack, had a nice bike, and he wished he had one like it as well. Ray always talked about the bike at dinner and hoped Santa would bring it to him for Christmas. His eight-year-old sister, Haley, chimed in, saying she wanted a Chihuahua, despite her mother's allergy.

Matt wondered how they could afford to give their children the gifts they wanted. They didn't have two cents to rub together, let alone money to buy the bike and a puppy. A thrill he remembered from his first bike ride flooded his mind. When he was a kid, it was a gift he never forgot. How could they ignore their children's excitement? They couldn't tell them they weren't getting those presents. As much as they loved their kids, what could they do to make them happy?

"Perhaps I can work as a Christmas helper," Maria suggested.

"No, Maria, you must take care of yourself. I'm not sure if we can afford to bring you back to the doctor if you have another asthma attack. You should stay at home and take it easy. I will meet Mr. Carlton tomorrow morning. Maybe I'll get that bonus he promised."

Matt left early the following morning. He walked to Mr. Carlton's office, but he wasn't there yet. His secretary wasn't there either. Matt glanced at the wall clock. It was only 6:35 a.m. He arrived early. Office hours wouldn't begin until 7 o'clock. As Matt sat in the waiting room, he flipped through a magazine. He looked around the office. Wall-mounted glass cabinets display some of their most popular toys. A large portrait of Mr. Carlton sat next to a landscape painting hanging on the wall.

Several minutes later, a sixty-year-old man with long gray hair entered the room.

"Matt, what are you doing here so early?" he asked.

"Mr. Carlton, do you have a minute? If it's okay with you, I'd like to speak with you."

"Sure, Matt, come in."

Mr. Carlton owns the Finnegan Toy Store. After inserting the key into the lock, he opened the door to his office. Mr. Carlton fumbled around the wall for the light switch, found it, and turned it on. He took off his hat, scarf, and jacket and hung them on the rack. He then opened the window shades to let in the sunlight. As Matt entered, he couldn't help but feel amazed at how nice it looked. Expensive furniture and artwork adorned the room. It displayed toys on shelves that covered the walls, while a large oak desk with a leather chair completed his office. The city view from the window was stunning, overlooking the street below.

"So, what's on your mind, Matt?" Mr. Carlton asked as he took a seat and turned on his computer.

"I'll get right to it, sir. Is it possible to get the bonus you promised us? It's almost Christmas, and I'd like to give my children their Christmas presents earlier this year." Matt felt like a young kid asking for a dime to buy candy. "I am sorry for being such a nuisance, sir, but I promised my son a bike and my daughter a dog. Buying them may be difficult or expensive if I wait too long."

Mr. Carlton raised an eyebrow at him. "If I give you your Christmas bonus sooner, everyone else will want one. I don't plan to give them out until Christmas Eve."

"Christmas Eve, sir? Don't you think it's late?"

"What?" Mr. Carlton asked, fumbling with something he was holding, not paying attention to Matt.

Matt felt like an idiot. He should have known better. Mr. Carlton loved his money, and counting it repeatedly was his favorite pastime at work. He considered himself a miser and held onto every penny. The man was thrifty, and he always tried to find the cheapest price to buy anything. Even his wife joked about it when she visited the factory. After bowing and thanking him, Matt walked away. Mr. Carlton stopped him.

"I've never said no yet, Matt."

Matt was confused. "Sir?"

"Come back here tonight. I have meetings all over town today, but I should be back in the office around 6 p.m. I'll give you your bonus, then."

In disbelief, Matt put his hands on his head and shook Mr. Carlton's hand.

"Thank you very much, sir. You don't know how much this means to me."

"While I may come across as strict, I assure you I do not embody Scrooge's qualities. Okay, get back to work."

Matt smiled as he stepped out of the office, leaving Mr. Carlton to work. Unbeknownst to them, Erica, Mr. Carlton's secretary, listened in to their conversation. Evil thoughts crept into her mind. As soon as Erica saw Matt walking out of the office, she hid behind the door. Through the crack between the hinges, she saw Mr. Carlton punch in the safe code. Erica held her breath, praying he wouldn't notice her. Her eyes followed Mr. Carlton as he opened the door and pulled out a few bundles, closed the safe, and turned the dial, unaware of the witness he had. A wide smile spread across Erica's face. She had never seen so much money in her life. After placing the cash in a small bag, Mr. Carlton put it in his desk drawer and locked it. Erica watched Mr. Carlton throw the key into a large jar filled with marbles. She entered his room.

"Good morning, Mr. Carlton," she greeted.

"Erica, I'm glad you're here. I'm headed to a meeting. Can you handle things while I'm gone?"

Erica nodded. "Yes, Mr. Carlton. Don't worry. I'll see you later."

MATT WAS IN THE EMPLOYEE locker room, preparing to leave. He called his wife and told her he would be late for dinner. Matt would meet with Mr. Carlton first, then pick up the bike from the warehouse. Fred, a warehouse supervisor, gave Matt an additional 25% off on top of his employee discount. Matt planned to adopt a dog later in the week. Erica, who appeared to be in a hurry, almost collided with him on his way to Mr. Carlton's office.

"Whoa! Slow down. What's the rush?" Matt asked.

"I'm late for my date," Erica said. "Mr. Carlton should be here shortly."

"How did you know I was meeting him?"

"Well, I just assumed."

Matt nodded. "Is the waiting area open?" he asked.

"Yes, it is."

"Okay, thank you."

Matt patiently awaited outside Mr. Carlton's office. He sat down and read a magazine. A few moments later, Matt stood up and paced back and forth. He glanced at the wall clock. It was 6:35 p.m. He had been waiting for an hour. Matt would have quit and gone home if he didn't need money so badly. He called his wife and informed her he was late and not to wait for him.

Mr. Carlton walked in just as Matt hung up the phone.

"Are you heading home, Matt? How long have you been waiting?"

"Yes, Mr. Carlton. I've been here for a while."

"I'm sorry for the delay. Today has been a hectic day for me. I'm glad you told me about getting gifts early. It slipped my mind that I had not yet purchased a gift for my wife, children, and family. I'll go soon. Our anniversary and Christmas are coming up, so I'm thinking about getting my wife a gold watch. It's a lot of money, but it's worth it."

"That's a nice present, sir. I'm sure she'll love it. I'm only giving my wife a sweater. Money is tight, and there are some bills to pay."

"Say no more. I have the money ready for you."

With his key in hand, Mr. Carlton unlocked the drawer and pulled out the bag he had placed there earlier. Upon opening it, he found it empty.

"What is this?"

"Sir?"

"Did you take the money in this bag?"

"No, sir. I did nothing. I didn't open that drawer."

"Wait a minute. My office door is open. Why is that? I always keep it locked."

"Mr. Carlton, I don't know what you are talking about. I did not enter your office. I was in the waiting area the entire time. Erica told me to wait there."

Mr. Carlton was so enraged that he heard nothing Matt had said. He had already judged him and found him guilty.

"I trust you, Matt. The only thing I can't tolerate is someone stealing from me."

"Sir, I stole nothing. I would not do that to you," Matt replied.

"Tell that to the police!" Mr. Carlton said as he dialed the phone.

"Mr. Carlton, please listen to me," Matt said. "I took nothing from you. You've known me for a long time. I would never steal from you or anyone else."

But Mr. Carlton had already convinced himself that Matt had done it. He chose not to listen to his explanations.

"Police are on their way. I'll make you pay for what you did. Nobody steals my money and gets away with it," Mr. Carlton said.

Matt couldn't believe what was happening. Mr. Carlton accused him of stealing. Matt could barely breathe because of his intense fear. He tried to explain again that he had nothing to do with the theft, but Mr. Carlton wouldn't listen. Matt knew he had to leave. He didn't want to go to jail. Matt ran out of the building, jumped into his truck, and sped out of the parking lot and onto the highway. As soon as he reached home, he felt relieved. Fearing the police would see him on the street, he slowed down and parked in an alley. His only option was to flee the city as soon as possible. Feeling like a cunning thief, he crept through the gate and into the backyard. Unlocking the back door, Matt groped in the dark. He stumbled and landed on the floor.

Meanwhile, Maria and the kids ate dinner early and went to bed at seven o'clock. She told Ray and Haley they would receive a surprise in the morning. Her thought was that the children would be delighted to find their Christmas presents under the tree.

"Can we see it now, Mom?" they asked.

"No, it's a surprise. Wait until the morning. So, go to sleep now."

Before saying goodnight, the children smothered their mother in kisses while laughing. Maria smiled and said goodnight. She turned off the lights and closed the door. Maria lay on the bed, her heart full of anticipation and excitement. She drifted off to sleep, dreaming of all the fun they would have in the morning. She awoke after hearing a noise downstairs. Maria sat up on the bed, her heart pounding. She listened and heard footsteps. Maria heard someone enter the room and stop in their tracks. She held her breath, afraid to move. Maria breathed a sigh of relief as her husband walked through the door.

"You scared me half to death," Maria said, trying to calm herself down. "Why are you late? Did you get the gifts for the kids?"

"Maria, please listen up. Something bad has happened. Don't ask questions. Take whatever you can. We have to leave now."

"Matt, you're scaring me. What happened?"

"I'll explain later. Grab whatever we need right now. We must get out of here as soon as possible."

Maria didn't know what was happening, but she trusted her husband. She would ask questions later. Maria pulled out a suitcase from the closet and stuffed their clothes inside. She shoved her piggy bank into her bag. Matt woke up the kids and told them to grab their sweaters. The family left the house, leaving only dust behind. Maria did not know where they were heading. She took a deep breath, trying to stay calm. She knew that whatever happened, Matt would take care of them. They were several blocks away when they heard police sirens.

"Matt, what's going on?" Maria asked, worried.

"Shh," he said. "Not now, Maria."

Matt turned his head to check on the kids in the back seat. He could see how terrified they were, not knowing what would happen to them. Matt sighed. What a mess he created! He couldn't get Mr. Carlton's expression out of his mind. Mr. Carlton believed he had stolen his money. He didn't even listen to what he said. It was all a misunderstanding, and Mr. Carlton was ready to throw him in jail.

Although Matt knew it was wrong, he had to flee to avoid arrest. He had to leave, and he wasn't willing to take chances. Matt drove fast, praying for safety. They arrived in Buffalo exhausted from the journey. They checked into a motel on a remote highway, relieved to have escaped. Matt knew he had to prove his innocence to Mr. Carlton. But how? Maria joined him in the truck when the kids were asleep.

"Aren't you cold? It's freezing out here," she asked.

"Just a little," he replied.

"Now, why don't you tell me what happened?"

Matt took a deep breath. He looked at Maria and shook his head.

"I was sitting in Mr. Carlton's office, and we talked. A split second later, he accused me of stealing his money."

"What? That is absurd!"

"Mr. Carlton called the cops to arrest me. That's when I freaked out and dashed out the door. The last thing I want to do is go to jail. I did nothing wrong."

"I believe in you, Matt. You are a good man. I know you didn't do it. But you should have told Mr. Carlton that you were innocent. You should have waited for the cops, and they'll find out your prints were nowhere near Mr. Carlton's office."

"Believe me, I tried telling Mr. Carlton many times that I didn't steal his money, but he wouldn't listen," Matt said. "You're correct, Maria. I made a mistake. I should have waited until the cops arrived, but I panicked. It's too late now."

"So, what are we going to do? We have no money. And the kids. What will we tell them?"

"Don't worry, I'll think of something. Why don't you go to bed? I'll be there in a minute."

Maria entered the room to rest while Matt remained in the truck. He made the wrong decision, but there was no turning back now. Matt had no choice but to face the consequences of his actions. Despite the odds, he was determined to turn things around.

Matt and Maria discussed their plans the next day. The motel was no longer an option since they didn't have the money to pay. Maria smashed her piggy bank against the wall and counted her paper money and coins. She came up with $180.52. Matt had $53.50 on him. Not enough to get by with two kids. Maria placed the coins in a plastic bag, packed their belongings, and checked out. They needed another place to stay. They drove until Matt pulled over to a park and let his kids play. Matt and Maria sat on a park bench.

"I'm sorry, Maria. This is not the life I promised you at our wedding."

"I know there are challenges to overcome, but as long as we stay together, we'll be fine. I'm sure of it," Maria said.

Matt wrapped his arms around his wife as he watched the children play. He smiled, knowing that no matter how challenging life got, they were always there for each other. Matt was thankful for his family's loyalty, trust, and love. He knew he could rely on them, and they would always have his back.

But proving his innocence would be an arduous task. He needed a miracle to clear his name.

CHAPTER TWO

Matt and Maria decided to leave the United States and start fresh in Canada. They knew this move was the right decision for their family. The conversation preoccupied them, and they were unaware that their daughter had distanced herself from them.

Haley's stomach flipped in a flutter of hunger when she smelled the barbecue aroma blowing in the air. The food became more enticing as she inhaled. The scent guided Haley to an old house. She noticed an elderly woman sitting on her porch.

"How are you, young lady? What are you doing here? Where are your parents?" the woman asked.

"They're in the park, and I'm hungry," Haley explained.

"We're serving barbecue chicken, corn on the cob, and baked potatoes for lunch."

"Yummy," Haley said, rubbing her tummy.

The old woman laughed. Just then, her husband called her, saying lunch was ready. He stopped, surprised to see Haley sitting on the porch steps.

"Why don't you bring the food out here? My new friend is hungry. What is your name, little girl?"

"My name is Haley. I'm eight years old!" she exclaimed.

"I'm Mrs. Ofilada, but you can call me grandma."

Meanwhile, Matt decided it was time to get to the border before someone recognized him. He called up his children, but only Ray appeared. There was no sign of Haley. They searched for her until they found her across the street, eating on the porch.

"Haley, you shouldn't leave like that. You scared us half to death," Matt scolded her.

"I'm sorry, Dad. I was hungry," she admitted, her mouth full of chicken. She smeared barbecue sauce on the left side of her mouth.

Matt shook his head, his heart heavy with remorse for his daughter's actions, and turned to face the old woman.

"Please forgive my daughter for intruding. I don't know what happened to her today. She usually behaves well."

"Forget about it. Take a seat. My husband prepared a lot of food. Please join us."

Matt stood speechless. Despite not knowing his family, this old woman invited them to eat. Matt considered refusing, but Ray had already sat down and helped himself to corn on the cob. He scratched his head. Matt couldn't blame his children. They hadn't eaten since last night, and they were starving. He took a deep breath and sat down. Maria joined them. They thanked the old woman for her hospitality and ate. The food was delicious, and they finished their plate in no time.

A smile spread across the woman's face. Her friendly and charming personality was clear. She stood up and said, "It's been a long time since I had guests. I'm glad I could share a meal with you."

The family thanked the old woman again and her husband for the food. They introduced themselves and enjoyed a fascinating conversation. Mrs. Ofilada appeared well-dressed for her age of seventy. She told them she used to be a theater actress and made a name for herself on the New York stage, where she won awards. Because of the injuries she suffered while on vacation, they forced her to retire early.

"Are you from around here?" she asked.

"No, we're from out of town," Matt replied. "We're just passing through."

Matt looked at his watch. "Thank you for the food, Mrs. Ofilada, but we should be on our way now before it gets dark."

"My husband bakes a cake. It's almost done. Why don't you just wait and take some for the kids?"

"We don't want to impose or take advantage of your hospitality," Maria said.

"Don't be silly. I enjoy your company. We have time to relax."

Maria smiled and nodded at Mrs. Ofilada. Matt checked his truck when he noticed the gas gauge was almost empty. He told Maria he would fill it up and return soon.

"Perhaps you should get hot dogs for our trip. The kids will be hungry later," Maria suggested.

"That sounds like an excellent idea," Matt agreed. "I'll pick them up on the way."

Mr. Ofilada directed Matt to the nearest gas station. Matt thanked him and went on his way. He arrived at the gas station and stepped inside the mini-mart to buy supplies. Matt was unaware of the danger he was about to face.

TILLY AND HER HUSBAND, Dusty, a globe-trotting multi-millionaire power couple, led a glamorous lifestyle but were also serious philanthropists. They were passionate about helping those in need. They supported many charities and organizations, and they were active in many social causes.

Tilly and Dusty's chemistry was undeniable. It was like two puzzle pieces fitting perfectly together. They were a match made in heaven. However, they always encountered a situation where they were solving a crime or embroiled in conflict.

A storm delayed Dusty's flight home from Asia, so he had to cancel his meeting in Buffalo. He tried calling to warn his meeting attendees but had trouble getting hold of them. Tilly, who was home in New York, cleared her calendar and offered to attend the meeting. Dusty was grateful for her help and thanked Tilly for her understanding. He was relieved that the meeting could still happen.

Tilly's private plane arrived early in Buffalo. She looked at her watch. It was only ten in the morning. They scheduled her meeting for 2 o'clock. Tilly needed to kill time, so she drove around town in a rented red Mercedes-Benz, taking in the sights and sounds of the city. For lunch, she had Buffalo wings and their famous Mighty Taco, a delicacy filled with meat, cheese, lettuce, tomato, and a special sauce. Tilly even tried sponge candy, a sweet, sugary treat that melts in your mouth with a sticky, chewy piece of candy. It was heaven. She purchased all the flavors available—dark, white, milk, and orange chocolate—for her husband to try.

Tilly stopped for coffee at a gas station before heading to the meeting. As she walked to the mini-store, she noticed a rusted truck in front of her and another white van beside it. She pushed the door open, and everyone turned to look at her. They looked fearful.

"Get inside," a man said behind Tilly.

When she turned around, she saw a man in a mask with a weapon pointed at her. She walked into a robbery in progress. Tilly had been in a similar situation before. After someone attacked her in the parking lot of her building a few months ago, her husband, Dusty, insisted she take self-defense and martial arts classes. Tilly initially despised it, but later found it refreshing. The self-defense class gave her courage and confidence in her ability to defend herself. She was much calmer now and ready to face any potential dangers.

Tilly walked to the back of the store to join the others. A few minutes later, police cars arrived and surrounded the store. They tried to persuade the robber to hand over his weapon and surrender, but he refused. Tilly watched the man pacing. As she looked at him, she noticed he was holding a toy gun. Tilly shook her head. She remained calm. As a martial artist, she wanted to test her skills. Tilly knew she had to end the situation before things got out of hand. She kept a close eye on the man as he moved around the room, stopping occasionally to check on them.

Meanwhile, Matt had entered the store earlier and was stuck inside with customers. It did not focus his attention on what was happening inside. Seeing the cops surrounding the store outside made Matt nervous. There was nowhere to escape. The police had blocked his truck, so even if they apprehended the man, he knew they would question everyone, including him. It terrified Matt because he thought a warrant was already out for his arrest. His thoughts turned to Maria and his children, who were waiting for him, and he knew he had to leave. His family needed him. But how?

Then it happened! Matt was so nervous and scared that he knocked over the stacked beer cans. It surprised Tilly, as well as did the other hostages. It hit the masked man in the head and knocked him out cold. Everyone ran, including Matt. The police cuffed and arrested the robber when he regained consciousness. Paramedics checked his condition while cops interviewed everyone at the scene. After receiving the statements, the officer took down their names and addresses before releasing them.

Tilly returned to her car and started it.

"Don't be afraid," Matt said.

Tilly heard a voice in the back seat.

"Who are you?" she asked.

"I'm the one who hit the robber with beer cans."

Tilly glanced in her rearview mirror and saw a man in his thirties looking fearful. She remained calm and relaxed. Tilly kept her eyes on the road and drove on, steadying her speed.

"May I ask what you're doing in my car?"

"The police blocked my truck, and I couldn't let them see me," Matt explained.

"I'm assuming the cops want you. Is that it?"

"I suppose you could say that."

"What do you want from me?"

"I regret involving you, but I have no other option. Can you give me a ride to the next street? You have my word; I won't hurt you."

"You just need a ride to the next street," Tilly asked. "You could have just walked."

"I could have, but I panicked. I was not thinking right."

Tilly felt at ease with this guy. Either he was stupid or smart. She wasn't sure which. Tilly trusted her intuition and went along with it. If the man was crazy, she would not hesitate to use her karate chop. She took the risk and hoped for the best.

"I'll get my truck once the cops are gone, and the coast is clear. Please, help me."

Tilly looked at him. Something about his voice made her believe in him. She continued driving until she saw a gas station. Tilly pulled into the parking lot and parked.

"I'm sorry for scaring you," Matt said. "I didn't know what else to do. Thank you again for the ride."

He stepped out of the car and walked around the corner. It relieved Tilly that the man had not hurt her. She pondered whether to call the cops, but there was nothing to report. The man didn't hurt her.

As Tilly left the parking lot, she noticed the man heading back to the mini-store. His head turned from side to side, looking around.

Curiosity got the best of her. What was he doing? Tilly didn't want to get involved, but her instincts told her otherwise. There was something about the man and his situation that piqued her interest.

Tilly called her secretary and canceled her meeting. She thought finding out the man's story was more important than judging a silly contest. Tilly stated that something had come up and she could not attend. After that, Tilly pulled the car to the side and called the man, leaving her secretary confused before hanging up the phone.

"I hope you don't mind me asking. What is going on? Why do you have a problem with the police? And why are you returning to the store? You're walking around in circles."

Matt stopped walking and turned to her.

"Look, I appreciate your concern, but this is not your problem. I've caused you so much trouble already, and I'm embarrassed as it is."

Her curiosity grew. "I'm an excellent listener. Perhaps I can help," Tilly said. The man seemed harmless.

Matt frowned. The woman was persistent. He didn't think she would leave him alone. Matt got into the car and complained.

"If you must know, yesterday was a marvelous day. I started my day by asking my boss about getting my Christmas bonus early so I could get my kids their presents. I was so happy when he said yes. The next thing I knew, I was a wanted man. My boss accused me of stealing his money."

Tilly frowned and looked at the man, attempting to read him. "Honestly, you don't look like you could hurt a fly."

Matt smiled at what the woman had said. He looked at her, and she seemed interested, so he told her everything that had happened. Matt felt a strange sense of comfort in sharing the details with her as if he were confessing his sins to a priest. Matt wondered why it was so easy to share his emotions with a stranger. He admitted he felt better when talking about it.

"Where are they now? Your wife and children?" Tilly asked.

"They're staying with this old lady we met this morning. We'll cross into Canada once I get my truck back."

"Is that your plan? Cross the border?"

"I hope so. We only have $100 left to spend on food and gas."

"To be honest, I don't think it's enough to get you to the border."

"I'm so confused right now. I can't think anymore. All I wanted was to give my children the gifts they wanted. Was that too much to ask?" Matt said, his voice trembling.

"I am an excellent judge of character, and I sense you are a good-hearted man. Please allow me to assist you. Let's get your truck."

"Are you sure? I can't take advantage of your kindness. You have helped me more than you realize, considering what I did to you earlier. I cannot justify my actions."

"I appreciate your honesty in owning up to your mistake. You were desperate. Your worry was about your family being stranded somewhere. I get it. I'll drive you back to the mini-store to get your truck. Your family awaits you."

"Why would you help me? You don't even know who I am."

"I know enough to realize you need my help. Your situation fascinates me."

Matt expressed his gratitude by nodding his head. "By the way, my name is Matt," he said as he shook Tilly's hand.

"My name is Tilly. Nice to meet you, Matt."

Tilly believed it wasn't a coincidence that Matt picked her to hitch a ride. Fate brought them together. It was a sign that she needed to help him.

CHAPTER
THREE

Tilly and Matt drove to the gas station. When they arrived, the cops had already left. Matt exhaled a sigh of relief when he saw his truck still there. He thanked his lucky stars that the police had failed to check his license plate number. Otherwise, they would have towed it.

Matt insisted Tilly meet his family. Tilly displayed hesitation but eventually gave her consent. She knew Matt had made a mistake and wanted to do his best to make up for it. Matt's gesture showed Tilly that he was sorry for causing her so much trouble. She kept an open mind and made the most of the situation. Tilly also saw it as an opportunity to get to know them better and learn more about Matt's family. She followed Matt's truck to the old lady's house.

It wasn't long before they arrived at Mrs. Ofilada's driveway. Ray and Haley were playing in the front yard when they saw their father.

"Where have you been, Dad?" Ray asked.

"Who is she?" Haley asked, pointing at Tilly.

When Maria saw her husband, she hugged him.

"You make me worry. You have been gone for a long time," she whispered. "I fear something might have happened to you," she added with a trembling voice.

"I'm sorry to worry you."

Matt introduced Tilly, and Maria looked confused.

"Hello, Maria," Tilly said, smiling.

"Nice to meet you, Tilly," Maria said as she extended her right hand.

"And these two monsters are our pride and joy. Kids, say hello to Miss Tilly," Matt said.

"Hello, Miss Tilly," Ray and Haley said.

"Good day, kids! Your father told me so much about you."

"And this lovely lady here is Mrs. Ofilada," Matt said.

The elderly woman smiled like a schoolgirl when Matt kissed her wrinkled cheek. She stepped inside the house and made lemonade for everyone.

Matt told the kids to play in the yard while they sat on the patio. He asked his wife to calm down before telling her what had happened at the gas station.

"Oh, my God!" Maria exclaimed aloud after Matt finished his story.

"Don't worry," Matt said. "Everything is fine, thanks to Tilly."

"Tilly, I apologize for my husband's actions. He didn't mean to do it. I'm sure Matt felt frustrated. I hope you can forgive him."

Tilly said she wouldn't be there if he didn't believe Matt.

"Thank you for helping him, despite what he did. I'm not sure what will happen to me and the kids if something happens to him."

Haley and Ray rushed to Matt and cried. Though they did not know what they heard or what they were talking about, they knew their father was in danger. Their tears filled their eyes as they tightened their embrace. Despite her desire to remain emotionally detached, Tilly found it difficult not to be overwhelmed by the pain experienced by the family. It broke her heart to see them suffer. After seeing their mutual affection, Tilly felt compelled to assist them. Her gut feeling was too strong to ignore. Tilly was determined to uncover the truth and help the family find justice.

"WAIT UNTIL YOU HEAR the good news," Matt said with a twinkle in his eyes. "Tilly offered to help us."

Maria frowned and looked at Tilly for a moment.

"I don't want to appear ungrateful, Tilly, but why would you do that?" Maria asked. "My husband put you in a difficult position when you first met him, yet you still want to help him?"

Tilly sighed. Even though Maria was right, she couldn't abandon them.

"I understand what you're saying, Maria," she replied. "But I can't just leave, Matt, knowing it affects your children. If I leave now, what would happen to you? I can't stand seeing your children cry. I can see how much they adore their father. Let's face it. Your family needs help, and I'm the only one who can provide it."

"Thank you, Tilly," Maria said. "You are right. We have no one. To tell you the truth, we don't know what to do. It was wrong of me to doubt you. It's just that we rarely get help from strangers or anyone else."

"I know Matt wouldn't run away from his problems. I do not think your old truck will make it to Canada, especially on a $100 budget. Ray and Haley need a warm place to sleep tonight. I know we just met, but trust me. Please stay in our apartment. There are plenty of rooms for you. We can discuss Matt's case when we get there."

"What do you think, Matt?" Maria asked.

"We don't have a choice," Matt said. "Tilly was right. Our truck may not reach Canada. We don't have any money for food or to pay for a place to stay. The children are cold and hungry. I have unfinished business here, and I'm not one to run away from problems. We need to think about our children, Maria. We have to end this. I don't want to remain a fugitive."

Maria knew Matt was right. Who was she to pass up such an opportunity? She took a leap of faith and took Tilly up on her offer.

"You'll love it there," Tilly said. "This is a great time to visit the city. The kids will enjoy ice skating in Central Park, and I'm sure you'll enjoy seeing the windows along Fifth Avenue. There's the Rockefeller Center Christmas Tree and holiday markets."

"We are going to New York, kids," Maria said. She had been there before and had fond memories. She was so excited to return and explore the city she loved.

"Yay!" Ray and Haley screamed with joy.

Matt sighed in relief. His family had lost hope, but the robbery at the gas station turned out to be a blessing for him. Thanks to Tilly. He had a shot at proving his innocence. They had the chance to get their lives back.

Matt expressed his gratitude to Mrs. Ofilada and her husband for their hospitality. When Tilly told Matt to leave his truck because they wouldn't need it where they were headed, Mr. Ofilada allowed him to park it in their garage. They promised to keep in touch and meet again soon. Matt and Tilly left the Ofiladas with a warm hug and gratitude.

While traveling in Tilly's rented car, Matt and his family were excited. It was their first luxury car ride. During the drive, the family enjoyed the picturesque scenery. Their anxiety increased when Tilly told them they were heading to the airport.

"Private plane?" Maria asked, her face beaming. "This is my first private plane flight. I bet it will be amazing."

It thrilled the family to experience something new. They boarded the plane and enjoyed the flight. Matt and Maria never expected that hours ago, they were at the end of their rope, and now they were having the time of their lives.

The kids' faces lit up with excitement as the plane took off. They noticed furry clouds hanging from the blue sky as they looked out the window. They felt like angels. The kids played video games on the plane while Matt and Maria sipped on the finest wine they'd ever tasted. This experience made them feel like kings and queens.

It was a quick trip. They had a limousine waiting at the airport. Tilly and the family entered when the driver opened the door. The children bounced from top to bottom on the leather seats in unbridled joy. Matt tried to stop them, but Tilly assured him everything was fine and they could have fun.

The car sped off, taking them to their apartment. In front of a 20-story luxury building, the driver parked the limousine. The doorman, who opened the car door, greeted them. The family entered the building through a revolving door. A security guard smiled and welcomed them. There was a white Christmas tree as tall as the sky, standing majestically in the lobby. They decorated it with thousands of twinkling lights and shiny ornaments. A star perched at the top, shining down on all who passed by.

They headed to the elevator when Carlos Angelo, a longtime elevator operator, welcomed them.

"Hello, Carlos," Tilly said, handing him a bag of chocolates she brought home from Buffalo.

"Thank you, Tilly," he said. "Are you staying for the weekend? Where's Dusty? Is he still in Italy?"

"He is on his way home. I'm just dropping off our friends. They'll stay in our apartment for a while," Tilly explained.

"Welcome to the building," Carlos said to Matt and Maria. "There is no better time to be in New York than now. If you need anything, you know where to find me."

"Thank you," they said.

The elevator ride to the penthouse was full of anticipation. They couldn't wait to see what awaited them on the top floor. As the family entered the opulent apartment, their jaws dropped. It provided a panoramic view of Lower Manhattan. They could see the Empire State

Building and all the other beautiful high-rise buildings in the area.

"I've always admired the view from here. New York City at night is a sight to behold," Tilly said. "Just make yourself at home, relax, and I'll see you in the morning. We will shop for winter clothing, boots, and jackets. The fridge has plenty of food. If you get hungry, you can eat whatever you want or go downstairs to a restaurant. Don't worry about charges. Order whatever you want, and they'll bill me later."

"Where are you staying?" Matt asked.

"We have a family home not too far from this place."

"Are you saying we have the entire place to ourselves?"

"Yes, you do," Tilly said. "Enjoy, and we will see you in the morning."

Maria and Matt hugged Tilly and thanked her for everything. The children also hugged Tilly and said thank you.

Tilly smiled and said, "It's my pleasure."

Before leaving, she handed Maria her phone number. Tilly smiled and waved goodbye. Knowing Matt's family was safe and warm in her apartment made her happy.

Matt and Maria looked around, excited to see their surroundings. Tilly's apartment was ten times larger than their previous one. There were six bedrooms, each with its own bathroom and walk-in closet. It had a large living/dining area, an eat-in kitchen, and wraparound city views of New York City's Greenwich Village. Everything they needed to feel comfortable was available to them.

The next few days were some of the most laid-back days Maria had ever experienced in her life. Her asthma did not flare up either. She could relax and breathe. Maria felt at home in the city and was grateful for her time there. She felt refreshed and rejuvenated.

Tilly hired an ice-skating instructor for the kids and took Maria to her favorite spa for a full-body treatment. Dusty took Matt and Ray to see the Knicks play, while Tilly brought Maria and Haley to see a Broadway production.

After everyone rested and enjoyed their time in New York, it was time to work. Tilly, Dusty, and Garrett, Dusty's private investigator, visited the family one evening. Matt told them everything that had happened, including his plan to move his family across the border.

Garrett remained silent for a moment, suspicious of the situation. As he listened, he rubbed his chin and nodded several times. There were three plausible explanations: Matt's boss was a liar, someone tried to frame Matt, or Matt was in the wrong place at the wrong time.

"Who knew you'd see Mr. Carlton that night?" Garrett asked.

"No one," Matt replied. "I met with Mr. Carlton early in the morning, and no one else was in the office except us."

"Someone must have been there."

"The only person I saw on my way to Mr. Carlton's office that night was Erica, Mr. Carlton's secretary. She seemed eager to leave the office."

"Garrett, you have your work cut out for you." Dusty smiled. "If anyone can get the information, it's you."

"Thank you for your confidence, Dusty. I'd better get started."

CHAPTER FOUR

G arrett worked undercover as a temporary office janitor at Finnegan Toy Store. On his first day of work, he stayed late and snooped around Mr. Carlton's office but found nothing out of the ordinary. He searched through the accountant's and office manager's rooms but found nothing useful. Garrett finished looking through the secretary's desk. He discovered a few receipts in the drawer but paid no attention to them. Garrett glanced around. He didn't know what he was looking for. Garrett couldn't think of another location he missed while hunting for clues. He had reached a dead end.

Garrett looked through the employee locker rooms but found nothing worthwhile. He closed the door, turned off the light, and called it a night until he realized he hadn't cleaned Mr. Carlton's office yet. Garrett knew Mr. Carlton would know if he didn't do his job. He didn't want to be fired on his first day, so he cleaned up. Garrett vacuumed the floor, dusted the furniture, and wiped down the windows. He was emptying the trash when he noticed paper remnants at the bottom of the secretary's trash can. Garrett took it out and discovered a $500 store receipt stuck to a piece of gum.

"Interesting," he said as he looked at it.

Garrett sat down, looking for something he might have overlooked. He opened the top drawer and found a slew of department store receipts hidden beneath the secretary's makeup kit. He also found a piece of paper wedged under the keyboard. Garrett pulled it out, and it was another receipt for an $800 Coach Rogue leather bag. By the date on each receipt, the secretary had bought clothes, makeup, and accessories several days ago and paid in cash.

There is something strange about all this. Garrett thought to himself. How does a secretary afford expensive items? Where did she get the money to buy all this stuff? She must have spent a thousand dollars in the store. Did Mr. Carlton give her the money? Are they having an affair? Or did she steal Mr. Carlton's money and frame Matt for it? And why would she leave all those receipts lying around?

Garrett needed answers to his questions. Even though he was certain he had the answers, he had to be sure. The next morning, he ventured into the break room to see if he could gather any information. He discovered Jim was an excellent gossip source.

Jim Garfield, a sixty-year-old sales representative, had been with the Finnegan Toy Store for 20 years. He knew more about the office than anyone else. He was well-versed in juicy gossip and gruesome details. Jim spreads rumors about other employees and brags to anyone who listens. He wanted to be the center of attention and look good in front of everyone. Garrett heard it with his own ears and formed his own opinion of him. What he needed now was to find the right moment to corner Jim and force him to reveal everything he knew about Erica—his prime suspect. Mr.

Carlton's office lacked security cameras. Nobody else could have taken the money. Except for his secretary, no one could access his office. There's no other explanation unless she was Mr. Carlton's mistress.

Garrett tried to get as close to Jim as possible, and it worked. Jim grew fond of him and enjoyed their conversation. Garrett didn't waste time. He invited Jim to an after-work drink. Jim accepted his offer and thought it was nice to have another friend at work after hours. They met at Hardy's, a pub close to Finnegan Toy Store. They walked to the bar and ordered a couple of beers. Garrett motioned for Jim to follow him and sit at one of the wooden tables in the corner. He had a bowl of nuts in the center. Garrett popped a few peanuts into his mouth as he talked about work.

"Let me tell you," Jim said. "Avoid Kurt. He works in maintenance. His wife dumped him, and if you tell him about Gus, he'll punch you in the face."

"Oh, really?"

"Yeah, his wife left him for Gus, his best friend."

Garrett smiled. He hit the jackpot. He believed Jim would provide the information he needed. Garrett motioned to the waitress to order two more beers, hot dogs, and nachos. He watched her walk away in her short skirt until she was out of sight.

Jim noticed it. "And if you want to get lucky, go out with Melanie. She's the office flirt. Just make sure you give her Godiva chocolate. That's her favorite. I promise you'll smile all the way to paradise."

Garrett almost choked on laughter as he swallowed a mouthful of beer. Jim burst out laughing and cried. Garrett decided it was time for action.

"Jim, who got the biggest Christmas bonus this year?" he asked.

"Why do you want to know that?"

"I was just curious. I've noticed that some employees look unhappy. They appeared to be in a foul mood. Everyone should smile because it's Christmas."

Jim shook his head. "I didn't notice."

"Come on, I'm sure you know."

"Would you believe me if I told you that is one thing I don't know? If you're curious, no one will tell you how much their Christmas bonuses are. Mr. Carlton is not generous, you know. It's more of an embarrassment than anything else. We're lucky if we get $200 from that penny pincher. He's Scrooge. He hasn't given me my bonus yet, but others have."

"Then allow me to ask you a question. Have you noticed someone dressing better than usual or purchasing expensive items, say, in the last two weeks? Come on, man, there's got to be someone you've noticed who looks like a million bucks."

"Well, Erica. She is Mr. Carlton's secretary. She wears expensive clothes and handbags to work."

"What's the big deal about that?" Garrett asked.

"Erica borrowed money from us all the time. She was always broke, even after payday. Erica liked to party on weekends, and when she returned to work, she didn't have a dime to her name. Now, she has designer handbags and clothes, as well as a fresh hairstyle. When we asked how she could afford it, she said she inherited money from a deceased uncle."

Bingo!

It gave Garrett a slight feeling of satisfaction to know that his suspicions about the secretary were correct.

Garrett had an NYPD connection. He was a detective before becoming a private investigator. He asked Darryl, a fellow detective, to investigate Erica Walters.

"There's not much to say except that she lives alone. I looked up her credit card history. Based on her purchases, I believe she likes expensive clothing and jewelry. She maxed out on her credit cards a few months ago, but she paid them off recently," Darryl said.

"So, no dead uncle, huh?" Garrett asked.

"No. Erica has no family, living or dead, according to the record. She grew up in an orphanage. Her foster parents raised her until maturity. Erica worked in fast food, rising through the ranks from flipping burgers to store manager. She took secretarial courses before landing a job at Finnegan."

"What about her bank account? Is there anything suspicious?"

"Erica Walters has $5,000 in her bank account. She made the deposit two weeks ago."

"It seems that two weeks ago was the common denominator. But Erica is clever. If she took the money, she either hid it or spent it on a shopping spree."

"Do you need anything else?"

"No, Darryl. That's it for now. I owe you, buddy."

"Don't forget to introduce me to your cousin, Amanda. You promise me."

"Don't worry, Darryl. She'll call you."

IT WAS ANOTHER LATE night at work. Garrett snooped around Erica's desk again. He had already drawn his own conclusions—she was the only suspect. After hearing footsteps approaching the door, he grabbed the mop and began cleaning up.

"Hey, are you still here?" Mr. Carlton asked.

"Yes, boss. Dirt builds up without proper cleaning."

"Good job," Mr. Carlton said, patting his shoulder, something he rarely did. He smiled, and his face showed genuine appreciation. "Keep it up. Your dedication and hard work won't go unnoticed."

Garrett thanked his boss for the compliment. "What brought you here so late at night, sir?"

"I have an early morning meeting, and I forgot to get my file."

"It's no surprise your company is doing well. You're such a workaholic, sir."

"You're correct. I've worked long hours and invested a lot of time and energy into getting my company to where it is today. I'm proud of what I've accomplished and committed to growth."

"Sir, I hope you don't mind, but I heard someone stole money from you. Did the police make an arrest?"

"No, they didn't. He fled the city before the police could apprehend him."

"How did it happen, sir? He must have followed every move you made to know you had money in your office and where to find it."

"How did you know it happened in my office?"

"It's no secret, sir. Everyone here talks about it."

"I still can't believe one of my trusted employees would do something like that. I considered promoting Matt."

"Matt?"

"Yeah, Matt. That is his name. He worked in production."

"Perhaps you made a mistake, sir? Maybe someone framed him?"

"Why would you suggest that? Who would do such a thing? Besides, Matt was alone in my office, and no one knew about the money except me."

"Even your secretary?"

"Erica? She's been my secretary for five years. She's the only person I trust around here."

"Nothing is going on between you, sir?" he teased.

"I am a devoted husband and father to my two children. I never considered cheating on my wife."

"Sorry, sir. I was messing with you. It's obvious that you adore your family."

"I've been married for 34 years. This Christmas marks our 35th wedding anniversary. Did I tell you that? We got married on Christmas Day. Matt gave me this idea about buying a gift for my wife. I took money from my safe and placed $50,000 in a bag. That night, I planned to pick up a gold watch for her and gifts for my kids."

"Fifty thousand dollars? That must be one hell of a marriage. Congratulations, sir. That's incredible. You are one fortunate man."

"I am," Mr. Carlton said, smiling.

"Now, back to the stolen money, sir. How did you know Matt took it? You said it yourself; you were the only one who knew about it. How did he know you had money on your desk?"

"Who else would have taken it? There is no one else in the office but us."

"I'm sure there's an explanation for it. When did you get the money out of the safe, sir?"

"It was seven in the morning. When I put my bag in the drawer with the money, I heard the clock strike at 7:00 a.m. I left for a meeting right after that."

"And what time did Matt leave?"

"A few minutes before seven. I saw him walk out of my office," Mr. Carlton said, rubbing his chin. "That doesn't sound right."

"Matt wouldn't have known about the money in the bag since he left," Garrett explained. "Had he taken the money, he wouldn't have stayed after hours to get his bonus. He would have gone home a long time ago, don't you think so?"

"Why are you interested in defending Matt? Have you ever been told you ask too many questions?"

"No, I don't think so, sir," Garrett said, looking embarrassed. "It's just that I want to understand what's going on. I watch crime shows on TV. It fascinates me."

"The problem is that you watch too many terrible crime dramas."

Garrett laughed. "I believe if someone asked for my opinion, Matt could not have done it. One: He left before you took the money from the safe. He didn't know you had money in your desk drawer. Two: Someone could have seen you open the safe without you knowing it. By the time Matt arrived to meet with you that night, whoever took the money may have already left."

"Perhaps, but it is up to the police to investigate. I leave it up to them to figure out who did it," Mr. Carlton said. "I have to go now. Don't forget to lock up when you leave."

"Yes, sir," Garret saluted.

Garrett remained in the room for a brief experiment after Mr. Carlton left. He discovered Mr. Carlton's office door latch was covered in sticky tape residue, showing someone had taped it to prevent it from locking. Garrett stood behind the door and peered through the hinged gap between the secretary's desk and Mr. Carlton's office. He could see it from where he was. Sitting at the secretary's desk, he imagined Mr. Carlton at his desk through the partially opened door. From where he sat, Mr. Carlton's every move was visible. No matter where he sat or stood, he could see everything around him. The suspicions he had about the secretary intensified.

After Garrett concluded his investigation, he notified Tilly and Dusty. Tilly agreed with Garrett's assessment of Erica. Her rushing out of the office on the night of the theft raised questions. Besides receipts found on her desk, there were questions regarding a shopping spree she undertook only days after the theft. Dusty, however, remained cautious. He suggested they wait and see what Erica was up to before making assumptions. But Tilly was impatient. Her top priority was to clear Matt's name before time ran out.

Tilly and Garrett crafted a trap to catch Erica with the help of the store manager. He was a crime novel and mystery reader and jumped at the opportunity. If Erica was innocent, Tilly would apologize, but if she was not, she would make sure Erica got what was coming to her. The store manager agreed to help them, and the trio set off to work. They couldn't wait to see if their plan worked.

CHAPTER FIVE

Tilly worked undercover as a sales clerk at the Bridgit Department Store, Erica's favorite weekend shopping spot. Garrett, disguised as a customer, remained in the background. The receipts found on Erica's desk show that she mostly visited the store on Saturday nights and shopped until closing. Garrett and Tilly used this information to implement their plan. Tilly waited for over two hours, but Erica was a no-show as closing time approached. Tilly's hope faded. Her husband waited for her outside the store. He pointed to his watch. She nodded at him.

"Just wait," she murmured.

As luck would have it, Erica walked in a few minutes later. Tilly recognized her from Garrett's photo taken when Erica wasn't looking.

"May I help you, Miss?" Tilly asked.

"No, thank you. I'm just browsing," Erica replied.

"Don't tell anyone, but if you are interested, we have the newest handbag arrivals from Paris for 50% off today only. Would you like to see them?"

"That is fantastic. Thank you. I'd love to see them."

Tilly smiled. Erica took the bait.

"You're so lucky," Tilly said, taking the two handbags Erica had chosen, along with a few other items. "I've always wanted a designer bag from Paris, but even with discounts, it would cost me several months' salary. You must be an executive at a large corporation to afford them."

"No, not really. I'm only a secretary," Erica said.

"Wow, you must make a lot of money. I only make minimum wage plus commission."

"They don't pay me much. I recently received some money and am treating myself to a new wardrobe, handbag, and shoes."

"Lottery?"

"No, but it feels like I hit the jackpot." Erica laughed.

During the check-out process, Tilly handed the purses and other items over to the cashier, where she scanned each item and entered the details into the system.

"That will be $960, Miss," the cashier said.

Erica handed her ten one-hundred-dollar bills. The cashier gave her the change and the receipt. Erica did not realize they recorded her on the store's video camera. Garrett and the store manager took Erica's money from the cash register after she left the store. They placed it in a Ziploc bag. The store manager turned Erica's payment and videotape over to Garrett as evidence.

"Mission accomplished!" Tilly said.

After leaving the police force and opening his own detective agency, Garrett spent his final year working with Detective Spencer. They worked together to solve a string of unsolved cases, gaining recognition for their investigative skills. The two remained close friends after Garrett retired and kept in touch regularly. Sometimes their cases crossed paths. Garrett enlisted the detective's help with some of his investigations. Detective Spencer provided valuable insight into the case, helping Garrett piece together the facts. Together, they solved several cases. The successful resolution of the jewelry robbery by Tilly and Garrett on their own accord instilled a sense of ease in Detective Spencer, leading him to collaborate with them. For two years, he never got a suspect in a case he thought was a dead end. The police chief and mayor praised him for his dedication, despite his minor role in resolving the case. Detective Spencer was grateful for the recognition, but Tilly and Garrett deserved it more. The three became close friends and have worked together ever since.

Detective Spencer reviewed Garrett's videos and the money Erica used to pay for her purchases at the store. Tilly and Garrett persuaded him to look into the case. Otherwise, they would send an innocent man to jail. Detective Spencer agreed to investigate further and promised to return with answers soon. Matt took the advice of Tilly, Dusty, and Garrett, and surrendered himself to Detective Spencer. They granted him bail while waiting for his hearing. Tilly hoped Matt could move forward with his life soon.

The detective conducted his investigation and sent the evidence for further testing. A call confirming Erica's fingerprints matched those on Mr. Carlton's bag prompted Detective Spencer to act immediately, without waiting for the forensic fingerprint analysis report to arrive. He coordinated with the Lake Placid Police Department chief to help him with the investigation. A helicopter took

Detective Spencer to the police station the following morning.

The chief of police and Detective Spencer drove to the Finnegan Toy Store. Their presence surprised Mr. Carlton. He asked if they had found the perpetrator. Detective Spencer said they had not, but they were close to an arrest. The news that the case was closing in was a relief to Mr. Carlton, but Erica's invitation to the police station surprised him. Erica refused to go, but Mr. Carlton convinced her to cooperate with them.

"You did nothing wrong. You will help the police with their investigation."

Mr. Carlton explained the importance of her testimony and promised to protect her. Erica agreed when Mr. Carlton's attorney accompanied her.

Upon arriving at the station, they escorted Erica and her attorney to a room. Detective Spencer and the chief interviewed her. They asked her several questions about the case. Her response sounded rehearsed. Detective Spencer grew more convinced of her guilt as he listened to her. He wanted to arrest her, but a computer glitch caused a delay in the transmission of the forensic fingerprint analysis report. There was no information on when it would be fixed. It angered the detective. It was impossible for him to make an arrest without proof. At Erica's attorney's request, they let her go since no charges had been filed against her. Detective Spencer instructed Erica not to leave the city if they needed to question her more. Erica nodded in understanding.

It took another day for the detective to receive the report that Erica's fingerprints matched those on the bag Mr.

Carlton had placed the money in. Erica's fingerprints appeared on the ten one-hundred-dollar bills she paid for the handbags at Bridgit Department Store, as well as Mr. Carlton's. Detective Spencer and the chief of police got a warrant for Erica's arrest.

They arrived at Finnegan Toy Store and found out Erica had called in sick. When the cops arrived at her apartment, she was not there. Her landlord let them in, and her place was a mess and her closet was empty. Erica left in a hurry. The police issued an all-point bulletin calling for her arrest.

After leaving Erica's apartment, Detective Spencer and the police chief drove down the street several times, looking for her car. The police checked all the local hotels, motels, and bus stations, but there was no sign of her.

A police officer in Plattsburgh, who was at a mini-mart, heard the report about Erica's car. He spotted it at Chase's gas station and called it in. Detective Spencer heard the report and looked it up on Google Maps.

"She's on her way to the border," he told the chief. "She's making a run for it."

The chief of police notified the border patrol.

ERICA DROVE NONSTOP after stopping in Plattsburgh for gas. She smiled. Erica would soon cross the border into Canada. Despite mulling it over for a while, her visit to the police station and her current circumstances prompted her to act now. She had enough money to get by for the next few months. Erica took a deep breath and sighed in anticipation, but the closer she got to the border, the more terrified she became. This was her first time leaving the country.

As she approached the border, her heart pounded. An American customs and border protection officer stopped her to verify her citizenship. Erica opened her purse, took her driver's license from her wallet, and handed it to the officer.

"How is the weather in Canada? I hope to wear my tiny bikini. I'm dying to go to the beach," Erica said, attempting to entice the man. The winter temperature in Canada was 22 degrees Fahrenheit, which she forgot or didn't know.

The man laughed and said, "You'll need more than a bikini to keep you warm in Canada. You'll want a coat for that beach!"

Erica realized her mistake and blushed in embarrassment. She groaned and shook her head. She should have known better.

The officer took her license, verified her identity, and discovered Erica had an arrest warrant. The agent told her to wait and walked to the office. He called it in. Erica felt her heart sink. She knew something was wrong. Fear and confusion overwhelmed her. She sat in the car, not knowing what to do.

Upon returning, the officer told her, "We need your passport."

"Passport? I'm sorry, but I don't have one," she explained.

"We need a current passport to enter Canada," the officer explained. "Please pull over to the side of the road and come with me."

"Why?" Erica asked. "What is this all about?"

"Just come with me, Miss. I'll explain inside the office."

"Am I under arrest?" she questioned.

"I am just asking you to come with me."

Erica parked her car and followed the officer as he held her arm, which did not make her feel better. He led her into a room and told her to wait. Erica's heart raced like crazy. She couldn't shake the feeling that something was wrong. Did they know she stole the money? It couldn't be. She was careful. How did they find her? The old, familiar knot in her stomach returned, and she walked back and forth, burning a hole in the floor.

Detective Spencer and the police chief arrived moments later in a helicopter. Erica looked down at the floor when she saw them. She knew they had caught her. There was a moment of silence between them.

Detective Spencer broke the silence.

"Erica, why did you leave? We told you not to leave the city. You didn't tell anyone in your office that you were going on a trip. They thought you were ill."

"I, uh, had an emergency. After a long day of work, I needed a break."

"To Canada?" asked the detective.

Erica did not respond.

"Let me get right to the point," Detective Spencer said. "Can you explain how Mr. Carlton's money ended up in your possession?"

It took Erica off guard. Her face remained impassive. "I don't know what you're talking about."

"It will be easier if you tell the truth. There are only two explanations for why you have the money: Mr. Carlton gave it to you or you stole it."

"I'm still not sure what you're talking about."

"All right, Erica, have it your way. There's no point in explaining it to you. Even if you pretend to be innocent, we have enough evidence to charge you."

"What evidence?"

"First, they caught you on surveillance tape. You paid Bridgit Department Store with cash from Mr. Carlton's safe. Second, I'm sure you know how much he enjoys counting his money. Everyone in the office said so. His fingerprints were all over them. That's how we know you took it. They found your fingerprints in the bag in which he placed the cash. Only Mr. Carlton had access to it. In your hurry to put it back in the drawer, you forgot to wipe it clean. Can you explain that?"

Feeling trapped and under intense stress, Erica knew they had caught her. There was no reason to deny it anymore. The proof was in their hands. In an admission, she confessed to stealing money from Mr. Carlton. Erica burst into tears.

"I didn't want Matt to get into trouble. He was in the wrong place at the wrong time. Matt made an excellent scapegoat."

Erica admitted to her wrongdoing. In her statement to the police, she explained why she did it. It was pure greed, motivated by the desire to live life to the fullest.

The police swarmed the scene moments later. They arrested Erica and charged her with felony theft. The officer informed her of her rights. When she said she understood, the police chief flew to Lake Placid by helicopter to take Erica into custody.

Detective Spencer hitched a ride back to the station. In a phone call, he informed Tilly that the investigation was over. Tilly was relieved to hear the news but still felt sadness. She couldn't help but think about how much Matt and his family had suffered. Tilly felt peace and closure, knowing justice had been served.

CHAPTER SIX

The court found Matt not guilty. After acquitting him of theft, the court allowed Matt to leave the courtroom and closed the case. Matt was relieved that it exonerated him and that he could move on with his life. He walked out of the courtroom a free man.

Matt and his family were present at Erica's sentencing hearing. The judge gave her one last chance to show remorse for her actions, but she did not. She remained silent. It frustrated Matt that Erica was not taking responsibility for her actions and making amends. Erica wasted her last opportunity to make things right.

The judge sentenced Erica to the maximum sentence possible. While Matt was relieved that justice had been served, he still felt sadness and disappointment. He hoped Erica would use her prison time to reflect on her actions and make better decisions in the future. They handcuffed Erica, and Matt watched as they led her away.

Matt and Mr. Carlton bumped into each other as they exited the courthouse. Mr. Carlton attended the hearing, and the discovery that Erica was the thief devastated him. He trusted her. Mr. Carlton couldn't believe Erica betrayed him like that. He felt like he couldn't trust anyone anymore.

Mr. Carlton chatted with Matt and apologized for misjudging him. He admitted he was wrong, and Matt was right all along.

"I should have known better. You are one of my most loyal employees. I should have trusted you, Matt," Mr. Carlton admitted. "Take the day off and work tomorrow. We have many orders to fill."

Matt frowned and stared at Mr. Carlton. Did he just tell him to go back to work? Mr. Carlton acted as though nothing had changed. It was business as usual for him. Matt felt frustrated and angry. He couldn't believe Mr. Carlton was so nonchalant about the situation. He felt taken for granted. Matt made a drastic decision. He couldn't work for that man anymore.

"I don't think so, Mr. Carlton."

"What are you saying, Matt?"

"When I was on the run, I had to endure hardships. Those I thought I knew were the first to cast stones at me, and a stranger helped me pick myself up. Where would I be if I hadn't met them? Do I have to be sent to jail for something I didn't do?"

"I said I'm sorry, Matt."

"Sorry doesn't cut it," he said. "I'm not looking for an apology."

"What do you want me to say?"

"Now is the time for me to find a new job, Mr. Carlton. It's time to go."

"Matt, it's Christmas. How will you feed your family? You need to consider their well-being. Think before you decide."

"I'm sorry, Mr. Carlton, but my decision is final."

"Please don't leave."

"The answer is no, Mr. Carlton."

"What if I gave you a promotion and a 30% raise?"

"If you had offered me this before, you would not have asked me twice. Things have changed. Money is nice, but it isn't an issue anymore. I'm trying to maintain my dignity while I still can. I'm sorry."

"Matt, please help me. Production is down, and—" Mr. Carlton couldn't finish what he wanted to say.

"I'm not interested to hear what you have to say, Mr. Carlton," Matt said. "I have my problems, and I can't help you."

"Okay, fine," Mr. Carlton said. "I'm in a pickle. If I didn't bring you back, all warehouse employees threatened to go on strike. So, help me, Matt. It's Christmas. We have many orders to fill, but no one is working."

"I'm sorry, Mr. Carlton. You are on your own. It's not my problem anymore."

Matt walked away with Maria and the children. Mr. Carlton watched them leave and knew he had lost a valuable and trusted employee. He got what he deserved. Mr. Carlton saw Garrett and Matt talking as he walked out. It puzzled him how the two knew each other. Garrett noticed Mr. Carlton's perplexed expression and approached him to explain everything.

"A private eye? That's a shame. I need someone like you in my company. Please call me if you change careers."

"You know what, Mr. Carlton? I believe we both deserve a break. Come on, let me buy you a drink," Garrett offered.

Mr. Carlton accepted. Garrett handed Matt the keys to his rental car.

"Here you go," he said. "You don't have to worry about me. I'll take a taxi to my hotel."

Matt thanked Garrett for everything he had done for him. Garrett hugged the children goodbye, and Maria gave him one last hug before walking away.

"Are you sure you want to resign, Matt?" Maria asked when they were alone.

"I must admit we could use the money right now, but one thing I've learned from Tilly is to have faith in myself. I should have quit years ago," Matt replied. "Don't worry, we'll be fine. I'll start looking for another job tomorrow."

"Well, what do you think, kids? Are you ready to go home now?" Maria asked.

"We're happy in our home in New York. It's big, and there's plenty of food there," Ray said, and Haley agreed.

"Kids, it's not our home, remember?" Maria said. "Tilly and Dusty were gracious enough to let us stay there, but it's time to return to the real world."

"Let's write to them," Ray suggested. "Maybe they'll invite us back."

"That's an excellent idea, kids," Maria said. "Write a letter, and I'll mail it tomorrow. I'm sure Tilly and Dusty would love to read your notes."

Upon arriving home, the family discovered an eviction notice taped on the front door. Matt ripped the note in half and inserted his key into the lock. It would not work. The landlord changed the lock, making it impossible for them to enter. Their furniture was still inside the house when they peeked through the window. Matt kicked open the door in frustration. He noticed their neighbors gathered outside; their eyes were red with rage. Matt considered these people friends, including Linda, who was close to Maria. Maria made brief eye contact with her, but Linda turned away as if she had a communicable disease.

"His innocent demeanor deceives," she warned. "He is a dangerous man and a bad father," she warned.

Their friends' sudden outburst disappointed Matt and Maria. They thought their friends would be more understanding and supportive. They felt let down and hurt by their friends' reactions.

"Everyone, please listen. How long have we known each other?" Matt questioned the crowd. "Over the past ten years, we have been friends, and our families have enjoyed picnics in the park or fishing at the lake. We have watched our children grow up together. You have known me for years. I have stolen nothing. A coworker set me up, and they found her guilty in court this morning. They arrested her."

"Leave this neighborhood or, better yet, move to another city. We don't want you near our children," they screamed.

"The court found me innocent. They cleared me of all charges. What more do you want me to say?" Matt asked.

No one listened to him. Matt felt like a stranger in his town. What Matt and Maria did not realize was that their friends and neighbors reacted that way for a reason. Nobody could forget the night the cops stormed into Matt's house. When they couldn't find anyone there, they questioned everyone in the neighborhood. The police even checked their homes and searched their cars. They were terrified and shaken up. Everyone was worried about what the police might do next. They felt violated and harassed. The police officers left, but the damage was done. The group formed a negative impression of Matt and agreed to avoid him at all costs. They don't want to experience the same thing again.

"You're the most awful father ever!" Linda screamed. "You stole money from a toy company. It's like taking candy from a baby. Stay away from our kids!"

"You are wrong! My dad is the best in the world," Ray said, tears streaming down his cheeks.

Matt calmed his son down but sensed the neighbors were hostile. He told Maria and the children to get into the car. It did not matter what he said; his friends concluded he was guilty. For the first time, he was afraid of what they might do to him.

"Dad, what about my toys?" Ray asked. "We have to get them."

"Can't you see?" Haley said. "We have no home, you Dum Dum."

"Haley, don't call your brother that. Everyone, please calm down," Maria begged.

When the family returned to their car, it wouldn't start, worsening the situation.

"What are we going to do?" Maria asked.

"Maybe the battery is dead. Stay in the car and don't get out. Make sure you lock the doors," Matt instructed.

Maria nodded. She felt her heart pounding in her chest. She prayed Matt could start the car again so they could leave.

Matt popped the hood release to see if he could figure out what was wrong with it. He was right. The battery died. There was a jumper cable in the trunk, but what use would it be without another car to use it on? The neighbors were still yelling at Matt, so he knew he could not ask them for help. When they started throwing things at him, Matt told Maria they needed to leave. Without a car, they didn't know which way to go. They could hear the crowd laughing as they walked.

"Where are we going?" Maria asked.

"I don't know, Maria. It's getting dark, and we shouldn't be here longer than necessary. It is likely that our friends and neighbors would harm us if given the opportunity. Now let's get moving."

As they walked down the sidewalk, a black limousine passed them. As the car backed up, the driver called Matt's name.

"Matt Calderon?" the driver asked as he rolled down the window.

"Yes?" Matt replied.

"Hello, my name is David. I apologize for being late, sir. I was supposed to pick you up in front of the courthouse hours ago, but an accident happened. The cops blocked the road, and I got stuck in traffic. The hotel manager gave me your home address. I had to take a detour to get here. I hope I didn't inconvenience you."

"Who sent you?"

"My instructions are to pick you up at the courthouse and take you to the Westside Hotel," the driver said. "If you need more information, ask the hotel manager when you check in."

Matt and Maria sighed in relief. There was only one person who could do this—Tilly. She saved them again. Tilly always showed up at the right moment. Maria sat in the back seat with the children, while Matt sat in the front seat with the driver.

Matt and Maria felt the sadness that weighed them down when they saw their neighbors staring in disbelief as they drove away. There was a lump in their throat and tears in their eyes. It was something they had to face, and they knew it would be difficult for them. As they left behind their lives, they had to say goodbye to the past and look forward to the future. It was a bittersweet sorrow, as they both expressed joy and sadness. Tilly's help brought them joy. Feelings of sadness because their friends betrayed them.

The limousine pulled up in front of the most luxurious hotel in town. The doorman opened the door for them. Upon entering, the family was taken aback. The lobby had a white Christmas tree in the center and a lush tropical garden with exotic plants and flowers. It also had flowing fountains and art collections in the area. It was truly a work of art. The manager greeted them and led them to their suite. The family's jaw dropped, and they breathed in awe when the door opened. There was a double sided fireplace in the room. There were pool tables, ping-pong tables, and air hockey tables scattered throughout the place. A large terrace overlooks a lovely interior courtyard. It moved them to tears when they noticed a Christmas tree, a bicycle, and a plethora of presents underneath. A Chihuahua ran up to Haley and licked her face until she laughed. She petted the dog, rubbed her ears, and hugged her. Then she dashed off with Ray to check the gifts under the tree with their names on them.

"My name is Bill, and I am at your service. Please contact me if you need anything. You have a dinner reservation at Ray's Bistro at 7:00 p.m. It's located downstairs next to the gift shop."

"We do?"

"Yes, sir."

"When did this happen? The limo, the room, the Christmas tree, and the presents?"

"All I know, sir, is that Mrs. Bonaventura's secretary made the arrangements yesterday. We have strict orders to serve you. The limo driver arrived at the courthouse to pick you up, but confusion ensued. I believe there was an accident, and he did not arrive on time. Fortunately, I found your name in the phone book and gave the driver your address. He picked you up at your house instead. We apologize for the inconvenience."

Matt nodded and thanked the manager. He took out his wallet and gave him his last few dollars.

"I appreciate it, sir, but Mrs. Bonaventura took care of everything. Have a pleasant stay." The manager exited the room and shut the door behind him.

"Matt, what's going on?" Maria asked, confused but excited.

"Leave it to Tilly to make us feel like royalty," Matt said. "It's Christmas Eve, and I can't believe she remembered Ray's bike and Haley's dog. Tilly is our guardian angel."

They could hear their children's laughter and see the excitement in their eyes as they tore the wrapping paper off their packages. It was the best Christmas they ever had.

A short time later, there was a knock on the door. Matt opened it, and the manager handed him a white envelope.

"This has just arrived, sir."

"Thank you," Matt said.

The manager nodded and walked away.

"What is it?" Maria asked.

Matt shrugged as he opened the envelope and read the letter.

We don't always understand why things happen to us or what their purposes are. What matters is that we are strong and present for our family. I've given you a second chance, Matt. Don't throw it away. Of course, if you have enough money to start over, you can better support your family. I hope this check will be helpful. Spend it wisely. We hope you enjoy our gifts. Merry Christmas. Please send our love to Ray and Haley. Always, Tilly. P.S. We know how much your children love New York. I have a job waiting for you at my company if you decide to move there. P.P.S. We learned you were being evicted just as we planned to surprise you with Christmas presents. That's why we moved it to a hotel. It's not home, but we hope it's close enough to feel like home.

Matt couldn't contain his happiness. He opened the envelope and found a one-million-dollar check made out to him. When he showed it to Maria, his hand shook, and they both looked at each other in disbelief.

"No way! This is insane!" Maria exclaimed, laughing hysterically. "Tilly told us that our lives were about to change. I didn't realize she meant to give us this much money. We have an angel in Tilly, our Mrs. Millionaire. This is a million-dollar chance she gave us."

"You can see a specialist now, Maria. There will be a cure for you. We can give our children an excellent education and a good life."

"I know, Matt, I know," Maria said as she wept.

"Tilly also offered me a job in her company. Children, we're moving to New York after all," Matt announced.

Ray and Haley's screams were so deafeningly loud that everyone in the corridor could hear them. They hugged each other and jumped up and down in excitement.

Matt's face lit up with happiness and peace. He picked up his wife, swung her around, and kissed her. Then he took his children and hugged them. Their laughter rang throughout the room. They knew their lives had changed for the better, thanks to Tilly and Dusty.

TILLY AND DUSTY STOOD in the shadows in the darkest corner of the Italian restaurant, not wanting to be seen. They could see Maria's radiant smile as she laughed aloud. Tilly and Dusty smiled when they noticed Ray and Haley's eyes widening when the food arrived. They watched as the two took their first bites, savoring the taste and exclaiming how delicious it was.

And what about Matt? They saw how he adored his wife and children and looked at them with a twinkle in his eyes. He was at peace—such blissful contentment. Tilly could see the joy on the children's faces. Maria even sobbed, and Matt had to console her several times. Then they both burst out laughing so hard that they cried.

It moved Dusty to tears while watching the family. It overjoyed him that his wife had helped another family in need. Dusty knew Tilly's mission and efforts were worthwhile after witnessing Matt's happiness and contentment. He wanted to be part of her charitable work more than ever. Dusty eagerly awaited their next adventure and meeting Tilly's next recipient.

"I love you, Mrs. Millionaire," Dusty said as he took Tilly's hand in his and led her outside for her special Christmas gift. Dusty arranged for a horse-drawn carriage to pick them up. He whisked his wife away on an enchanting ride through town on a chilly night under the full moon.

"There's only one thing missing to make this a perfect Christmas," Tilly said.

"What is it?"

"Snow."

And miraculously, snow fell all around them.

"Now it's perfect. This is the best white Christmas ever!" Tilly laughed.

Dusty kissed his wife as the driver took them through the Christmas-decorated city. Hundreds of multi-colored lights lined the streets, hanging from sidewalk to sidewalk, with bright red bows and bells tied to each lamp post, creating an impressive lighting display.

A truly magical night!

———— ⟨◦⟩ ————

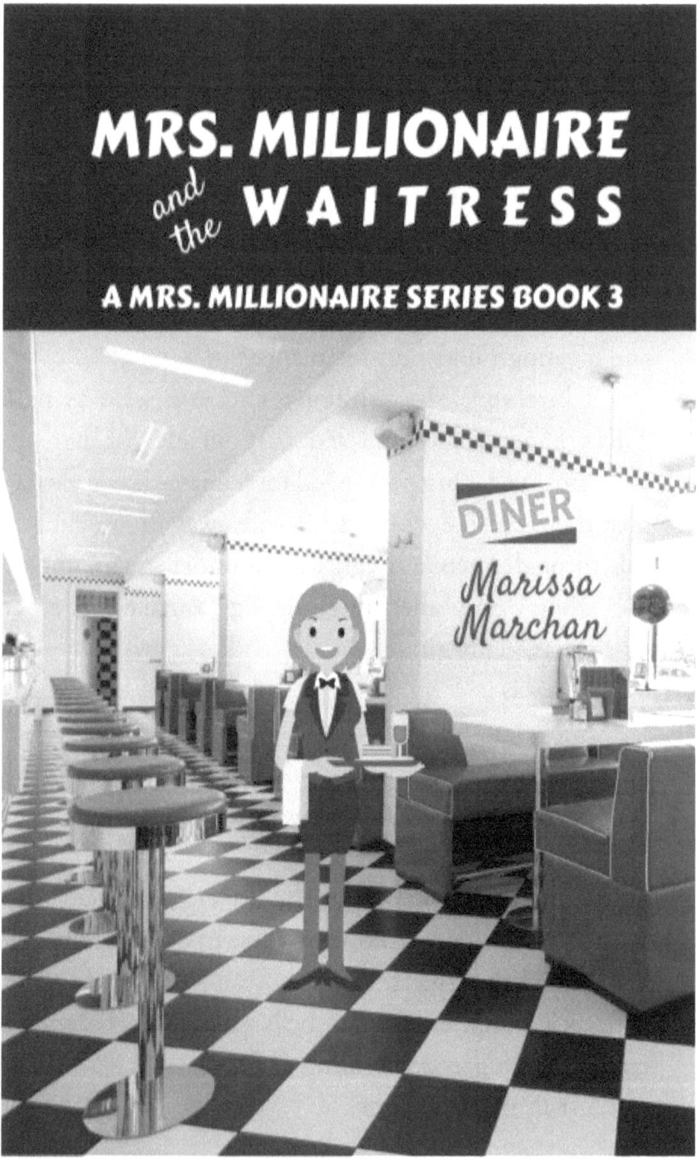
MRS. MILLIONAIRE
and the WAITRESS
A MRS. MILLIONAIRE SERIES BOOK 3
DINER
Marissa
Marchan

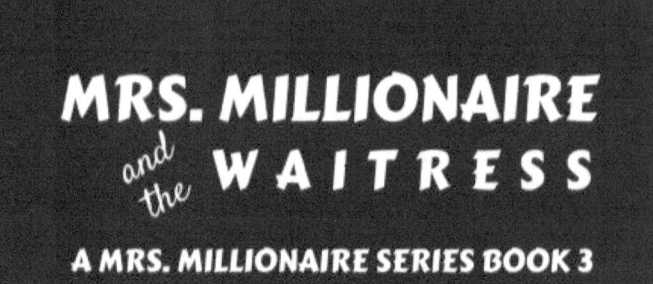

MRS. MILLIONAIRE AND THE WAITRESS

CHAPTER ONE

It was a busy Sunday morning at Mel's Diner, a local favorite in Victorville, California. It was a small desert town on the way to Las Vegas. People regarded Mel's Diner for its exceptional classic American dinner dishes and personable staff. It was a popular stop for travelers and locals alike.

Chaos ensued as the crowded diner served a popular Sunday brunch special. The bell clanged on the door as a stream of people arrived. A line of customers waited to be seated, and children ran amok while their parents watched. Laughter and conversation filled the restaurant. The aromas of brewed coffee, bacon, eggs, blueberry pancakes, cinnamon French toast with warm maple syrup, and sausage wafted through the air.

The servers gathered the dishes, balanced the trays, and cleaned the tables while the hostess greeted and seated the guests. Lucy, the youngest of the three servers, poured coffee into customers' cups while sitting at the long counter. She smiled at them as she spoke. Soon after, she heard the cook yell, "Pick up!" at the top of his lungs while ringing the bell.

"Hold your horses. I'll be right there!" Lucy said.

She stacked the plates on her arms to deliver the food, called out each order, and nodded to the person who ordered it. After placing the plates on the table, she asked if there was anything else the customers needed before returning to the kitchen to pick up another order to serve. Afterward, she assisted with clearing the tables and replenishing salt and pepper shakers and napkin holders in anticipation of the next set of patrons. She hadn't finished cleaning up when construction workers arrived. Lucy sighed. She knew she had a long day ahead of her.

After several hours of working nonstop to serve food and beverages, the restaurant finally calmed down. Lucy collapsed into a chair, exhausted. She took a deep breath and thanked God for giving her the strength to work her shift. Lucy gathered her things and headed home.

Waitressing was perceived as a straightforward job. They considered it a position that did not call for substantial skill or knowledge. What people didn't know was that it was hard work. It was physically demanding, with long hours and tight deadlines. You had to multitask, including taking orders, serving customers, clearing tables, restocking the kitchen, and handling customer complaints. You had to stay focused and organized.

Lucy worked long hours for little pay, not to mention the physical fitness and balance required to carry trays to and from tables. She had to deal with rude customers and low-tippers. The kids threw food at her, and many customers yelled at her, particularly outsiders. But the customer was always right, and Lucy had to smile even when they weren't.

Sometimes she wanted to give up, but she had responsibilities. She had a family who relied on her income.

Everyone in their small town knew Lucy's family had taken advantage of her generosity. They knew money was tight, but they continued to buy things on credit and expected Lucy to take on the never-ending debt without complaining.

Marge, Lucy's best friend and supervisor at Mel's Diner, tried to convince her to speak up and tell her family that enough was enough. Marge was a shoulder to cry on and a source of moral support. Lucy knew Marge was right. She didn't seem to be a family member. Lucy was an outsider, and she was afraid to talk to her family. That was why it was so difficult, because they were the only relatives she had left, her only living flesh and blood. Lucy did not know what she had done to deserve their treatment. She worked hard to please them and even let her family walk all over her for years.

Lucy suspected her inability to defend herself occurred after her father's death two years ago. She felt obligated to live a miserable life for the rest of her life. Lucy would have quit her job long ago if it hadn't been for her employer, regular and loyal customers, and the rest of the diner's staff. They treated her as one of their own, more than her family could provide for her.

Lucy had to rush home after her day shift to prepare for her second job as a cocktail waitress at Harley's, a popular local nightclub. Lucy lied about her age in order to get a job there. She wasn't old enough to drink, let alone serve alcohol, but she needed another job to supplement her income.

Lucy took a quick shower and changed her clothes. The makeup she wore made it impossible to tell how old she was. She double-checked herself in the mirror to ensure she looked her best. The bar owner sometimes held special events at the club. This time, it was the boss' daughter's birthday. Lucy had to look stunning and be extra friendly to customers. She counted on the tips she would make that night.

Lucy did not know she came from a prominent family with a silver spoon in her mouth. But how did this happen? How did her family keep her unaware of her privileged background? Were they trying to protect her from the expectations of others? Or was it something else?

Lucy had a happy and comfortable life as the only child in a wealthy family until her mother died. Lucy was too young to remember her. She was only two years old when it happened. Her father, Nicholas, had been heartbroken for a long time. So when an attractive young widow with two children from a previous relationship came along and started moving on him, Nicholas fell for her charms, and they married soon thereafter. Patricia was a heartless gold digger who enjoyed parties and the good life.

Nicholas, encouraged by his new wife, never told Lucy the truth about her dead mother, so Lucy grew up believing her stepmother was her actual mother. When Nicholas arrived home early from the office one day and discovered his wife was punishing Lucy for no apparent reason, he ignored the warning voice in his head. Patricia convinced him of Lucy's proper behavior training, and this continued until she reached her teenage years.

Lucy was by far the most beautiful girl in high school, in every sense of the word. She was intelligent and popular, and her peers voted for her as homecoming and prom queen. Lucy dated the school's most attractive, wealthy, and popular students, whom the other girls coveted. But she wasn't just a pretty face. Her intelligence matched her beauty, making her the envy of everyone at school. Lucy was smart, kind, and concerned about others, and it was the combination of these qualities that shaped her into the charming young woman she became. Her father was so proud of her, but he was unaware that Patricia and her two children despised his daughter.

Lucy's life turned upside down when her father died of heart failure while watching television. He addressed his last words to his daughter, Lucy, which enraged his wife and stepchildren. Jealous of the love and affection her husband gave to his daughter even at his last breath, Patricia fired the housemaid after the funeral. She forced Lucy to do chores in the house. Patricia told Lucy that her father left them penniless. It was the day Patricia found a copy of her husband's life insurance policy inside a briefcase. It named Lucy as the sole beneficiary.

Patricia, filled with rage and anger, falsified the documents and, with the help of a lawyer friend, became the beneficiary of everything, including Lucy's trust fund. She moved to a luxury apartment overlooking Spring Valley Lake as soon as the money appeared in her bank account. She left the house without informing Lucy. Patricia splurged on an expensive sports car, designer clothes, and expensive handbags. Her son, Ricky, and daughter, Venus, flew to Paris and stayed in luxury hotels. They bought expensive clothing, gourmet dinners, and chauffeured trips around Europe without a care in the world. Their mother paid for it.

Patricia and her children abandoned Lucy. She returned home from school and found herself alone in the house. Her mother's and siblings' rooms were empty, and their clothes were missing. Lucy screamed and cried all night, but no one heard her. She didn't know why her family had left her. They didn't even leave her a note. Lucy opened the fridge after calming down and discovered nothing to eat. Lucy looked through the cupboards and found vegetable cans and ramen noodles. She searched through the house, but all she found was change. Lucy knew she was on her own, with no one to help her. But she was a fighter. That's what her father told her. It hurt Lucy, but she vowed to make her life worthwhile.

Lucy was only a few months away from graduating and more than a month away from her seventeenth birthday. With her father's death and her family abandoning her, she dropped out of school to find a job to survive. This was much to her teachers' chagrin because she was on track to be valedictorian. Lucy's ambitions took a back seat to supporting herself. She planned to return to school when she could.

Lucy told no one about her family's abandonment. The thought of being taken away from home by child welfare frightened her. Lucy worked part time at Hardy's Pet Store in the morning and Kayla's Yogurt Shop in the afternoon. They paid her minimum wage, but it helped pay bills and buy food and other necessities. Seeing her friends hang out at work after school was unsettling for a young teenager. She knew they made fun of her behind her back. It was very depressing, but Lucy couldn't do anything about it. She did what she had to do.

Patricia lived the life she'd always wanted, crossing the state line to gamble at casinos. She won at first, but became addicted and lost a lot of money every time she visited, which was almost every day. As her losses increased, she became desperate and unable to stop gambling. She lost everything, including her apartment, car, and everything else, to pay off her debts.

For a moment, Ricky's and Venus' lives seemed fine. The two rented a two-bedroom apartment near the beach. They went to nightclubs and socialized with strangers. They dined out at fancy restaurants and bought expensive clothes. The two felt free and alive, far away from their troubles. They acted like spoiled rich kids, partying and drinking until they ran out of money. They called their mother to ask for more money, but Patricia told them to pack their belongings instead.

"Your vacation has ended. You must return home," she told her children.

Ricky and Venus refused to leave, and the apartment manager evicted them because they could not pay their rent. With nowhere else to go, Ricky and Venus had to take the next flight home.

Lucy returned home from work one day, surprised to see light coming from the house. As she entered, she noticed a few pieces of luggage in the entryway. Lucy walked into the kitchen, surprised to see her mother and siblings eating pizza at the dining table. There were no greetings exchanged. The sudden situation left Lucy unsure of how to react. Patricia noticed her presence and looked up with a forced smile. Lucy's siblings kept their heads down and ate. Lucy wanted to vent her anger about living alone in the house but quickly calmed down. She couldn't stay angry for too long. Lucy's excitement overtook her, and she hugged everyone.

"I can't believe you're home! Where have you been? You were away for a long time. I was worried about you. Why did you leave? And what compelled you to return?" She asked nonstop.

Patricia and her children never responded. Their reaction to seeing Lucy was not pleasant, and they never explained why they had returned home. Lucy didn't expect them to answer. She was just relieved to see them again. The house was too empty and lonely without her family. Lucy was certain to resume her education now that they were home. She welcomed them back into her life without hesitation.

Patricia and her children's quick spending made their return home bittersweet. After tasting the good life, they didn't feel obligated to work, so they slept all day and stayed up all night.

CHAPTER TWO

Lucy was kind, loving, and understanding. After Patricia told her she would not return to school without explaining why, Lucy was disappointed but respected her mother's decision. Even when Patricia told her she should continue working until her siblings found jobs, she never held grudges. Lucy had to quit working part time at the pet store and the yogurt shop because she could not support her family on her nominal salary alone. She accepted a full-time server position at a nearby restaurant with higher pay, including tips. Lucy lacked experience, but she knew Marge, a regular customer at the pet store. She hired Lucy on the spot.

Lucy returned home from work to find a large flat-screen TV in the living room.

"Where did you get that?" she asked.

"We bought it," Venus replied, sitting on the couch and eating popcorn while watching TV.

Lucy smiled. "Does this mean you have a job?"

"No, I didn't get a job," Venus replied, smirking.

"So, where did you get the money to buy a TV?"

"It's so simple these days to buy something with store credit."

Lucy sighed. She shook her head and said nothing. She walked to the kitchen to prepare dinner.

A month passed, with Ricky sitting in front of the television all day. Venus was on the phone with her friends, and their mother was out with her friends. Lucy returned home from work to find Ricky in the living room. She noticed an envelope from Easy Credit addressed to her. She opened it and choked when she saw a $1,500 charge for a television set. Lucy became enraged. Her brother and sister had purchased the TV with her credit, and she now had to pay for it. Lucy took a deep breath and relaxed before speaking to Ricky.

"The income I earn is not enough to provide for our family. I can't even afford food, let alone television. We need to return it," Lucy said, standing in front of him. "Did you hear what I said?"

"Yeah, I heard you the first time," Ricky said, but he never took his attention away from the television.

A frustrated Lucy went to her room and sobbed on her pillow, not being able to get help from Ricky. How would she pay for the TV? How could she make her family help her? It was the longest night of her life.

As if that weren't bad enough, they fired Lucy from her second job at Harley's the next day when they discovered she was underage. She felt overwhelmed and helpless. Her life seemed to slip away from her.

Lucy worked an extra shift at the restaurant, day and night, to earn more money to cover for the TV. One day, Venus told her she needed a cell phone. She stated it was critical for her to have a phone she could carry anywhere.

The TV was such a frustration for Lucy, but now Venus demanded to get her a phone. The only way Lucy could find peace was by giving in to her sister, who complained all the time. She bought a refurbished phone from a computer store. Lucy's high school friend worked there, so he gave her 50% off. She felt guilty for caving into Venus' demands, but she knew it was the only thing that would end the conflict. Lucy was thankful for the discount given by a friend in the store. It was ironic that neither of her siblings ever thanked her.

Meanwhile, Patricia joined a senior citizens' club at the town hall ballroom dance. She acted like a teenager, wearing heavy makeup and a different outfit every night. When Patricia fell head over heels in love with her dance instructor, thirty years her junior, Patricia spoiled him with clothes and everything he wished for. She even stole Lucy's emergency cash from her drawer. When Patricia's money ran out and she couldn't buy her boyfriend what he wanted, the young hustler threatened to end their relationship. Patricia didn't want to lose him, so she promised to get the money for him. She returned to Lucy's room and found a gold necklace her father had given her. Patricia took the jewelry and sold it.

TILLY AND HER HUSBAND, Dusty, a globe-trotting multi-millionaire power couple, led a glamorous lifestyle, but they were also serious philanthropists. They were in Los Angeles for an annual fundraising event for one of their foundations, benefiting the Children's Orphanage of America. The event raised enough money to construct a playground and an additional wing to give the children more space. It was such a success that a private event organizer invited the couple to attend a benefit concert in Las Vegas over the weekend. This event was to benefit a variety of causes, including helping street children, literary advocacy, drug treatment programs, and mental health. Dusty and Tilly agreed to attend. They planned to see a show while they were there.

It was a lovely Saturday morning, the perfect day for a drive. Tilly packed their belongings and left early to avoid rush hour traffic. They allocated extra time for driving so they could take in the scenery before the charity event started at 6 p.m.

Unfortunately, the rental car overheated and left them stranded in Victorville. Dusty called up a tow truck, and the driver arrived. They had their vehicle towed to the nearest auto shop, where a mechanic checked it. There was no major problem, but he lacked parts. The employee called the auto parts store, and the next delivery was on Monday.

"Sweetheart, we'll be late for the charity event," Tilly said.

The mechanic heard what she had said.

"If you need to get to Las Vegas, there is a bus leaving this afternoon. There is also a car rental a few blocks away," he added.

"I appreciate sharing that information. Where can you get food in this area?" Dusty asked. "I'm hungry."

"There's Mel's Diner across the street. The best food in Victorville."

Dusty thanked the man and said they would eat first and return later. He instructed the mechanic to call the other auto shop for the parts.

"I'll do my best," the man said.

"Let's eat," Dusty said to Tilly, taking her hand as they crossed the street.

A homeless woman stood outside the café with her face against the window. Hank, the diner owner, shooed her away as she upset the customers.

Lucy was taking orders from Tilly and Dusty when she saw what Hank had done to the poor lady. She excused herself and headed to the kitchen. Lucy returned with a brown bag of food, which she handed to the woman. Lucy hugged her and walked back inside to work.

Tilly smiled as she observed everything. "Did you notice that? People no longer do things like that for others."

Dusty agreed with a shrug of his shoulders. "Yeah, our waitress is something else."

Dusty ordered the traditional meatloaf, while Tilly had a tuna melt. Soon, the food arrived. Tilly hadn't finished her sandwich when she noticed a young woman wearing cut jeans and a heavy metal T-shirt with gelled and pointed hair enter. Tilly took pleasure in watching people. She maintained her focus on where the girl was going. When the woman saw Lucy, she walked up to her and whispered something in her ear.

"Excuse me, sir. I'll be back to take your order," Lucy informed the customer.

The gentleman looked annoyed as he nodded his head and looked at the menu. Lucy motioned for Venus to follow her to the back room. Tilly was on her way to the restroom to freshen up when she heard the women conversing.

"Are you going to give me the money or what?" Venus asked.

"I told you I couldn't give you money. I didn't get paid yet."

"How will I explain this to my friends? They're waiting for me."

Lucy looked out the window and noticed a yellow convertible with two girls in the back seat and a young man driving.

"Just tell your friends you're broke. They will understand if they are your friends."

"Easy for you to say. You have no life."

"I don't have a life because I'm too busy supporting you all."

"Enough with the lecture, Lucy. You are not my mother. If you give me the money, I'll stop bothering you."

"Venus, even if I wanted to, I didn't have money."

"You always say that. You are stingy!"

"Venus, I work hard to have a roof over our heads and food on the table. I haven't had a day off in a long time. Why don't you get a job and help me out instead of asking for money?"

"Oh, just shut up and forget about it."

Venus exited, slamming the door behind her.

"Wait, is that your sister?" Marge asked.

Lucy nodded.

"Listen, Lucy. I'm telling you. Your family abuses you. Tell them to back off and find work so they don't have to rely on you all the time. Stop being such a sweetheart."

Lucy nodded again. If only Marge knew she was afraid of being thrown out of the house by her family. She knew they would do it in a heartbeat. Where would she go? She then returned to the gentleman to finish his order.

Tilly shook her head after witnessing their heated arguments. She wished she had siblings so she could discuss things with them. Being an only child was difficult for her. Tilly returned to her seat when her husband perused the mini dessert menu. Dusty ordered a cheesecake for him and a chocolate cake for her. The taste was so good that Dusty ordered another. Tilly saw a young man enter the diner as she wiped her mouth.

"Speak of the devil," Marge said louder than she realized, drawing Tilly's and Dusty's attention. "What brings you here, Ricky?"

"I'm looking for my sister. Is she here?"

"She's with a customer. What do you want?"

"If you don't mind, I need to speak with her."

"Like I said, she's with a customer right now. Wait until she finishes," Marge said.

Ricky nodded and sat in the waiting area, agitated. When he saw Lucy walking towards the kitchen, he stopped her.

"What are you doing here, Ricky? I thought you started work today." Lucy asked.

"It didn't work out. My boss fired me."

"Fired? On your first day?" Lucy asked.

"I left because of a disagreement with the owner."

"For God's sake, what happened?"

"He insisted I clean the office toilet. I refused because I don't do toilets."

"Ricky, I pulled some strings to get you that job. You're a janitor. Cleaning toilets is part of your job."

"It's your fault. You didn't tell me."

"Ricky, that job pays $12 an hour."

"Don't make me feel guilty, because it won't work. I'm here to ask you for $20. My friends and I wanted to hang out, and they told me it was my turn to bring the booze."

Lucy sighed in frustration. "I'm sorry, but I don't have any money."

"What do you mean, you don't have money? You are selfish."

"Selfish? I'm exhausted and need help. I've been working hard to support our family." Lucy sounded like a broken record.

"Enough with your lecture, Lucy. So, are you going to give me the money or not?"

"As I told Venus earlier, I don't have any money to give you."

"What will I tell my friends then?"

"Tell them they fired you from your job, and you have no money."

"I can't tell them that. It would embarrass me too much."

"I'm sorry, but I have nothing to give you. You should leave. I'm still working, and Hank stares at me strangely. We both know I need this job."

It enraged Ricky when he left, and he slammed the door behind him. Tilly and Dusty heard everything. They looked at Lucy and felt sorry for her. The girl looked younger than her siblings, but that didn't stop them from taking advantage of her.

CHAPTER THREE

Dusty called the auto shop to check on their car. The mechanic said he attempted to contact several auto parts stores in Victorville and even Barstow, but they were closed or did not have the parts. When the store reopened on Monday, he would call them back.

"What shall we do until then?" Tilly asked.

Dusty answered, "I don't feel like going to the fundraiser. Let's tell Mrs. Lewis we won't be attending. I'll contact the rental company to request a replacement car. Let's find a place to stay tonight."

"And then what?"

"We're already here. We can explore the town in the morning if you like."

"I think that's a wonderful idea," Tilly said.

Lucy walked up to their table and interrupted their conversation.

"Is there anything else I can get you?" Lucy asked as she poured coffee into their cups.

"It seems we're stuck here. Are there any recommendations for where to stay?" Dusty asked.

"There's a motel a block away. It's a cute little place, but it's clean. Homer, the manager, is friendly. Tell him I sent you."

"Thanks, we'll check it out."

"You're not from around here, are you?" Lucy asked.

"No, we had car trouble on our way to Las Vegas," Dusty explained.

"I see."

Moments later, an older woman walked into the coffee shop. She approached Lucy and whispered something in her ear when she saw her. Dusty and Tilly raised their eyebrows. Another family member?

"Please, not here, Mom. You could get me fired."

"I'll leave if you give me some money," Patricia said.

"I'm sorry, Mom, but I have no money. There was nothing left after paying the bills."

"Lucy, my boyfriend is waiting for me. Don't embarrass me. Either you give me the money now or I swear I'll do something drastic that you won't like."

Marge heard their loud conversation and told them to keep their voices down since the customers were staring.

"Mom, I beg you, please leave. You'll get me in trouble at work again." Lucy sobbed. "I need this job."

"You know I will not leave, Lucy, until you give me the money, or should I continue to embarrass you in front of everyone in this room?"

Lucy looked around to see if anyone had heard what her mother had said. She dropped her head in shame when she noticed Tilly looking at her. Lucy wondered why her mother humiliated her in front of customers with such a fuss. If she had money, she would have given it to her, but she didn't. It was difficult for her to comprehend why the job she had worked so hard for was being threatened by her mother and siblings all the time.

When Patricia grew impatient, she grabbed Lucy's hand and walked outside. Dusty and Tilly watched Lucy's mother slap her face in the parking lot. Tilly looked away in disgust as Patricia screamed at her daughter. Dusty felt anger welling up inside him as Lucy's tears streamed down her face.

"This is too much!" Tilly exclaimed.

She was about to walk outside to help Lucy when Dusty stopped her. He said it was a family matter, and they should not get involved in their business.

"All right, but if that woman slaps that young waitress again, I'm not letting her get away with it. I'm going to call the cops."

Patricia walked to her car, leaving Lucy crying. She wiped away her tears before entering the diner. Lucy drew Marge aside and then took the tip money from a glass bowl and gave it to her mother, who followed her.

"Why do you keep making things difficult?" Patricia asked as she took the money from Lucy's hands.

Watching her mother get into a car, Lucy wiped her tears with her backhands before walking to the restroom. Tilly followed her. Lucy was washing her face, rubbing her fingers under her eyes, and wiping away tears. Tilly couldn't help but sympathize with her. She put her arms around Lucy and hugged her. Lucy looked up at Tilly and smiled, grateful for the gesture of support.

"It's okay. Don't cry," Tilly said as she handed her a handkerchief.

"Thank you," she said, smiling.

"Try not to be bothered by it. Things will work out," Tilly assured her as best she could.

Lucy looked up into Tilly's face and saw her sincerity. She handed her napkin back, saying, "Thank you. I feel so much better now." She introduced herself as Lucy.

"You are welcome, Lucy. My name is Tilly. Nice to meet you."

"I apologize for my behavior." Lucy laughed as she described the drama as a family affair.

When they exited the restroom, they ran into Hank in the hallway. Before leaving for a fishing trip with his buddies, he told Lucy that if there was an emergency, she should call him right away. Hank asked Lucy to review the cash receipts and sales slips at the end of each day because Marge was having trouble balancing the cash flow. He gave Lucy the key to his office, main door, and desk. Hank told her to put the money in the drawer. He would deposit it when he returned. Lucy nodded and placed the key in her pocket. Marge didn't appear offended by Hank's decision. She admitted that math was not her favorite subject.

As soon as Hank left, Lucy took two apples and peach cobblers from the bakery display case. She topped them with vanilla ice cream and handed them to Dusty and Tilly.

"It's complimentary. This is my way of saying thank you for making me feel better earlier," she said.

"Lucy," Tilly said. "Could you please sit down for a moment?"

Lucy pulled up a chair and sat down next to them. "I know what you're about to say," she exclaimed. "Why do I allow my family to do this to me?"

"I know it's none of our business, but I have to know," Tilly said. "Aren't they your siblings? The girl and the boy who were here earlier?"

It was difficult for Lucy to tell her life story to a virtual stranger, but she felt the need to do so. She had suppressed her feelings for a long time. If she didn't let the rage out, she would explode.

"Isn't that surprising?" Lucy asked. "Being the youngest, you'd think they'd want to take care of me instead of bossing me around."

"And what about the older lady?"

"She's my mother," Lucy replied. "Sometimes I get the impression they don't want me. The way they treat me makes me feel like an adopted child."

For a while, Tilly and Dusty remained silent. They were both perplexed. Based on what they had seen earlier, they could conclude that Lucy's family did not care for her. Tilly had more questions, but when the customers arrived, Lucy excused herself and stood up to greet them. She seated them at an empty table before handing them the menus.

After seeing that Lucy was busy, Tilly and Dusty checked into the motel Lucy recommended before it got dark. They left a $100 bill for their meal, and Lucy was grateful for the generous tip.

MEL'S DINER BUSTLED with customers that night. After playing bingo in the hall across the street, a group of senior citizens ate dinner there. The servers were busy, but they smiled as they served everyone. As they waited for their food, the seniors chatted and laughed. Everyone cheered when the food arrived and thanked the servers for their service. Their conversation continued until it was time for them to leave.

The last customer left half an hour ago, and the staff went home. Lucy stayed at the office to balance the daily sales. She slid the cash box into the drawer and locked it. She double-checked the kitchen door and closed all access points before turning off the lights and locking the front door before leaving.

Nobody was home, and the house was dark. Lucy entered her room and placed her hard-earned money in a piggy bank, where she hid it in the closet. She was saving it for the night classes she planned to take to get her high school diploma. She would not spend a penny of this money on anything except her education and future. Lucy put the office keys on top of the dresser and took a quick shower. After changing into her pajamas, she turned on the TV in the living room. Lucy checked the kitchen for food. There were none. She sighed and shook her head. She remembered the paper bag Marge had given her earlier in the day.

"Good old Marge," she murmured as she opened the bag, revealing a bowl of chili and a corned beef sandwich.

Lucy placed a tray in front of the television and microwaved the chili. She had barely sat down when the door opened and Ricky walked in. He demanded money from her. When Lucy said she didn't have any money to give him, Ricky became enraged. He dragged her to her room.

"I know you have a stash of cash here. Hand it over before I hurt you."

"Stop it! Why are you doing this?" She burst into tears.

Ricky began searching Lucy's room, but he stopped when he saw Mel's key chain on the dresser.

"What are these keys for?"

"Don't touch that. It belongs to my boss."

"You mean Hank trusts you that much? What's going on between you two?"

"Stop it, Ricky. He's an old man. Show respect."

Their attention suddenly focused on their mother, who was returning from a night out.

"What's going on here?" she asked, raising an eyebrow.

"I asked Lucy for money, but she refused."

"Here you go again, Lucy. You're always causing trouble," Patricia remarked.

That was the last straw. Lucy couldn't take it anymore.

"Why does everyone look at me like I'm a money bag? I work hard to provide for our family. I pay the bills and buy food. Could you please explain why I am the only one with a job? I'm your daughter, too, Mom. What have I done to deserve this treatment?"

Ricky and Patricia stared at Lucy in disgust and left the room, leaving Lucy crying.

Lucy arrived at Hank's office early in the morning to prepare the deposit slips for him. Hank would be returning the next day from his fishing trip. Three hundred dollars were missing from the cash box, and she was the only one with the key. Lucy knew Hank would hold her responsible for it. What would she do? She accounted for the cash receipts and locked the drawer last night, so no one could have stolen it.

"Honey, are you okay?" Marge asked as she entered the room. "You look pale."

Lucy stared at her, terrified.

"Lucy, what is the matter? Why do you look like someone just died?"

Lucy couldn't stop crying. "Marge, I'm not sure what happened, but $300 is missing from our sales receipts."

"What? How did that happen?"

"I'm not sure. All I know is that I reconciled the receipts last night to ensure everything was ready for Hank."

"Money can't just walk away," Marge said, but she frowned when she noticed Lucy's red eyes as if she had cried all night. "Did anything happen at home again?"

"It was nothing," Lucy said.

Marge looked at her. "Lucy, you know you can tell me anything, right?"

Lucy couldn't lie to her. "Last night, my mother and Ricky ganged up on me because I didn't give them any money."

"Do you think your mother or Ricky had anything to do with the missing money?"

"Of course not. She's my mother, for goodness' sake. Why would she do that? She knew I'd be the first to be blamed. They know how important this job is to us."

"Okay, if you say so."

"How do I explain the missing money to Hank?"

Marge looked at her, shaking her head. "I'm not sure, but we need to come up with something quick."

Fortunately, the hall across the street had bingo night, filling up the diner. Lucy, Marge, and the diner staff worked late and pooled their tips to make up for the cash shortage. However, they were still short of a hundred dollars. Marge answered the phone when it rang, listening and nodding before hanging up.

"Marge, who was it?" Lucy asked.

"Lucy, we solved your problem. That was Hank on the phone. He won't return until Tuesday. That will give us another day to come up with the rest of the money."

The staff cheered and applauded. Relief washed over them. It was a close call.

CHAPTER FOUR

Lucy returned home, and the house was pitch black. As usual, no one was there. When Lucy flipped the switch, she sensed something wasn't right. It didn't take long to discover that someone had ransacked her room. Lucy opened the closet door to check on her piggy bank. She felt her heart racing and her hands trembling. Someone smashed it and took the money. Lucy became hysterical and threw things around. Her dreams of a diploma were shattered. As she walked into the living room, she looked for any other stolen items, but nothing was missing. Ricky's and Venus' rooms showed no evidence of a break-in.

As Lucy entered her mother's bedroom, it appeared to be in shambles. Her clothes and shoes were all over the floor, but she realized her mother was just sloppy. Upon checking the house, she found everything in order. Her room was the only one targeted. That much was clear. But why?

Lucy returned to her mother's room and found something from her childhood. It was her favorite book, a fairy tale her father read to her as a child. Her mother hid it beneath other items on the shelf. Lucy picked it up and clutched it to her chest, tears streaming down her cheeks. Having lost her father, she longed for him.

Lucy took the book and walked to her room. She opened it and leafed through it. Lucy remembered her father talking about a treasure hunt, and all she had to do was find it. She didn't understand what her father meant when he said that. Curiously, Lucy examined the book and noticed the back cover was thicker than the front. She took the scissors and cut along the edge. There was something behind it. There was a folded piece of paper inserted underneath. She opened it and found her birth certificate. How could someone hide it so well in that book? And why? Upon examining it, her birth certificate did not have Patricia's name on it, which puzzled her. It was Alicia.

It was a shock to Lucy. She struggled to believe that Patricia wasn't her real mother. Why would her father deceive her? Why would everyone lie to her? And why did her father bury it in her favorite book? Lucy trembled, unsure of what to do. Her father could no longer answer her questions.

After returning to Patricia's room, she opened the drawers in search of something that might shed light on this surprising development. There was a large envelope under the mattress. She found a copy of her father's marriage certificate, which shows that he married Patricia three years after she was born. Her heartbeat became even faster, and she struggled to breathe.

She sifted through the papers until she found the adoption certificate. Her father adopted Ricky and Venus a year after marrying Patricia. This meant she had no blood relationship with them. It all makes sense to her now. Patricia wasn't her biological mother, and her children were Venus and Ricky. It explained why she never felt at ease with any of them. They had mistreated her because she was not one of them. They never loved her. The only family she knew was a complete fabrication. They made her feel guilty, so she continued to work to support them. Lucy felt foolish and angry. She felt betrayed. Long, hysterical screams filled the room, and Lucy realized they were coming from within her.

Lucy considered confronting them about her discovery but lacked the courage. She wasn't sure if she was ready for the truth. Things had changed in her life, but she had difficulty processing them. There was one thing for sure: Lucy had never felt emotions like this before. There was a missing piece within her. Lucy felt lost and confused, not knowing what to do or how to feel.

As she lay on her bed, thinking, she noticed a stack of photo albums piled high in the corner. They were her baby pictures. She hadn't seen them for a long time. A book fell from her grasp as she leafed through it, and something fell out. It was her father's will.

PATRICIA ARRIVED HOME at midnight. She'd been out with her friends at a local pub again. Lucy was sitting on a chair in the dark. When she turned on the lamp, Patricia jumped.

"Why are you still up?" Patricia asked.

Lucy said nothing.

"So, what is this? Silent treatment? Are you trying to make me feel guilty for arriving home late?"

Lucy sighed before speaking. It was time to confront her family.

"I discovered you are not my biological mother," she said.

Patricia's eyes widened, and it left her speechless. Lucy took her by surprise.

"What are you talking about?"

"Do you know why my father hid my birth certificate in my fairy tale book?"

"How did he—?" Patricia couldn't finish her sentence.

"Now I know why you won't let me see it. You know I will find out the truth," she said.

Patricia said nothing.

"And Ricky and Venus are your children. My father adopted them," Lucy continued.

"How did you find out?" Patricia stammered.

"With these!" Lucy said, waving the papers in her hand.

Patricia was furious when she recognized it. "It's my property! You have no right to invade my privacy. What were you doing in my room?"

"Someone trashed my room and stole my money. It bothered me they searched your room, too, so I checked. Guess what? I found the adoption papers and marriage certificate under your bed. You've lied to me for years. You made me believe you were my family."

They exchanged awkward glances.

"I also discovered my father's will," Lucy said, breaking the silence.

"You're a liar! Your father did not leave a will," Patricia stated.

"I'm sure you know nothing about it, but my father left it for me to find. He hid my birth certificate inside the book he gave me as a child. Given how much you hate me, it surprised me you didn't throw it out. I found the will left by my father in an unlikely place—my baby pictures. He knew you wouldn't look there. My father also established a trust fund for my education. I went to the bank, and they confirmed you withdrew the money. My father made me the beneficiary of his life insurance policy. I called them. Guess what? They issued a check for $350,000 two years ago. I don't recall receiving the check, but it cleared the bank. The insurance company stated they would look into the matter. Do you have any knowledge of that?"

Patricia couldn't keep the truth hidden any longer. Lucy held the evidence.

"All right, fine. I kept the truth from you. So what? What do you want me to say?" Patricia rolled her eyes.

"Perhaps you can tell me the truth."

"Do you want to know? Fine, I'll tell you the truth!" Patricia screamed. "You were a year old when I met your father. He was everyone's dream. He was tall, handsome, and wealthy. The only problem was that he was married to your mother. It overjoyed me when she died. I wanted to be close to your father, so I applied to be your nanny and gave the best performance of my life. He hired me on the spot. Whenever he came home, I would walk in revealing clothes and wear strong perfume to attract his attention. He soon proposed to me because I was such a wonderful actress. We married, and I lived the good life I deserved. Your father treated my children well and even adopted them, but he loved you more than they did. Well, I despised you then, and I still despised you now."

"I was a toddler. How could you dislike a small child? Did you even try to love me?"

"Who would love someone like you? You're an annoyance. The only reason I kept you was to help us cope with the life we're used to."

Lucy burst into uncontrollable tears. "What have I done so wrong that you despise me so much? I've done everything you've asked of me, and you're still treating me like a servant. Did you ever love my father?"

Patricia looked down at the floor. "It was a marriage of convenience, at least for me. I was born to live a good life. As for you—" Patricia said, unable to finish what she was about to say.

"What about my father's insurance check? My trust funds?"

"They were mine and my children's. Do you want to know what we did with it? I moved into a luxury apartment and purchased a sports car. I had the life I deserved. Ricky and Venus had the time of their lives living in Paris."

"Was that the reason you all left me?"

"I've been itching to get away from here for a long time, especially from you. You will never be one of us."

"All my life, I've struggled to feel like a stranger in my home, and for many years, I've wondered why you treat me differently. I guess I know why this is the case. You kept everything from me so you could work me to death to support you and your children. My father left me everything he had because he knew you were an evil stepmother deep down in his heart. That's why you took everything away from me. I will never let you walk all over me again."

Patricia clenched her teeth as Lucy stared at her with her piercing eyes. They were both furious. Patricia yanked Lucy's hair, and the last thing Lucy remembered was being hit on the head. Everything became dark.

IT WAS TUESDAY MORNING. Hank returned from his fishing trip and drove straight to the diner. He parked his truck in the alley and took a fish icebox. Hank was about to open the door when he noticed the back door was unlocked. The diner wouldn't be open for another three hours, so no one should be there. Hank set the chest down and looked inside to investigate. He grabbed a frying pan hanging from the wall as he walked through the kitchen. No one was there, which relieved him. The kitchen was clean. Hank assumed one of his employees forgot to lock the door. The incident enraged him, and he planned to fire the employee. Hank turned on the lights, took the icebox inside, and placed it on the counter. After returning to the truck, he grabbed the fishing rods and went to his office to store them. It shocked him to find his office in shambles. When he discovered the drawer was open and the cash box was missing, his heart raced. He called the police to report the burglary.

Meanwhile, Lucy awoke with a severe headache and prayed that the pounding in her head would stop. She looked around, wondering why she had slept on the floor. Her eyes appeared swollen and red when she looked in the mirror. She remembered everything that had happened the night before. The confrontation with her stepmother did not go well. She felt a large bump on the back of her head as she touched it. Did her stepmother, Ricky or Venus, harm her?

Lucy looked at the clock. It was nine o'clock. She was late. She didn't care that she wasn't feeling well. Lucy jumped to her feet, changed into her uniform, and drove to the diner. It would irritate Hank to see her late. As she approached the diner, she frowned as she noticed people standing around in the parking lot.

Lucy was unaware of the glances and reflections she received from the diner staff when she entered the restaurant, and she felt a sudden coldness from them. Marge avoided her as well. It appeared something was going on.

"What happened here?" Lucy asked, but no one replied. She received a scathing look from Marge.

"We helped you replace the missing money from the cash box, but that wasn't enough, so you stole the rest of our salaries!"

"What are you talking about, Marge? I didn't take any money. I wouldn't do that."

"Well, someone did."

Lucy turned around when she heard Hank's voice behind her. His eyes glared at her, filled with anger and suspicion.

"Hank, you don't think I have anything to do with this, do you?"

"The police said there was no evidence of a break-in, and you alone had access to the restaurant and my office."

"Hank, are you accusing me of stealing?"

"Yes, I'm accusing you. Money doesn't matter to me, but my baseball card collection and the Rolex watch my father gave me on his deathbed do."

"Please believe me. I am not a thief."

"How could you? I trusted you," Hank said, not listening to Lucy.

"I balanced the receipts for the past few days, and I even made the deposit slips last night for you so you could take them to the bank today."

"Is that right?"

"Yes, Hank, that's the truth."

Hank took Lucy's hand in his and walked into the office. Marge followed them.

"Where is the money you're referring to?" Hank asked.

The sight of files and paperwork strewn about the floor shocked Lucy.

"I don't understand."

"Stop acting, Lucy."

"Please believe me, Hank. I didn't do it," Lucy said.

She turned her head to look at Marge, but she did not respond. Her silence hurt Lucy. Lucy felt Marge was quick to judge her for something she didn't do. Tears welled in her eyes.

"Please, everyone. You are making a mistake. I would never commit theft, particularly against you. You are my family. Why are you doing this to me?"

"Let's end the drama, Lucy," Hank said. "We have caught you. Admit it."

Lucy felt her heart sink. She cried as she left the room, feeling lost and confused. She made her way to the back room to get her things. Nobody wanted her to be there. But where would she go? She was sure her stepmother would not let her inside the house. Lucy was emptying her locker when the police entered the room.

"Are you Lucy?"

"Yes?"

"We need you to come with us."

Lucy walked with the police without incident. She felt like a criminal, even though she had done nothing wrong. She was just a victim of circumstance. Lucy felt scared and helpless, not knowing what the police would do to her. Her life was spinning out of control, and all she wanted was to go home.

CHAPTER FIVE

Tilly and Dusty shopped at the Factory Merchants Outlet in Barstow after the rental company sent a replacement vehicle. Their search for souvenirs took them a few hours as they browsed the different stores. They bought a variety of items, including T-shirts, magnets, and key chains. The couple intended to stay in Victorville only for the night. However, their trips to museums, county fairs, and farmers' markets allowed them to relax. They enjoyed their time in Victorville so much that they stayed longer. Dusty and Tilly loved exploring the area and the small-town vibe. It surprised them to find that the town had so much to offer. The people were friendly, and the couple felt at home.

The time came for them to return to Los Angeles a few days later. They packed their bags and left tips for the staff. They stopped at the diner to say goodbye to Lucy and gift her a basket of expensive perfume, lotion, and chocolates. When they arrived at the parking area, it surprised them to see a crowd forming.

"What's going on here?" Tilly asked.

"There was a burglary here last night, and they brought Lucy in for questioning," Marge explained.

"Lucy? Why her?"

"Who else would take the money? The police found no signs of a break-in. Lucy was the only one with access to the owner's office. She had the keys."

"I don't believe Lucy would do something like that. She's one of the nicest people I've ever met."

"Well, I thought so, too, but we don't know her well, do we?"

The comment Marge made about Lucy made Tilly frown.

"I thought Lucy was your friend."

"I thought so too, but I'm glad I found out sooner than later."

"Have you ever considered that someone in her family might have something to do with it? You know her family well, and I've only seen them once. She had a horrible family that didn't love her. They were only interested in taking money from her. With the office key, it would have been easy for them to steal it without her knowledge. I don't know her family, but I know Lucy has a heart of gold. She wouldn't do what you accuse her of doing."

Marge did not respond and remained silent.

"You assume quickly. You know Lucy better than I do, but her heart is true. She is not guilty."

Marge looked at Tilly, and she knew she was right. Lucy trusted her more than her own family, and she betrayed her. But Marge was too proud to admit her mistake.

From Marge's actions, Tilly knew something was on her mind. And she waited for her to say something to her, but none came. She gave Marge a knowing look and walked away. Marge stayed silent, regretting her decision not to speak.

Tilly walked back to the parking lot, where her husband was waiting in the car. She shared with him the information she had gathered and how Lucy was taken by the police. Dusty felt surprised. He, like Tilly, never believed Lucy could steal anything. Lucy was the sweetest person they'd ever met, and she didn't have a mean bone in her body.

"Lucy is probably worried about being alone at the police station," Tilly speculated. "I bet her family wasn't concerned. I have the impression that her detention is of little importance to them. Is it okay if we go to the police station to check on Lucy? I just want to make sure she is okay."

"I was about to suggest the same thing," Dusty replied, hurrying away.

When they arrived at the police station, they approached the information desk and asked the officer if they could see Lucy.

"Someone will be with you shortly," the officer said.

Dusty and Tilly sat in the waiting room. A few moments later, an officer appeared.

"I understand you want to see someone here."

"Yes, we are here to see Lucy. They brought her in for questioning this morning. Have you let her go yet?" Tilly asked.

"No, we haven't."

"Does she need a lawyer? Are you intending to charge her anything?"

"She may not leave, but we do not detain her."

Tilly frowned. What did he mean by that?

"Could we see her?" she asked.

The officer directed Tilly and Dusty to one of the interview rooms.

"Lucy!" Tilly said so as soon as she saw her.

Lucy turned her head, and as soon as she saw a familiar face approaching her, she threw her arms out in a hug. She burst into tears.

"Lucy, what happened?"

"I don't understand what is happening to me," Lucy sobbed. "They've questioned me like a criminal."

"The server told me about a burglary at the diner last night."

"That's what they told me."

"Lucy, did anything unusual happen last night? The police found your fingerprints at the crime scene."

"I'm not surprised. For the past few days, I've used Hank's office to balance daily receipts. He told me I could use it."

"Lucy, it wasn't just your fingerprints. The waitress—I think her name was Marge—said they found Hank's keys on the floor, the keys he gave you before fishing. The cops believe you dropped it when you robbed the place last night."

"That is insane. I would never do such a thing. I had the keys with me last night, but when I looked in my bag a while ago, it's gone."

"Perhaps you dropped it as you left the restaurant?"

Lucy paused for a moment.

"No, I had them with me when I left."

"Are you sure?"

"I'm sure. I locked the place, put the keys in my handbag, and went home."

"Did anything happen after that?"

"Several things happened to me last night. I came home to find my room ransacked. Someone stole my piggy bank. An argument broke out between me and my mom. I was struck from behind, causing me to lose consciousness. When I woke up this morning, I was lying on the floor," Lucy said, rubbing the back of her head. "I'm not sure who it was, but I believe it was my brother, Ricky."

"Why would your brother hit you in the head?" Tilly asked.

"It's complicated," Lucy said. "I believe he took the keys from my purse when he knocked me out. He was the only person who knew I had Hank's office keys."

"I believe you, Lucy. Just hang in there a little longer. I'll speak to the officer about getting you out."

Lucy nodded and hugged Tilly again.

"Thank you so much. You don't know me well enough, but I'm glad you're here. I'm not sure what I would do if you weren't here. I can't handle it by myself."

"It's fine, Lucy. Everything is going to be okay," Tilly assured her.

"WHAT ARE YOU DOING here? How did you get out of jail?" Hank asked when he saw Lucy enter the diner.

"Don't worry, Hank. I'm only here to empty my locker. I'm leaving as soon as possible."

Lucy glanced at Hank with disappointment. "I can't believe you think I'd steal from you. You told me you trusted me."

"The evidence is clear, Lucy. Your fingerprints were the only ones found in the office."

Lucy felt devastated.

"If you had only given me the opportunity to explain myself, I would have told you I had used your office to balance the daily receipts. Why would I wait until closing time to take the money or return to the diner and steal the money when I could have taken it with me when I went home?" Lucy explained.

Hank said nothing while processing Lucy's words.

"I was grateful that you trusted me when you gave me the keys to your office. You're like a father to me. But making you think I could steal from you disappoints me more than being humiliated," she said, before turning her head to face her friends. "And you, Marge, Hector, Sylvia, and Jane, how quickly you accused me of the crime. I thought you were my family."

Everyone remained silent. Lucy thought it was pointless to talk to them. She cleaned out her locker in the back room. Lucy gave everyone one last look before leaving the restaurant, heartbroken. Lucy walked to the parking lot, where Tilly and Dusty were waiting for her.

"It is important not to let this situation get to you, Lucy. Your friends may have abandoned you, but my husband and I are still here to help you prove your innocence. We believe in you," Tilly said.

"Thank you, Tilly and Dusty. What hurts the most is that I discovered last night that the woman I thought was my mother was actually my stepmother. My biological mother died when I was two. My father remarried the following year. Ricky and Venus are my step-siblings," Lucy explained.

"What? How did you know? And they kept all these secrets from you? Why?" Tilly asked, confused.

"I couldn't believe it either. My father hid my birth certificate, will, and insurance documents for me to find."

"Oh, my God. What happened?" Dusty asked.

"My stepmother forged the documents, cashed my father's life insurance check, and used my trust fund to live in luxury while I had to quit school to support myself when they left me. After their money ran out, they returned home, and I have been supporting them since. I confronted my stepmother. It didn't turn out well."

"What did she do?" Dusty asked.

"My stepmother pulled my hair, and Ricky or Venus must have come home and walloped me because I passed out. I woke up this morning lying on the floor with a bump on my head. I went to the diner, and the police arrested me."

"Oh, my God!" Tilly exclaimed. "What a day you've had, Lucy. What are you going to do now? Where will you go?"

"My father left the house to me in his will. I don't know if my stepmother knew that. I have a copy of the deed. It listed the house as owned by him and my biological mother. Perhaps he foresaw these events. I am sure my stepmother would not let me back in the house. I have nowhere else to go."

"What about insurance money and trust funds?"

"They spent it. That's why my stepmother and her children returned. They lost everything."

Tilly shook her head, feeling sorry for Lucy. She was too young to experience such hardship in life. However, her intuition kicked in again, and she became suspicious of the strange events that occurred.

"Lucy, we are returning to Los Angeles today. We have an early flight to New York tomorrow. However, since you have nowhere to go and you still have to appear in court, we will extend our stay here. We will stay with you until this is over," Tilly assured her.

Lucy wept. "Why are you so nice to me? You don't even know who I am, but you're here to help me. The things you do for me are so much more than I have ever received from my family."

"Let's just say we like you," Tilly said. "I am only a few years older than you, but you have already endured many challenges in your life. When my husband and I first met you, we knew you were special. You have a golden heart. Your father raised you well. It's unfortunate that people take advantage of your sweetness. What are your plans once this is over, Lucy?"

"I turned nineteen a few weeks ago," Lucy stated. "I thinking about leaving the state. Perhaps I could sell my parents' house and move somewhere far away from here. I will finish school and attend university."

The words Lucy had spoken to Tilly and Dusty filled their hearts with warmth. She was young but full of hope and ambition, despite all the bad things that happened to her. They wished her all the best and promised to be there for her if she ever needed them.

"I'm sure you'll be fine, Lucy," Tilly said. "But it's time to uncover the truth and clear your name. We don't have enough time, so we need to act quickly."

"How will we do that?" Lucy asked.

Dusty cut them off from their conversation. "I guess this is a job for our friendly neighborhood private investigator."

Tilly and Dusty laughed, while Lucy looked confused.

CHAPTER SIX

There was a jingle of bells on the door of the pawnshop on Melrose Street as the detective entered.

"May I assist you, sir?" the clerk asked.

Garrett, Dusty's private investigator in New York, took out his wallet and showed his identification card. Garrett worked tirelessly and had gotten a tip from a source about a pawnshop in Los Angeles that he might want to check out. Several days of searching and following leads led to this discovery.

"I need to speak with the owner," he said.

The clerk nodded and walked to the back office.

An Asian man with a long white beard emerged moments later. "May I help you, sir?" he asked.

"We believe you sell stolen goods here."

"I'm not sure where you got that information, but I run a legitimate business."

"Are you sure?" Garrett asked, turning his head and looking around.

"I'm sure. What is this all about?"

Garrett was a mild-mannered detective with a gentle demeanor, but he was also cunning and intimidating, not afraid to bend the rules to catch the bad guy. He walked past the owner and into the back room. Here, he discovered an employee labeling some items. The owner followed Garrett into the back room.

"Wait a minute. You can't go back there."

"What are those?" Garrett asked, pointing to some items on the table.

"Someone pawned those items but never reclaimed them. The deadline has passed to repay the loan, so I am now selling them."

Garrett scanned the pieces and noticed a vintage Rolex timepiece. He picked it up, read the inscription, and showed it to the owner.

"Who sold this to you?"

"A young kid came in here a few weeks ago with a sad story about his sick father. He claimed it was a family heirloom passed down from father to son, but he needed to sell it to pay hospital bills."

"How much did you pay him?"

"I'm a business owner, and I recognized its value. I gave him $500 for it."

"Is he a regular?"

"No, it was his first time here."

"Is there anything you can tell me about this kid?"

"He was in his early twenties, a young man with a pleasant look and a laid-back demeanor."

"Would you recognize him if you saw him again?"

"Yes, is that enough assurance for you?"

"If you see him, please call me day or night," Garrett said as he handed him his business card.

"What's in it for me?" he asked.

"For starters, I will not ask the cops to raid your place and check your merchandise for hot items. You may have a legitimate business, but publicity would be detrimental in any case."

"Alright, that's good enough for me."

"If I were you, I wouldn't sell the watch. It's stolen. The cops will want to see it," Garrett told the man while taking pictures of it.

"Thank you for your advice. I'll put it somewhere safe," the man said.

Garrett left the store when his stomach grumbled. He looked at his watch. It was past 2 p.m. He noticed a coffee shop across the street and got something to eat. His phone rang just as he bit into his hamburger.

"Is this Garrett?" the caller asked in a whisper.

"This is Garrett. Who is this?"

"This is Al from the pawnshop. This is about the antique Rolex."

"Oh, yes, Al. What can I do for you?"

"The kid is back. You just missed him. He's in my shop right now. He's selling rare baseball cards. Are you interested?"

Garrett hit the jackpot. That was the last stolen item from the diner.

"Good, keep him there. Don't let him walk out of your shop, do you understand? There's money in it for you."

"Yes, I understand," Al replied as he adjusted the surveillance camera before returning to the front of the store.

"So, what do you think? Are you interested?" Ricky asked.

"What?"

"The baseball cards? Do you want to buy them or not?"

"Yes, I'm interested," the man replied. "This is a rare collection. Where did you get them?"

"I have had them since I was a kid."

"I need to make sure it's genuine," Al said. "We're talking big bucks here."

"Big bucks? How much?"

"A few thousand, maybe, but I have to make sure they're real. I don't want to defraud my customers, you know. There's a good chance they'll come after me if I sell them fakes."

"Yeah, I get it. Why don't you take a picture of the cards, and I'll return with the rest when you have a buyer lined up?"

"No, just stay. It shouldn't take me long," the store owner said. He stalled, but he couldn't think of a way to keep Ricky in the shop for much longer.

"They are not forgeries, that I can assure you of."

"I'm sorry, but I can't take your word for it. This is business. Please give me a minute to check it."

The store owner walked into the back room. He called Garrett, but he never picked up. Al sighed. He did not know how long he could stall the kid.

"Have you checked them out?" Ricky asked when Al returned.

"I called my go-to guy, and he'll be here soon. Can you please wait a few minutes?"

Ricky grew impatient. "Give me your phone," he said.

"Excuse me?"

Ricky snatched the owner's cell phone and photographed the cards. "Call me when you have a buyer."

"Wait a minute, kid," he said. "If you are not here when my man arrives to appraise those cards, he will leave. I can't know if the cards are genuine, I can't buy them from you. Good luck selling the cards."

"Okay, fine," Ricky said. "I will grab something to eat across the street. If he comes in, call me."

Ricky had just stepped outside when the police surrounded him and ordered him to put his hands up. He surrendered with his hands raised. Ricky could feel his heart pounding in his chest as the cops advanced, handcuffed him, and put him in the back of a police car. Ricky knew he was in serious trouble.

Garrett commended Al for keeping Ricky until law enforcement arrived. Al was pleased with the outcome and did not ask for rewards. In a statement, the police thanked him for his help in apprehending the criminal.

PATRICIA GASPED AS she leaped from the sofa and grabbed the remote control to increase the volume. She saw Ricky handcuffed and thrown into the back of the police cruiser. The ticker tape at the bottom of the screen read, "Live Breaking News."

During a sting operation in Los Angeles, police arrested her son live on television. Patricia was both enraged and concerned. She called her lawyer friend but declined to represent her son.

Ricky did not post bail and remained in jail. He spent the night in his cell, worried about what was going to happen. Ricky hoped the judge would set him free, but he knew it was possible that he could face a longer sentence. He lay awake, praying for the best possible outcome.

Patricia never missed a visit to her son, but seeing him in prison was difficult for her. She struggled to hold back her tears when they said goodbye, and she often stayed in the car after the visit, collecting herself. When Ricky entered the courtroom in handcuffs during his court hearing, her heart shattered into a million pieces.

Ricky looked around. He saw his mother and Venus crying in the front row. Lucy sat in the back. Ricky glared at her, but when he noticed Lucy staring at him with sadness in her expression, he felt guilty. He glanced away and trembled. He knew he had made a mistake. His eyes welled up with tears.

What have I done?

Ricky had to admit that Lucy treated him as an older brother with kindness and respect, but he took it for granted. He took advantage of her gracious nature and never expressed his gratitude. It was all his fault. It was time to mature. Ricky felt remorseful about what he had done. Lucy had endured enough at their hands. He knew he had only himself to blame for his decisions and actions.

The court found Ricky guilty of theft, and the judge sentenced him to a year in prison. Ricky glanced at his family as they led him away. Patricia rushed forward to hug her son, but the bailiff stopped her. She couldn't help but cry.

Hank was relieved to get his items back from the police, but he regretted accusing Lucy. He felt embarrassed and ashamed. Hank wanted to apologize to her and let her know she got her job back, but it was too late. No matter how hard he tried, he couldn't reach her.

Lucy did not press charges against Patricia for stealing her trust fund. She knew there was no way for her to get the money back. The insurance company continued investigating how they issued a check directly to a minor and who cashed it.

Lucy and the sheriff visited Patricia in her home one day.

Patricia yelled, "Get out of here!" when she saw Lucy walking toward the front door.

The sheriff served Patricia with an eviction notice.

"What the hell is this?" she screamed. "This is my home."

The sheriff shook his head.

"There is no truth to that statement. They registered the deed to the house at the county recorder's office. It belonged to Lucy's father and biological mother, and he left it to her in his will."

"No, this is impossible. My husband owns this house, so it now belongs to me."

"If you don't leave this house, we'll arrest you for trespassing," the sheriff warned.

"You wouldn't dare."

"You have one week to vacate the place."

Patricia and Venus screamed. "This is not happening!"

Patricia approached Lucy and slapped her across the face. Lucy fell to the ground, holding her cheek.

Venus grabbed Lucy by the arm and yelled, "It's all your fault!"

The sheriff restrained Patricia and Venus by holding their arms. He was about to handcuff and arrest them when Lucy shook her head and told him she was fine. She would not press charges for aggravated assault.

"Are you sure?" he asked.

Lucy nodded. Touching her face with her open hand, she stood in front of her stepmother with all her courage.

"You spent my father's money and lived in luxury. I worked hard, scrimped, and saved so we wouldn't be hungry. All the while, you made me believe my father left us penniless. You even stole the money I had set aside for my education. I have no sympathy for any of you. You deserve everything that is happening to you right now."

Patricia and Venus remained stoic and showed no remorse for their actions.

"The next time you touch me, I'll press charges against you."

"How dare you talk to me like that?" Patricia asked. "I am not easily threatened by someone like you."

Lucy bit her tongue to avoid rash remarks. She tried to stay calm. "You have one week to vacate the house," she said as she walked away without looking back.

"Come back in here!" Patricia yelled. "We're not done talking yet!"

Lucy pretended not to hear her and got into the sheriff's car, and they drove off. Patricia leaned over, picked up a handful of stones from the side of the road, and tossed them into the car. However, it had already turned onto the next street, leaving Patricia behind. She watched the car disappear into the distance, a fleeting look of frustration on her face as she continued to scream.

The fire alarm sounded off at midnight. Multiple fire engines arrived at Lucy's home, sirens blaring. When they arrived, the house was already on fire. Patricia danced around the street, clapping, while Venus wept. Her mother seemed to have lost her mind. It was Patricia who started the fire in Lucy's bedroom when she burned her baby pictures. It caught fire and spread rapidly. Their neighbors watched as firefighters battled the flames. The house suffered destruction.

The police arrested Patricia and took her to the hospital for a mental health evaluation. They left Venus alone, with nowhere to go. It forced her to live in a temporary shelter until she could find a permanent residence.

Lucy stood outside her parents' house, which lay in ruins after being burned to the ground. Tears welled up in her eyes as she looked around at the charred remains of her childhood home. She couldn't believe Patricia could do something like this. She took everything from her. Lucy took one last look at the house, haunted by painful memories.

"There's nothing left for me here, Tilly. My stepmother took everything from me. I have no job, no money, no home, and the people I thought were my family have abandoned me. The most unfortunate circumstance was the failure of my stepmother to maintain the home insurance. I gave her money to pay for it, and she wasted it. I have nothing left."

"Oh, Lucy," Tilly said. "I can't believe you are only nineteen years old and have made so many sacrifices. Your courage and kind heart touch our hearts. We'd love to help you if you allow us. Considering you don't have any family left here, would you like to stay with us in New York until you return to school?"

"Are you serious, Tilly? I don't know what to say."

"Say that you will."

"You are the only family I have now. I would love to finish school, and I promise I'll work hard to get a job and pay for my education."

"Oh, Lucy. That is unnecessary. Dusty and I will handle everything. All we want is for you to study and achieve your life goals. This is for your future."

Lucy burst into tears. She could feel Tilly's sincerity as she stared at her.

Dusty hugged Lucy and said everything would be fine from now on. "Tilly and I will treat you as if you are our younger sister. We promise to care for you. You will never be alone again. We are your family."

"I thought this day would never come. I thought I'd be a waitress for the rest of my life. Thank you both for giving me a second chance and a fresh start in life."

"I think part of the reason we stayed in Victorville was because of you," Tilly explained. "We fell in love with you because of your kind heart."

Lucy hugged Tilly and Dusty and thanked them for welcoming her into their family. They smiled and embraced her warmly. Tilly and Dusty promised to always be there for Lucy and love her unconditionally. Lucy felt relieved and grateful for their kindness. She recognized that when one door shuts, another opens. She was lucky indeed!

Lucy received special commendations from her teachers and the principal for her service at the school. She had more than enough high school credits to take the proficiency test required to graduate. Lucy was a natural and aced the tests. It thrilled her to graduate and move on to the next stage of her life. Lucy's acceptance into college marked the start of a bright future.

A CHILLY BREEZE BLEW as Lucy drove away in her white Mercedes-Benz, courtesy of Tilly and Dusty. She felt like the luckiest girl in the world. Lucy drove down the road, feeling the cold air brush against her face. She smiled, grateful for the unexpected gift. Lucy was excited about moving into her dorm, starting her first college adventure, and meeting new people. She felt a sense of anticipation as she left, knowing that the next chapter in her life was about to begin. Lucy was unaware of the remarkable life that awaited her. Tilly set up a one-million-dollar trust fund for her until she turned twenty-one to ensure her education and future.

The wind blew against Tilly's face as she stood on their apartment balcony, looking out over Manhattan's glass skyscrapers. Tilly knew Lucy was ready to start her journey, and she had faith she would make the most of her opportunities. She was sure Lucy would succeed and be happy.

Tilly sensed her mother's presence near her, or even her mother's arms embracing her. Tilly knew she had made her mother happy as she added another accomplishment to her list. As she prepared to meet the next beneficiary of her foundation, she was grateful for the opportunity to give back. She knew she had achieved something remarkable and this was just the beginning.

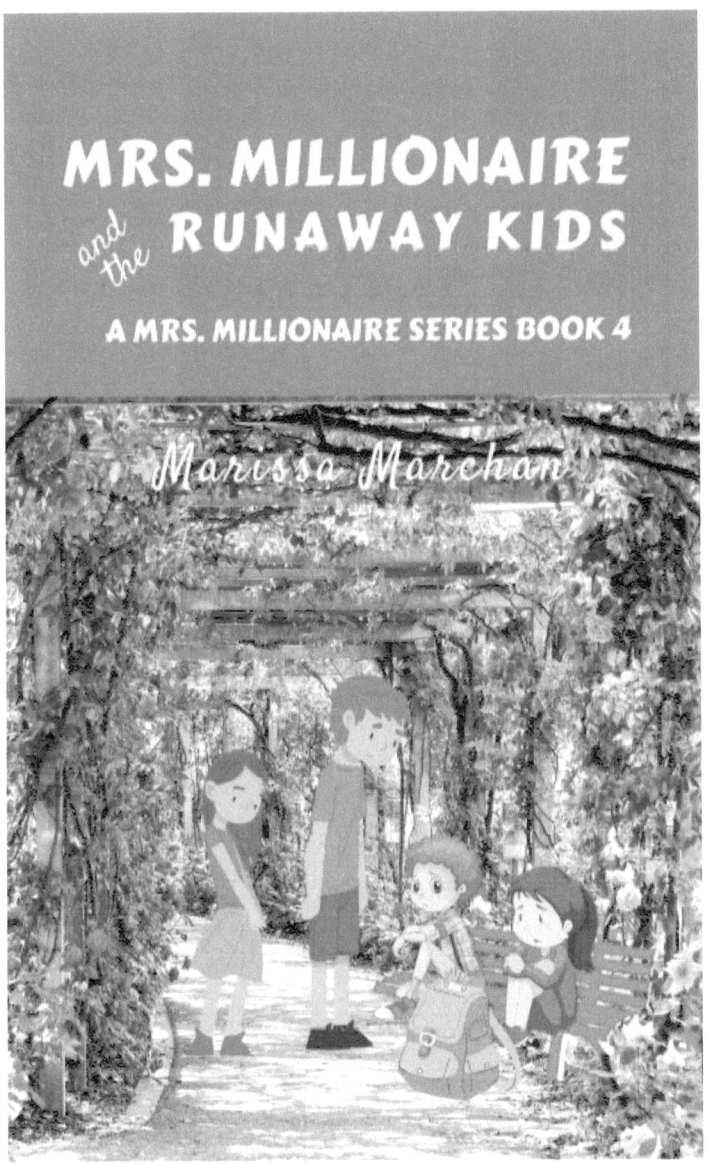

MRS. MILLIONAIRE AND THE RUNAWAY KIDS

CHAPTER ONE

I t was a chilly night. The streets remained deserted, and the air became thick with fog. A distant storm rumbled far away. Four souls slept in Brooklyn Park. They huddled together, sharing warmth and protecting each other from the cold. The wind penetrated their bones. They shivered and groaned, praying for morning to come soon.

Jonathan, Jeffrey, Chasity, and Chrystal were siblings who ran away from home. They had been living on the streets for a month without anyone noticing them, and no one seemed to care. Why would anyone talk to filthy, dirty, and rag-clad children?

It all began on a stormy day. It started bright but turned gloomy, threatening downpours. The rain fell, the wind became gusty, thunder rolled, and lightning flashed.

"Mom, we're home!" the kids said as they tossed their backpacks on the floor.

It forced all schools in the district to close because of inclement weather. As the storm approached, the school bus drove the students home.

Upon entering the living room, the children discovered their father, Dexter, sitting on the sofa. It filled his eyes with tears.

"Dad? What's the matter?" Jonathan asked.

A tear came down their father's cheeks, and he hugged them. As he sobbed, he told them that their mother had died early that morning. A long cancer battle took its toll on her. She was 35 years old. The children knew their mother was sick, but they did not know she had cancer. They didn't know what that meant, but if they knew, they could have looked it up. Perhaps they could have done something. They could have saved their mom. There was nothing they could do but cry.

"It's all right, Daddy," Chasity said. "Everything will be alright."

They hugged each other, and their father seemed at peace. Dexter didn't know what to do. He always relied on his wife, Martha, to make family decisions. While Dexter earned the money, she handled the finances, budgeting, school activities, and chores for the children without complaint. He also depended on her to be there for him, to listen, and to provide support and advice. Martha was the backbone of the family, and without her, Dexter felt lost. She was everything to him.

They held a private service for relatives and close friends. They scattered Martha's ashes over the mountains following the service. Her friends and family gathered to watch her last journey. Everyone shared stories about Martha's life and shed tears. It was a sad day but filled with happy memories. Her loss devastated Dexter, but he knew she would always remain in his heart.

Dexter and his children drove home after the funeral. Everyone remained silent. Chrystal dashed into her parents' bedroom when they returned home, convinced that the whole day had been a dream. She realized she was alone in the room. She couldn't believe her mother was not coming back.

"Mom!" she screamed.

Jonathan, Jeffrey, and Chasity sobbed and comforted one another. Dexter was sitting in the living room, his face buried in his hands, his shoulders shaking, and he cried. Would he cope without her? He felt emptiness and loneliness in his heart. Dexter felt like he had lost a piece of himself. He took a deep breath and wiped away his tears. He had to be strong for his children. Dexter ran to them and burst into tears. He embraced them and found peace despite the pain. He promised to remain strong for them.

It took a long time for Dexter and the children to recover from Martha's death. After a year of mourning, Dexter started a new life. Nolan, Dexter's college roommate, offered him a job in Bridgeport, Connecticut. He and the children moved there: Jonathan, the oldest child, was twelve; Jeffrey was eleven; Chasity was ten; and Chrystal was eight. Dexter was the executive chef at an upscale country club in Toledo, Ohio, but needed a fresh start. He set aside his culinary passion when he became a supervisor at a textile mill. Dexter was determined to make the best of the situation and worked hard to make the most of his new career.

It was stressful for the kids to move to an unfamiliar town. Ohio was their only home. It was difficult for them to leave their friends and family behind. They had to start over at a new place.

They rented a small, two-bedroom apartment on the second floor of an old building. There was only one bathroom, a small kitchen with an eating space, and a living room. Even though Dexter told his children it was only temporary, they weren't happy about it. One positive outcome of their relocation was that they made new friends in the neighborhood.

As Dexter entered the building, he was nervous. It was his first day at work. He was keen to make a good impression on his boss, Mr. Arlington. Nolan showed him around the office and introduced him to the staff. Dexter felt excited about starting his job and making a positive change. Introducing himself as their new boss, Dexter walked around the warehouse, shaking hands with everyone. They greeted him with a warm welcome, and everyone was eager to hear what he had to say. He thanked everyone for their kindness and enthusiasm.

Dexter and the kids adjusted to their new life. He worked hard to provide for his family, and the kids enjoyed their change of environment. They soon made friends in the neighborhood and at school. As time went by, they felt more and more familiar and comfortable. In no time, Dexter and the children became integrated members of the community. They felt a sense of belonging and found a place to call home.

Dexter had no vices. He had no desire for alcohol or cigarettes. Dexter would go to the grocery store as soon as the alarm went off, signifying the end of their shift. He enjoyed cooking nutritious meals for his children. They worked together on chores and laundry. The family soon appreciated their simple life in Connecticut. Anyone who knew them would agree that Dexter was an outstanding father to his children. He always spent time with his kids, teaching them valuable life lessons. He was a role model and an example for others to follow. His dedication to his family was unwavering.

After a few months, Dexter earned his employees' trust by treating them fairly. He would cover for someone who needed time off to care for a sick child, wife, or parents. They respected Dexter. This resulted in happier and more productive workers.

However, Dexter's popularity at work became an issue for one of his coworkers. Diego envied him and competed with him since Dexter joined Arlington Textile. Diego expected a promotion, but Dexter got it instead. From then on, he despised him.

One day, the general manager assigned Diego to tour investors. Diego was ecstatic. He believed it was his turn to shine. Diego answered all their inquiries and won everyone over. The group headed to the gift shop to get a novelty of the company's hat, T-shirt, tailored socks, various publications linked to the textile sector, and other souvenirs. Diego's agitation was noticeable when faced with investors' tough questions about his qualifications and employment. He was not a people person. Diego made several people uncomfortable. It just so happened that Dexter was in the warehouse, talking to the delivery guys. They laughed and talked. When Diego and the investors entered the loading dock, one person recognized Dexter. He approached and shook his hand. Dexter introduced himself and greeted the other guests. The investors informed Dexter of their worries and concerns, and he responded with elegance, honesty, and courtesy. It left a lasting impression on them. Instead of following Diego, they followed Dexter around the warehouse. He discussed the machinery used in warping, beaming, and weaving operations. Dexter even introduced them to the weaving team. They discussed weaving process procedures, from loading bobbins to spinning and weaving to finishing the woven fabrics.

When everyone left, Diego stood alone in the room, gritting his teeth. He returned home in a rage because he felt Dexter humiliated him. Diego was furious at Dexter and wished to retaliate. He devised a plan to discredit him, and after accomplishing this, he was sure they would fire Dexter and promote him instead.

His plan came to fruition at the right time. The company secured a multi-million-dollar account from a New York Garment District plant. Dexter handled the details, such as overseeing delivery and staying in touch with vendors. Dexter delegated tasks to each staff member to ensure everything ran smoothly. He assigned Diego to inspect all arriving and outbound shipments.

One night, after everyone left for home, Diego remained behind. He walked to Dexter's office and logged into his computer. It was easy to get in because he had watched Dexter for several days and memorized his password. Dexter was far too trusting. He didn't realize Diego was cunning. Diego accessed the work order files and canceled five orders due Friday, two days away. Before leaving, he turned off the computer and wiped his fingerprints off the keyboard. It worked just as Diego predicted. The shipment did not arrive, and Mr. Arlington was furious.

He asked loudly, "What happened? I left you in charge, so nothing could go wrong. Do you know what you've done?"

Dexter explained he had spoken with their delivery driver, who assured him the shipment would arrive on time.

"Dexter, I just spoke with him, and he said we canceled the order two days ago. How do you explain that?"

"Canceled, sir? I did not cancel the order."

Dexter dashed into his office and checked his computer. His boss had a valid point. It showed he had canceled five deliveries.

"There must be a problem with the system, sir. I did not do this."

"We checked with IT. There was no computer error."

"Someone is trying to sabotage me," he said. "I'm always careful. I don't make mistakes, especially ones of this magnitude."

"Why would anyone do that to you, Dexter?" Mr. Arlington asked. "Instead of accepting responsibility for your mistakes, you accuse others. This is unacceptable. Your stupidity costs us a lot of money. I want you to pack your belongings and leave. You're fired!"

Diego's mouth curled into a sinister grin. His heart soared with excitement when he heard it. Finally, he got rid of Dexter.

"But, sir," Dexter tried to reason with his boss, but he was uninterested.

"You heard what I said, Dexter. Now get out before I call security."

Mr. Arlington would not listen to anything he had to say, no matter how hard he tried. With his head down, Dexter returned to his office and packed all his belongings into a box. He stormed out, shocked by what had just happened. Who would do something like that? Why would someone want to sabotage him?

Dexter arrived home late. He found his children sitting at the table, doing their homework.

"Daddy, I got an award today," Chrystal remarked, holding out her certificate, but Dexter remained silent. "Are you feeling okay?" she asked.

"Dad, we ran out of milk," Jonathan said.

Dexter nodded, acknowledging what they had said, before paying the babysitter as she left. He cried as he gazed at his children. Dexter hugged them and told them he had lost his job.

"What happened, Dad? Weren't you the boss there?" Jonathan asked.

"Not anymore. My boss let me go. Someone gained access to my computer and erased the orders. Everyone blamed me, but I didn't do it."

"Why would someone do that to you, Dad?" asked Chasity.

"I don't know, and I can't prove my innocence. They told me to leave the building. Don't worry, kids. I'll get another job. We're going to be fine."

"You'll find work again, Dad. You'll see," the kids said.

Dexter headed to the unemployment office the next day to file a claim. Unfortunately, they refused to pay his unemployment benefits because his employer fired him for just cause. He appealed the denial, and after a hearing, they upheld the decision to deny him benefits. Dexter's world crumbled around him.

Every day, Dexter looked for work—temporary, casual, anything to support his children—but no one hired him. His savings ran out, and he couldn't pay his bills. Dexter returned home with an eviction notice taped to the door. Dexter knew he had to do something, but he didn't know what to do. They faced homelessness and uncertainty. Dexter yelled and punched the wall, venting his frustration and anger. He walked to the store and purchased a bottle of vodka to escape his problems while the children were at school. Dexter drank it and passed out on the couch. He woke up with a pounding headache and dread.

From then on, vodka was for breakfast, lunch, and dinner. He consumed alcohol, disregarding his children's needs. It soon wrecked his life as his addiction spiraled out of control. Dexter stopped cooking, cleaning, and laundering for the family. As his drinking worsened, Dexter's physical and mental health declined. His priorities shifted from his family to drinking. This had a profound impact on his children, who had to learn to fend for themselves.

CHAPTER TWO

The kids got off the school bus and walked a block to their apartment. Jonathan retrieved the key from his pocket and unlocked the door. The boys found their unconscious father on the kitchen floor.

"Dad, are you okay?" Jeffrey asked, shaking him by the shoulder, but he did not respond.

"Can you hear me?" Jonathan asked.

But their father still didn't answer.

Chrystal remembered watching a movie where they threw cold water at an unconscious man, so she splashed it on her father's face. Jonathan was about to call 9-1-1 when he saw their father resuscitated. It took the children a while to help him get up onto the couch. Chrystal and Jonathan were relieved when their father opened his eyes. He seemed dazed and confused, but not dangerous. During the entire struggle, the landlord, who was trying to collect unpaid rent, witnessed everything. He left the apartment without saying a word.

Child Services visited the family the next day. The landlord called them in after reporting the incident. When Jonathan opened the door, the social worker told the children she needed to see their father. Jonathan let her in and took her to their father's room. They found Dexter asleep on his bed, intoxicated. The social worker revived him, but he was so disoriented when he stood up that he tripped, fell, and hit his head on the cabinet. It knocked him unconscious. The social worker dialed 9-1-1 as blood flowed from his head.

It didn't take long for the ambulance and police cars to arrive. Child Protective Services placed the youngsters in a temporary shelter until they could make other arrangements for them. The children didn't want to go and cried as police officers escorted them away. The CPS worker tried to reassure them that everything would be fine, but the kids were unconvinced. They were taken to their new home with mixed feelings of hope and fear. Every day, the children waited for their father to pick them up. He never came. There was no one willing to tell them anything, so they became concerned.

Jonathan heard the office manager and social worker conversing while going to the bathroom. According to them, their father was in a coma, and doctors were unsure whether he would ever wake up. Since there were no known relatives for the children, they placed them in foster care. They had to split them into separate households.

Jonathan heard it. He knew they were talking about his family. His siblings were in the garden when Jonathan sprinted up to them. He told them what he had heard. The children could not believe their father was in a coma, and they would never see him again.

"What is a coma?" Chrystal asked.

"I'm not sure, but it seemed serious," Jonathan said. "Dad is no longer here to protect us, so it is up to us to look out for one another. If he doesn't wake up soon, they'll separate us."

"No, I don't want to leave. I want to stay with you," Chrystal cried.

"I don't want to be apart from you either, no matter how much you annoy me," Jonathan joked to relieve stress. "It's time for us to develop a plan."

One day, the kids watched *Annie* on TV, a story about an 11-year-old orphan who escaped to find her parents. Forty-five minutes into the film, the children had the brilliant idea to run away so they could be together. As they planned to return to Toledo, they had to escape.

The kids were quite perceptive. They kept a record of all employee actions and breaks, as well as their eating and resting habits. After watching the staff for a few days, Jonathan devised a plan for when and how to flee. They agreed to visit their father one last time. Since they didn't know where they'd taken him, they planned to spy around the office. Once the manager left for lunch, the kids rushed to work.

Chrystal was short enough to remain unnoticed. While Chasity was on the lookout, Chrystal entered the room and searched for anything that could help them find their father. Chrystal was desperate until she noticed a tray with red files on it. She opened one and stared at it. She couldn't read the big words yet, let alone the cursive, so she took them and gave them to her sister. Chasity snatched it from her hand, and the two crouched behind the stairs. The folders had names written on them, and she looked through them one by one. Chasity found a folder labeled 'Curtis Children.' She had to read it twice before understanding what it said. Mother deceased, father Dexter Curtis, at Loyola Hospital, 1900 Stewart Street, and condition: comatose.

Chasity's hand trembled as she scribbled the address. Before returning to the office, they double-checked that the coast was clear. As Chrystal put the folders back on the tray, she spotted a small open bag of wrapped candy on the desk and picked it up. When she saw some money on the tray, she placed it in her dress pocket. The two sisters breathed a sigh of relief as Chrystal strolled out of the office and into their rooms, unnoticed. The youngsters tried to figure out how to get to the hospital now that they knew the address. Even if they escaped the building undetected, they lacked the money to board a bus. As the siblings debated what to do, Chrystal remembered the candy in her pocket. She took one and ate it.

"Where did you get that?" Chasity asked.

"I found it in the office. I like candy."

"Don't be stingy. Share it with us," Jonathan said.

Chrystal took the bag from her dress pocket and handed it over to Jonathan. He reached inside, expecting candy, but found twenty dollars and some change.

"What's this?" Jonathan asked.

Chrystal smiled and said, "I found it."

"Good job, Chrystal!" the kids laughed.

Jonathan looked around to ensure no one could hear them.

"Listen, there is a good chance someone is looking for the money. Just eat the sweets and don't leave the wrappers behind. Take it with you, and we'll throw it outside. Until then, we must hide the money somewhere safe. We'll take it when we're ready to leave. Do you understand?" Jonathan said.

The kids said okay. They hid the money under a flower pot and buried the candy wrappers in the flowerbed. The children figured no one would look there. They checked to make sure no one had seen them and left.

IT WAS A BUSY SUNDAY morning. Staff from the children's shelter were on hand to answer questions from anyone interested in volunteering, giving, fostering, or caring for them. They served refreshments and appetizers. Jeffrey was getting food on the table when he heard Mrs. Drummond, the office manager, conversing with a couple.

"I am sure you will be proud of the children you foster. Because of their father's health condition, they need a suitable residence. I understand you have three children at home." Mrs. Drummond asked.

"Yes, we have three children," the mother said.

"So having more children wasn't a problem for you?"

"We have a large house. The kids will get along well. Unfortunately, we can only bring two children. We'll return tomorrow to pick them up. We'll ensure their rooms are ready."

Jeffrey heard it loud and clear. He knew they were talking about them. Jeffrey hurried outside and informed his siblings of what he had heard.

"I don't care whether those people live in a mansion. It will be a disaster to live in the same house with three other children," Jeffrey said. "They're coming for us tomorrow. We must follow our plan. It's our last chance. Otherwise, we won't see each other anymore."

Jonathan looked around the area. He wondered how they could flee without being seen. There were people at the entrance and in the courtyard.

"We'll have to find a way out."

"Maybe we can climb over the wall and escape," Jeffrey suggested.

"I said without being seen, Jeffrey," Jonathan responded. "We are not tall enough. They'll catch us right away."

"What if we sneak out when no one is looking?" Jeffrey asked.

"We'll never make it," Jonathan replied. "Wait a minute. Hold on."

Jonathan noticed a white delivery truck parked in the driveway, delivering food to the shelter. He had an idea. Jonathan retrieved the money from under the flowerpot, put it in his pocket, and called his siblings to tell them about his plan. Everyone agreed. The children climbed into the truck one by one, avoiding being seen as they walked to the driveway.

"Where is Jeffrey?" Jonathan asked when he noticed he was missing.

Chrystal and Chasity both shook their heads. "He was here a minute ago."

"He will ruin our plans," Jonathan said in anger.

Meanwhile, Jeffrey was in the kitchen, stocking his backpack with food and beverages. When he heard footsteps approaching, he dropped his backpack and pushed it under the table.

"What are you doing here?" the cook asked.

"I got hungry," Jeffrey said as he bit into the fried chicken.

"Just take it with you and go back outside to play."

When the cook left, Jeffrey grabbed his backpack and crept out the back door. He saw Jonathan gesturing for him to hurry. They got into the truck and hid in the rear behind the boxes. After a few moments, the kids realized they were on the move and relaxed a bit, thinking they had escaped unseen.

The driver drove for half an hour before stopping. He exited the truck and opened the back door. The children held their breath as they heard the driver climb up and footsteps approaching. Jeffrey and Jonathan realized the driver had seen them when he reached the back of the truck. The kids scrambled out of the truck and ran off. Confused, the truck driver scratched his head and drove away.

Standing in front of a mini-market, the children didn't know how far they were from the children's shelter.

"Excuse me, sir. Do you know where Loyola Hospital is?" Jonathan asked a passing man.

"It's not far. Turn right onto Stewart Street, three blocks down, and continue. You can't miss it."

"Thank you, sir," Jonathan said.

"What a stroke of luck! Dad is close. Let's move!" Chasity stated.

The kids walked. The closer they came to the hospital, the faster they ran, and then they burst into a full sprint. When they reached Stewart Street, they turned right, just as the man had said. He was right. The hospital was so big that you couldn't miss it. They walked another block before arriving at the hospital's entrance.

"Listen, I don't think they'll let us in," Jonathan said. "They'll be suspicious if we walk inside together. Wait here."

Jonathan stepped inside and looked around. He followed an elderly couple heading for the elevator. He found a staircase next to it. Jonathan knew what to do. His siblings approached him after he exited the building.

"Why don't you walk with an adult and make people think we're with them? But don't get too close—just enough for the hospital staff to assume we're with our family. When we get inside, we'll meet on the stairs by the elevator, okay?"

"Got it!" exclaimed the children, both thumbs up.

Chrystal followed an old couple into the hospital. Chasity and Jeffrey did the same thing. Jonathan was the last person to step behind an older woman as she approached the information desk.

"What room is Mr. Ed Mahoney in?" she inquired.

The clerk was untrained and didn't ask for ID. She checked the computer. "He's in room 312."

"Thank you," the woman replied as she searched through her handbag on her way to the elevator.

"Mr. Mahoney is my grandfather," Jonathan told the receptionist. "My grandmother forgot we are here to visit her friend, too. Would you mind checking it for me, please?"

"What is his name?"

"Dexter Curtis."

"Oh, their rooms are right next to each other. He's in 313."

"Thank you," Jonathan said.

He followed the old lady to the elevator. Jonathan walked alongside her but left her when he saw the stairway sign. His siblings waited for him. Jonathan told them what he had discovered, and they proceeded up the stairwell to the third floor.

CHAPTER
THREE

M any people waited in the waiting area, but there were no children. Jonathan soon realized why. It filled the waiting room with coughers and sneezers. The floor didn't allow kids to be there because of the risk of disease exposure.

The children walked down the hallway one by one. Nobody spotted them sneaking in while the busy staff dealt with an emergency. The kids walked along the corridor, reading the room numbers.

"309, 310, 311... there it is, room 313," Jonathan said.

The children entered the room and noticed they had hooked their father up to monitors with an IV infusion flowing into his veins. It shocked the children to see their father in such a serious state. He had an oxygen mask on his face. His complexion appeared pale, and his breathing was strained. The children felt their hearts sink as they realized their father was seriously ill.

"Are you okay, Dad? Can you hear us? We're here," Jonathan murmured, squeezing his father's unresponsive hand, tears streaming down his cheeks.

Jeffrey, Chasity, and Chrystal joined him. They gathered around the bed, praying that their father would wake up.

None of them could bring themselves to leave him, uncertain whether it would be the last time they said goodbye. The four of them stood in silence, and all they could hear was their father's breathing and the heart monitor's beep. They knew their time with him was running out. They feared that the nurse would catch them and call the police.

"Maybe that's what they meant when they said a coma. Dad has been sleeping for a long time," Chrystal said.

"Say your goodbyes now," Jonathan said. "We need to leave."

"Dad, we want to say we ran away. We're heading back to Toledo to see our friends. I'm sure someone will take us in," Jeffrey said, wiping away his tears.

"We came to say goodbye because we do not want to be separated by the social worker or the shelter," Chasity said. "We want to be together. You always tell us that no matter what happens, the family stays together. We love you, Dad. Please get better."

One by one, the children kissed their father goodbye. It filled them with sadness and fear. They believed their father would pull through, but they knew the situation was serious. They took one last glance before leaving the room. As soon as they reached the bottom floor, they exited the building.

"Where are we going, Jonathan? I'm scared," Chasity said as they headed along Stewart Street.

"I don't know. We need to stay strong and stick together. I am sure we'll be okay."

The children walked for hours with no particular destination in mind. When they stopped to rest, they noticed the sun was setting. They realized they had walked all day and were far from home. They felt scared and alone.

"I'm hungry," Chrystal stated.

"I'm hungry and thirsty," Chasity said.

"We only have twenty dollars with us," Jonathan said. "There's a food truck over there. I'll buy us a hamburger, but we have to split it four ways."

"That's not enough," Chasity said. "We should look for something else. We could go to the grocery store and get some snacks. Or maybe we could try that pizza place down the street. There are more options than just hamburgers."

"You are not listening to me," Jonathan said. "We only have $20. We have to stretch it as far as we can. Hamburgers are the only affordable option."

"Don't worry, guys. We got food," Jeffrey remarked.

Everyone turned to look at him.

"What are you talking about?" they asked.

"I've carried my backpack the entire time, and you haven't noticed?"

Jonathan saw Jeffrey's bag for the first time. He laughed. "Good for you, Jeffrey. What do you have there?"

"I got our clothes, and I grabbed food on the way out."

"Jeffrey, you are amazing!" Chrystal and Chasity said as they hugged him.

There was a spot beneath the tree where the kids sat down. They ate hot dogs, fried chicken, and Hawaiian punch. Everyone laughed and had fun. They looked like they were having a picnic. It made Jeffrey so happy to see his siblings appreciate what he did for them. He felt so loved.

It was dark, and the kids were tired. They cleaned up the mess before sleeping in the bushes. No one would see them there. Jonathan noticed a police car patrolling the area. He whispered to the others and told them to keep quiet. They huddled together, praying the police wouldn't see them. As the patrol car drove by, their hearts pounded faster. The police passed by without noticing them. The kids breathed a sigh of relief and agreed they needed another place to sleep if the police returned. Jonathan looked around and spotted a bread truck parked outside a mini-market. He saw the driver exit and grabbed a dolly to deliver.

"I think I located our ride," he added, pointing to the truck.

"Seriously?" Jeffrey asked.

"It worked for us before. Maybe it'll work again," Jonathan speculated.

The kids snuck into the back of the truck. They hid behind the boxes, and moments later, they felt the truck moving. Chasity picked up a bag of bread and ate. Her siblings followed suit and finished the bag. They giggled with excitement as they bounced around. The truck rumbled down the highway, and the kids settled in for the long ride. They had been on the road for hours when the truck slowed down. Noises from the bustling streets awakened them.

"Where are we?" Chasity asked, rubbing her eyes.

The children stepped outside after opening the back door. The sunlight hit them, making them squint. They looked around the busy street.

"Where are we?" Chasity asked again.

The cold trembled in her voice. They were in front of a bakery. There was a laundromat next to it with a sign reading "Brooklyn."

"Where is Brooklyn?" asked Jeffrey. "How do we get to Toledo?"

"No idea," Jonathan said.

Moments later, the truck driver returned. They watched him drive away.

"Oh, no! I left my backpack in the truck," Jeffrey said.

"Well done, Jeffrey. We have no clothes or food," Jonathan said.

"Sorry, I forgot I had them."

"What are we going to do? I'm hungry," Chrystal said.

"We still have $20, but we have to be smart about spending it. We have to stretch our money as far as possible. Let's see if we can find something filling and cheap."

Chrystal was holding something in her hand when Chasity saw her.

"What do you have there?" she asked.

Chrystal stuffed the bread in her mouth, her cheeks bulging. She swallowed in a hurry, feeling the bread slide down her throat. "Nothing," she replied, her cheeks still full. "It's just some bread," she said, her voice muffled by the food.

Chrystal's pocket was full of bread when Chasity pulled it out.

Taking the bread and sharing it with Jonathan and Jeffrey, Chasity said, "You could have shared it with us."

"I was planning to, but I got hungry," Chrystal said.

The children laughed as they ate. Thanks to Chrystal for taking the bread and relieving them of hunger. Walking down the busy street, the children watched the traffic. Fish, meat, and vegetable markets were everywhere. At the plaza, they saw some children playing. They stopped to watch them for a moment before continuing on their journey. They were getting tired and their stomachs rumbled.

There was a hotdog stand selling plain hotdogs for $.99. They each bought one and sat down to eat. The man gave the children a bottle of water, which they shared. As they finished, Jonathan asked the hotdog vendor how to get to Toledo. He said he didn't know, but told the children to ask the police for directions. Jonathan thanked the man and left.

The children spent their first night in Brooklyn sleeping on park benches and washing themselves in public restrooms. It was their temporary residence for the next few days. Chasity and Chrystal sang beautifully, while Jeffrey and Jonathan danced to everyone's delight. People put money in their cups, but nobody asked why four kids lived on the streets.

A MONTH SLIPPED BY without the children showering. They were dirty and smelly, and their clothes were tattered and torn. They still slept in the park but had to move around so the police didn't catch them. The children had to keep an eye out for patrols and try to find new spots every day. They had to endure the rain and cold, and they were often hungry and tired.

Being separated from their father was difficult for the children, especially since they did not know whether he had recovered. The children were freezing, hungry, and filthy.

They had to rely on each other for support and strength. They had to find the courage to keep going.

"I thought we were heading to Toledo," Chrystal asked.

"How many times must I tell you? We need money for bus tickets," Jonathan explained.

"How much do we need?" Chasity asked.

"I'm not sure," Jonathan replied. "It's possible we'll need $100."

"We need a miracle, you mean?" Jeffrey said.

"Yes," the kids said.

One day, a kind stranger bought the kids hamburgers and sodas. They ate and drank happily, grateful for their unexpected gift.

The stranger smiled and said, "Enjoy your lunch, kids," before walking away.

The children were so hungry that they didn't notice a police officer standing alongside them.

"Ahem!" He cleared his throat. "Children, what are you doing here? Where are your parents?"

It surprised the children and rendered them speechless.

"Officer, our parents should arrive soon. They left to get more food," Jonathan answered.

The officer examined the children's filthy and ragged clothing. "Homeless, huh? We'll wait for your parents, then I'll drive you to the shelter. Children should not be out on the streets."

The kids exchanged glances, as though they were debating what to do. The officer did not leave and sat on the bench with them while they waited for their parents. Two hours later, the children's parents still hadn't returned, and the police officer became suspicious.

"Are you sure they're coming back?"

"I'm sorry, officer. Our parents sometimes take a long time to get us food, but they should be here soon," Jonathan explained.

The cop didn't believe him, so he dialed his phone. He asked Child Protective Services to pick up the children. When the police turned his back on them, the kids took off. The police officer pursued them, and the youth hid behind a garbage can. The cop didn't see them and ran towards the next street. When Jonathan saw him return, they needed another place to hide. By this point, the only way the kids knew to get away from the cops or anyone else was to hop on the back of a truck.

There was no truck around, but Jonathan spotted a white van parked in the alley. He tried the door handle, and it was unlocked. He opened the side door and told his siblings to crawl inside and hide in the third-row back seat.

The children observed the cop scratching his head and running to the next street. They chuckled. The youngsters laughed and high-fived each other, celebrating their successful escape. They heard voices as they about to step out of the van. They crept back inside.

Tilly and her husband, Dusty, a globe-trotting multi-millionaire power couple, led a glamorous lifestyle, but they were also serious philanthropists. When they were not busy running their businesses, they volunteered for their charitable foundations.

Dusty parked their van in an alley to pick up their favorite Italian food for supper. They were in Brooklyn for their monthly outreach and food delivery program to local homeless shelters. It had been a long day, and all Tilly wanted to do was eat spaghetti and take a hot bath. She couldn't wait to get home and relax. She and Dusty had worked hard all day, and now it was time to reward their efforts.

"Tilly, I made this for you. Your favorite dessert," Alfredo said.

Alfredo and Dusty had maintained a close friendship since their time in Italy. Dusty introduced Alfredo to Tilly at his mother's birthday party. Alfredo catered for the event. Tilly and Alfredo hit it off and soon became close friends. They often hung out together, and Alfredo cooked something special for Tilly whenever they were in Brooklyn. Tilly loved Alfredo's desserts and always requested them.

"Tiramisu? Alfredo, you spoil me. I think I gained 10 pounds in the last week from eating your delicious dishes."

"I enjoy cooking for you, Tilly," Alfredo remarked. "However, Dusty here is far too thin. He needs more pasta."

"I think I'm fine," Dusty said while rubbing his stomach.

"Nonsense!" Alfredo said. "You need to eat. I made you a big plate of pasta with all your favorite toppings."

"Who am I to refuse your food?" Dusty laughed.

"I'll see you both next time you visit Brooklyn, okay?"

Tilly hugged Alfredo, and Dusty shook his hand before saying goodbye. They returned to the van and placed the food in the back seat.

"Are we heading home now?" Tilly asked.

"Yes," Dusty replied. "We dropped off the last food container at the shelter. It's been a long day for us, and I'm exhausted. Your reunion with Alfredo seemed endless. He never stopped talking or ran out of things to say."

"Oh, you noticed that too, huh? He is a fantastic storyteller."

They both laughed.

Meanwhile, the children didn't notice the van moving. They smelled the food, and their bellies grumbled. The scents were heavenly. Chrystal reached for the bag and attempted to open it, but Chasity swatted her hand away and yelled no.

"But I'm hungry," Chrystal remarked.

"Shh, they'll hear us," Chasity said.

It was too late. Tilly thought she heard voices. Looking back, she saw only food bags in the back seat.

"Did you hear something, dear?"

"What do you mean?" asked Dusty.

"I thought I heard voices from behind us," she whispered.

"What?"

Dusty pulled off the road and parked. He stepped around the van and unlocked the sliding door, shocked to see four children huddled in the third-row seat.

"What are you doing there?" Dusty asked.

"I'm sorry, sir. The cop was after us, and we saw your van was open, so we jumped inside," Jonathan explained.

"Wait, what? Why was the officer chasing you? And where are your parents?"

The kids remained silent.

"All right, we have to take you home. Where do you live?" asked Dusty.

The kids shook their heads.

"We don't have a place to live," Chrystal said.

"What do you mean, you don't have a place to live?"

"Our mother died, and our father is in the hospital," Jonathan explained. "They evicted us from our apartment. The social worker took us to a shelter, but we fled because they intended to separate us. We're heading back to Toledo. We have friends there."

"Toledo?"

"That's where we used to live. And now, we live in Connecticut," Jonathan said.

"Connecticut? How did you end up in Brooklyn?"

"It wasn't easy, ma'am. We had to hide in the back of a truck."

"Oh, I see," Tilly said. "But, children, I know you think what you did was right, but it wasn't. It's dangerous. It's a good thing nothing terrible has happened to you. Promise me you will never do this again."

"We promise," Jeffrey said.

"Okay, kids, you're coming with us. It's late, and I'm sure you're hungry and sleepy. We'll discuss it in the morning, okay?"

The kids exchanged glances. They weren't sure if these people would take them back to the shelter. What have they done this time? Should they run? However, the smell of the food in the paper bags was delicious. They were so hungry that they took a risk and stayed. One thing was certain: As soon as they finished eating, they would run away.

CHAPTER FOUR

Dusty arrived in front of their apartment building in no time. Four dirty children emerged and greeted the doorman when he opened it. The smell of the children made him cover his nose. He ushered the children into the building, trying to ignore their stench.

"These are my nieces and nephews. They played in the mud," Tilly said as she pushed the children inside.

"Wow! This is a very large building," Jonathan remarked, and his siblings agreed.

The lobby was enormous, with marble floors and a grand staircase. It adorned the walls with paintings and sculptures. Chrystal looked up at the chandelier, which was made from millions of tiny glass pieces, and lit up the entire lobby. They stepped into the elevator and felt the smooth ride to the top floor.

As they entered the lovely residence, the children's jaws dropped. It featured a view of Lower Manhattan. They could see the Empire State Building and all the other amazing structures. There were six bedrooms, each with its own bathroom and walk-in closet. The apartment featured great living and dining space, an eat-in kitchen, and panoramic views of New York City.

"Is this your house?" Chrystal asked.

"Yes, when we're in town," Tilly said. "There is another house near here where we always stay. It's an old house with a cozy feel. We love it there."

"Whose house is it?" Chasity asked.

"It was my parents' house," she said. "It's where I grew up."

Tilly felt lonely after talking about her childhood home. She missed her parents.

"Kids, wash your hands before eating. I'll get dinner ready in a few minutes," she continued. "I'm sure you're all hungry. Afterward, you need a long bath."

The kids walked to the kitchen to wash their hands. Chrystal turned on the faucet and grabbed a hand towel. She dried her hands and handed the washcloth to her siblings to do the same. They washed and dried their hands before sitting down to eat.

"Make sure you use soap. I don't think you've washed your hands in over a year," Tilly said.

Chrystal laughed and said, "Yeah, I guess you're right. We've forgotten to do that."

"Let's all remember to wash our hands with soap before and after eating from now on, okay?" Tilly said.

"Yes, ma'am," the kids said.

Dusty laughed so hard that he choked, and the kids laughed at him. They sat down to eat. Tilly was relieved Alfredo had given them an additional order of spaghetti because she wasn't sure there would be enough to feed the kids. They were really hungry. Otherwise, she'd have to order pizza.

The children smiled and laughed as they enjoyed their meal. Dusty and Tilly looked satisfied as they watched them. There was no food left on the kids' plates after eating. They licked their lips and wiped their mouths clean. Tilly and Dusty grinned when they burped.

"Children, I want you to rest for a few minutes, then take a long bath. Please leave your clothing in the hallway so we can burn it later. They're disgusting," said Tilly.

Dusty prepared the tubs in each bathroom and poured a bubble bath, and suds soon appeared. He told the children to soak, scrub, and wash their ears. Meanwhile, Tilly called her friend at the general store down the street and ordered toothbrushes, underwear, shorts, and T-shirts for the kids. She gave her the children's ages and instructed her to hurry.

Tilly's order arrived moments later. Dusty thanked the delivery man for his prompt service as he opened the door. Dusty gave the man a generous tip as a thank-you. The man thanked Dusty and left, smiling. Tilly walked into the kitchen and opened the boxes to make sure everything was there. It did.

The children were still in the tub, laughing and giggling as soapy bubbles floated around. The warm water soothed their skin. They splashed and had fun, making a mess in the bathroom.

After the children finished bathing, they put on their pajamas. They loved the fabric's smoothness and warmth. Tilly gave the kids toothbrushes, and they took them to the bathroom to brush their teeth and rinse their mouths. They felt cozy and relaxed, ready for bed.

Tilly led them to a big room with two king-size beds. There was nothing better than lying in bed and wriggling your entire body to the sounds of silky sheets against your skin and pillows that smelled so divine.

Tilly walked to the kitchen to get a nightlight for the kids.

"I love it here," Chrystal said.

"Me too," Chasity said.

"I understand what you mean, but we still need to be cautious. Keep your eyes and ears open to anything. We don't know what they plan to do with us," Jonathan explained. "We want to make sure they do not send us back. You know what we need to do if they do."

Dusty and Tilly entered the room shortly after and tucked them in. Tilly plugged in the nightlight, and it lit up the room with a soft orange glow.

"Thank you very much, ma'am and sir," the children said. "We didn't expect such a comfortable bed after sleeping on park benches."

"I'm pleased you like it. Tonight, you need to rest. Tomorrow, I have a surprise for you. Now let's rest. Good night, kids," Tilly said.

The youngsters knelt on the bed and kissed Tilly and Dusty till they tumbled off the bed, giggling. But soon they quieted down.

"Good night, sleepy heads. We'll see you all in the morning."

Tilly and Dusty left the room. The children snuggled up in their beds and drifted off to sleep, excited about what Tilly had in store for them tomorrow.

"It appears we have a puzzle to solve. We need to help the children. We need to find out what happened to their father," Tilly said when the two were alone in their room. Tilly thought for a moment and continued, "Let's start by asking the children. So far, we know their mother died and their father is in the hospital. CPS was involved and ran away."

"I'll call CPS in Connecticut tomorrow and let them know the kids are staying with us and provide them with any information they may need," Dusty said.

"Ask them what hospital the father is in so we can check his condition," Tilly said.

Tilly and Dusty took the kids shopping for clothes, shoes, and other fun items. The children were ecstatic when Tilly told them they could buy whatever they wanted. Chrystal, like Chasity, purchased a handbag and purple glitter for hair art, nails, and face painting. Tilly bought Chrystal and Chasity matching earrings. Jonathan bought a blue shirt and Vans shoes, while Jeffrey settled for a backpack and a camera.

After shopping, Tilly and Dusty brought the children to an indoor theme park with slides, bumper cars, roller coasters, a mini-golf course, and a Ferris wheel. The kids were so excited to explore all the attractions. They had a blast and played for hours. After they were done, they ate pizza for lunch. The children spent the rest of the day playing water gun races, balloon darts, and milk bottle games. Tilly and Dusty were happy to see the children smiling. They enjoyed themselves, and they returned home exhausted.

Tilly and Dusty had a heartfelt talk with the children in the evening while eating pizza and chicken wings. It was what the youngsters requested. Pizza was their favorite food. Tilly wanted to know why they fled and what happened to their father. The children took a long time to open up, and they told them everything that had transpired. They claimed it all started when their father lost his job.

"Dad told us that someone in their office hacked into his work computer and caused him to lose his job. He looked for work but found none. Dad became depressed and drank," Jeffrey explained. "He had an accident at home when he hit his head, and now he's in a coma, whatever that means."

"Our father wanted to clear his name, but they wouldn't let him return to the building. He couldn't find any evidence to prove he was innocent," Jonathan said. "We know him. He adores us. He didn't do what they said he did. Our father is an honorable man."

Dusty and Tilly exchanged glances.

"It is too late to help your father," Dusty said. "The damage has been done, and we cannot reverse it. They fired your dad from his job. There is nothing we can do about it."

Jonathan replied, "The reason our father turned to drinking was to clear his name. He was innocent."

"But kids, I don't know what we can do to help," Tilly said.

"Can you look into it, anyway? For our father?" Jeffrey asked.

"Don't worry, children. We will do everything we can to help your father."

TILLY AND DUSTY SAT down with the kids a few days later. No one said anything while Tilly stared at them. Then she broke the silence by saying, "You don't have to travel to Toledo anymore. We have located your father at Loyola Hospital. They moved him to a private room, and we hired a nurse to care for him. Would you like to stay with us for a while? You are welcome to visit your father whenever you want."

"Really?" Jonathan asked.

"Yes, really," Tilly responded. "We spoke with Child Protective Services, and they consented to let us be your temporary foster home until they locate your relatives in Toledo. We will ensure you feel comfortable and safe here. Dusty and I will be here for as long as you need us. We are here to help you and your father get better."

"Oh, we like that a lot," the kids remarked as they hugged Tilly and Dusty.

"As soon as we receive all your documents, we will enroll you in school. Would you like that?" Tilly asked.

The children smiled. "Yes, of course! We can't wait to learn!"

"In the meantime, it's time for bed. Don't forget to brush your teeth," Tilly said.

The kids dashed into their room, changed into pajamas, and hurried to the bathroom to brush their teeth. They hopped into bed and slid under the lovely blankets when they finished. Tilly and Dusty came later to check on them. They stood there, staring down at the sleeping children as if they were little angels. Tilly asserted it forced the children to mature quickly because of circumstances beyond their control.

"It's important to them to clear their father's name. I don't know what we will discover, but the children need our help, and we're here for them. We'll make sure of it," Dusty said.

"Should I contact Garrett, or do you want to do the honors?" Tilly teased her husband and giggled as they headed to their bedroom to sleep.

Garrett was Dusty's private investigator who helped them with personal matters, even working undercover to get the answers they needed. Tilly and Dusty trusted Garrett with their lives. They knew he was reliable and dependable. He always kept them safe and had their backs no matter what.

Dusty had to pull some strings to get Garrett hired as a security inspector at Sec-Ur, a security and alarm system handling Arlington Textile's account. Dusty's business associate, Mr. Davis, owned Sec-Ur.

Garrett became friends with the mill guards after checking their surveillance footage.

"Do you have any issues?" Garrett asked.

"No, we have a state-of-the-art system," the guard said as he watched the TV screens. "We keep surveillance videos for 120 days."

"Do you mind if I check?"

"Sure."

"Please allow me to test your computer knowledge and experience. Are you interested?"

"That sounds fun. Yeah, I'm up for it."

"All right, let's start with an event three months ago. I learned about it from your company's newsletter."

"Three months ago?"

"Can you recall anything unusual that happened?"

The guard shook his head. "That was a long time ago. I can't even remember what I had for breakfast this morning," he laughed.

Garrett showed the man what he had on his phone. The article on Arlington Textile's website talked about losing a big account and the company's recovery.

"Oh yes, that's right. I remember now," he said. "They let go of a supervisor three months ago. I was out of town when it happened. When I returned the next day, I found out they had fired Dexter, who was a supervisor at the warehouse. This took me by surprise. He was a wonderful, pleasant guy. They accused him of causing problems with orders. He would never make a mistake like that. He was diligent and precise in his work. Everyone knew that."

"Wouldn't you say the man was okay?"

"Yes, of course. Dexter brought us coffee every day. He always smiled, greeting us when no one bothered. He was a pleasant person to be around."

"Did security review the surveillance videos?"

"Not that I'm aware of. There was no reason to."

"Then let's look at the security video, shall we? Let's choose a date randomly. How about March 4th, the day before Dexter's termination? Let's look at the data from that day."

The officer activated the application and accessed the footage. Garrett reviewed several videos but found nothing unusual.

"Where is the video from this angle?" Garrett asked, pointing to the warehouse camera.

The guard uploaded it, which also had nothing on it, but something caught Garrett's eye from afar. He paused the video and expanded the image. Garrett noticed a man entering Dexter's office after everyone left. The time stamp on the security video showed 7 p.m. Warehouse hours close at 6 p.m.

Garrett asked the IT Department to check the security database to see who used the computers after hours on March 4th. Dexter appeared to be logged into his computer when the man entered his office. However, Dexter's security badge showed he had left the premises at closing time. Arlington Textile had a tight security system, requiring employees to swipe their badges when entering and exiting the building. A guard identified Diego as the man on the tape when they enlarged the image. As confirmed by IT, Diego swiped and left the building at 7:15 p.m. on March 4th. Garrett identified the perpetrator.

CHAPTER FIVE

Six months after being in a coma, Dexter awoke. He was confused and disoriented, but he tried to make sense of the situation. His memory slowly returned, and he remembered his life before the accident. Dexter remembered his children and asked about them. The doctor informed him they had contacted his family and they would visit him soon.

Dexter opened his eyes and saw his children standing by his bedside. It filled the kids with joy to see their father awake.

"Children!" he mumbled.

"Dad! You're awake!" Chrystal shrieked as she embraced and kissed him. Jonathan, Chasity, and Jeffrey followed.

"How are you all doing?" Dexter asked, concerned.

"Dad, you've been here for six months. You sleep a lot," Jonathan remarked.

Dexter was shocked to hear he had been in the hospital for that long. He didn't realize how serious his actions were, which got him hospitalized—that someone had to take care of his children without him was heartbreaking. Dexter felt guilty for not being there for them. He did not know how his children managed without him and expressed concern for their welfare, as he feared they were not receiving proper care.

"Who looks after you?" he asked.

"After your accident, Social Services took us away. We waited for you to come, but you never did," Jonathan explained. "I overheard them talking about putting us in foster care and splitting us up after you fell into a coma. We didn't want it to happen, so we escaped."

"To where?"

"We planned to return to Toledo, but we didn't have the money, so we hitched a ride on a truck. We ended up in Brooklyn."

"Brooklyn? Brooklyn, New York?" Dexter's eyes welled up with tears the entire time he spoke. "What were you thinking, kids? You could have gotten lost. Something horrible could have happened to you."

"Nothing has happened to us, Dad. We are fine," Jeffrey said.

"We slept on park benches. Jonathan and Jeffrey danced, while Chasity and I sang. People gave us money, Dad. We had money to buy food, mostly hotdogs," Chrystal explained.

"Shh!" Jonathan hushed her.

Chrystal ignored him and continued. "We had to run from the police after they chased us."

Jonathan smacked his forehead. Chrystal never paid attention to everything he said. He talked with everyone earlier, and they agreed to keep that information secret from their father to spare him any worry. Chrystal couldn't resist blabbing about their experiences.

"What?" Dexter exclaimed. "Oh my God!"

"Don't worry, Dad," Jonathan said. "We ended up in Tilly and Dusty's van. They took us in, and we have stayed at their house ever since. They even sent us to a private school. When they found out about your situation, they moved you to a private room and even hired a nurse to look after you."

Dexter couldn't believe someone had stepped in while he was in the hospital to help him and his children.

"Who are Tilly and Dusty?"

Tilly and Dusty walked up to Dexter and greeted him. It was such a relief to see him awake and speaking.

"We're glad you're awake, Dexter," Dusty said. "While you were here, we temporarily fostered the children."

"CPS found your relatives in Toledo, who came here to visit you. Once they found out we put you in a private room and saw the kids were happy in our care, they allowed them to remain with us. The children visit them once in a while," Tilly said.

Despite his best efforts, Dexter couldn't hold back his tears. "I hope they didn't cause you so much trouble."

"There is no need to worry," Dusty said. "Your kids are remarkable. They showed respect, politeness, and enthusiasm. They do well at school and receive praise from their teachers. You raised them well."

Dusty told him everything that had happened in the previous six months while he was in a coma. He said the children visited him on weekends and talked about their schoolwork and awards. Jonathan tried out for football and made the team. Since Jeffrey was a computer whiz, they enrolled him in a workshop.

Dexter smiled at Dusty's words. He was proud of his children, and he felt relieved that they were doing well. Dexter knew Dusty had done a great job caring for them while he was away. He could see his children were happy because they laughed and talked together. There was a sense of connection between them.

Tilly mentioned that Chasity and Chrystal were attending ballet class and performing admirably.

"Your children need you, so you should make things better for them," Dusty said. "They are wonderful kids. You should be proud of them."

Dexter's eyes welled up. He felt a surge of pride for his children. He thanked Tilly and Dusty, but not without apologizing first, and told them his story. After being fired from his job, he said he had become depressed. He turned to drinking to cope with stress when he couldn't find work. Dexter felt guilty for not providing for his family because of his mistakes. He was grateful for their kindness and support. Having learned his lesson, Dexter promised to never repeat the same mistake and never drink alcohol again.

"I love my children very much. Please believe me," Dexter said. During his drinking, he said he did not realize the consequences of his actions. Dexter drew a cross on his chest and said he would never drink again.

"That's great to hear, Dexter," Dusty said. "It's okay to drink, but in moderation. We believe in second chances, and your children do too."

"Thank you, children," Dexter said as he wept. "I promise to work hard to give you a better future."

"We love you, Dad," the children said as they hugged him.

"Dexter, the kids told us about what happened to you at work and wanted us to help you," Dusty said. "We told them we couldn't do anything for you, but they were determined to clear your name. We are thrilled to share with you some wonderful news. Garrett, our private investigator, found the evidence you sought. It turns out that one of your coworkers removed some work orders from your computer to discredit you. It was the reason they canceled the delivery. Garrett provided Mr. Arlington with proof to back up his claim. After Garrett presented this information to Mr. Arlington, Diego confessed, and Mr. Arlington fired him."

"Are you saying Diego deliberately ruined my life? Why would he do that?"

"In his confession, he expected a promotion, but they offered it to you. He was jealous and swore vengeance."

"Just for a job, he ruined my kids' lives and mine."

"Dexter, not everything is lost."

Everyone looked at the man who had just entered the room.

"Nolan!" Dexter said when he saw his former college roommate.

"Please accept my apologies, my old friend. When they fired you, I should have stood by your side. I knew you'd never make a mistake like that. It was my responsibility to defend your right to fair treatment. I let you down, and I'm sorry for that."

"Thank you, Nolan. I appreciate that."

"I am informing you that Mr. Arlington apologizes for the incident. His presence today is impossible, as he is in New York for a meeting. He wanted me to tell you he is taking steps to ensure it never happens again. You'll be back on the team once you are better, Dexter. All is well. Your warehouse team, along with everyone else, is waiting for your return."

Dexter's eyes were brimming with tears. Tears of happiness were shed at that moment. He was finally found innocent. Thanks to Tilly and Dusty.

"I'll return later, okay? Just rest," he replied as he shook his friend's hand and left.

"Dexter, we talked to the doctor, and they want to take some tests to make sure you're okay. The road to recovery is still long. They will refer you to physical therapy to regain muscle mass. You'll need to stay here for a short while, and once the doctor says you're fine, he'll release you," Tilly said.

"Oh, I see."

Dexter's eyes were sorrowful. It should have been a relief to him, but where would they go after his release? Where would they live? The last thing he remembered was their eviction from their apartment.

Dusty could sense his anxiety.

"I hope you don't mind, Dexter. We spoke with the kids, and they all expressed a strong desire to stay in New York. They love their new school. We would like you and the children to stay in our apartment while you recover. If you're okay with it, we hired a cook and nurse to care for you and the kids," Dusty said.

Dexter paused for a moment to consider his offer. No way could this be true. Was everything that happened to him and his children a dream? Were there still good people in the world? What made him think he could rely on them? Then again, without Tilly or Dusty, where would they be? The offer was too tempting for them to refuse.

Dexter had too many questions and guesses but couldn't say no. Without money, he and the children would have to live on the streets after the doctor released him. He was worried about what would happen to them. Dexter needed a job and a home but wasn't sure how to make that happen. He trusted his gut instincts and took a chance. Their situation was dire, and they needed all the help they could get.

Dexter smiled back at his children. They appeared healthy and cheerful. Tilly and Dusty did an excellent job looking after them. He looked over and saw honesty in Dusty's eyes. He turned to glance at his children.

"Are you certain this is what you want?"

"We are sure, Dad. Running away was the best thing we've ever done," the children said.

"I regret not fulfilling my duties as a responsible father to you. My depression was so overwhelming that I forgot about you. I give you my word that it will never happen again, as God is my witness. I'm sorry for disappointing you. Can you forgive me?" Dexter asked.

"All we care about is that you're awake now, Dad. We'll be together again," Jonathan said.

Dexter cried when his children smiled and laughed. He turned to Dusty and accepted his offer.

"Are you sure, Dusty?" Dexter asked. "We don't want to burden you. That's five more mouths to feed. My kids eat a lot."

Tilly laughed. "I'm sure we can manage, Dexter. Don't worry."

"If the kids say yes, I guess we're moving to New York. We'll stay till I get better and find work," he said.

"Sounds like a smart plan, Dexter," Dusty said.

"Thank you, Tilly and Dusty. I don't know how we'll repay you."

"Please get well soon. Your children need you."

Dexter cried as he held the children in his arms. He let them down too many times. He would work hard to improve his children's lives. It was a promise he made to himself as he looked forward to the future.

Nolan was not surprised when Dexter declined Mr. Arlington's offer to return to work. He wished Dexter the best of luck in his future endeavors and told him to keep in touch. Nolan was confident Dexter would succeed in New York.

Dexter had to undergo several weeks of physiotherapy before he could walk on his own. Through a gradual process, they introduced him to various exercises to restore his strength and mobility. The physiotherapist encouraged him to practice the exercises, and as he progressed, they assigned him more challenging tasks. With dedication and perseverance, Dexter regained independence. Soon, the doctor released him.

The nurse escorted Dexter to the front of the hospital, where his children, Dusty and Tilly, awaited him. The driver opened the door and assisted Dexter into the vehicle. Dexter knew Dusty and Tilly were wealthy, but he couldn't imagine getting picked up in a limousine. The driver closed the door; the limousine pulled away, and Dexter was on his way home. It overwhelmed him with emotion as the reality of the situation set in.

Taking off on a private plane gave him happiness and excitement. He watched the world below him, feeling awe and wonder. A brand-new life in New York City sounds great to him. Dexter felt a wave of excitement as he thought about all the possibilities in the city. He knew this would be the start of an adventure that would change their lives forever.

Several months had passed, and Dexter seemed healthier than ever. He was more active and motivated. His skin was brighter, and his immune system was stronger. He increased his exercise regimen and improved his energy levels. The doctor was pleased with his progress.

There was no end to children's happiness. They had a wonderful life and were thankful for their father's recovery. As soon as Dexter could return to the kitchen, he experimented with various recipes. Dexter found his passion again, and the family enjoyed healthy meals together.

Tilly and Dusty tasted his cooking whenever they visited the family. His food was delicious, and Dexter always prepared something special for them. He was generous with his ingredients and often gave Tilly extra to take home. Dexter and the children celebrated every milestone with enthusiasm and joy. Everyone was thankful for their newfound happiness. The children were well-liked at school and had good grades.

Jonathan enjoyed sports and was popular with girls. He was a natural leader, often organizing social activities with his friends. His teachers praised him for his dedication and enthusiasm. They often chose him to represent his class in extracurricular activities.

Jeffrey emerged victorious in the class president's election. At a young age, he worked hard to ensure everyone felt heard and respected. His explanation was that he watched too many TV shows and got many ideas from them. He was a mentor to his peers and always willing to help. The example he set inspired his classmates.

Chasity was shy at first, but Jeffrey encouraged her to speak up. He helped her find her voice and gave her the courage to take risks. She auditioned for a play and got the role. They signed Chasity up for another play after her first success. Chasity thanked Jeffrey for his guidance and support. Jeffrey told her she could do anything she put her mind to. That's how supportive he was of his sister.

Chrystal was always the first to raise her hand and answer every question. Her teacher always praised her for her good behavior. Her classmates loved Chrystal for her charm, and everyone wanted to be her friend.

One day, Tilly and Dusty brought the family for a fun day out in the city. It surprised Dexter and the kids to see an enormous amusement park. The children were excited to explore all the rides and games. Dexter took pictures as the kids rode each ride. Tilly and Dusty helped them win prizes at the games. After the amusement park, they headed to the ice cream shop and had a big family ice cream sundae. The family had a wonderful day together.

What they didn't know was that Tilly and Dusty had another treat for them, and they couldn't wait to show it. As the limousine approached Times Square, it stopped in front of a two-story building on Broadway. The driver opened the door, and the family got out, along with Tilly and Dusty. As they walked into the building, Dexter noticed construction was going on. He saw several people walking around in hard hats and construction vests. He wondered what they would use the building for. It took Dexter a moment to realize how large the area was. A fine dining restaurant would be suitable for it, he thought.

Tilly and Dusty took the children upstairs. Dexter followed behind. There was a large living room, an open kitchen, an entertainment room, and a children's playroom. Tilly showed the children the bedrooms.

Dexter's heart pounded. He felt anticipation, knowing something big was about to happen. He was not sure what it was, but he was sure it would be something special.

"Are we living here, Tilly?" asked the kids.

"Yes, this is your new home, and the most exciting part is that it's close to school."

"Yay!" exclaimed the kids. "We love it."

"That's not all," Tilly said. "You are a very talented chef, Dexter. We sampled your food, and it was fantastic. Dusty and I are confident that you will make a name for yourself in the future. You mentioned you wanted to follow your heart and continue working as a chef, so here it is. You and the children will live upstairs, and downstairs is your restaurant."

Dexter wept and hugged his children.

"Tilly, I don't know what to say, but we can't accept it. It's far too much. Besides, I can't afford it. It's New York City. We're in Times Square. I don't even have a cent to my name."

"This place means a lot to me, Dexter," Tilly said. "When my parents moved to New York, this was the first home they purchased. This place was meaningful to them. It's been empty for years. I'm sure you'll make many lovely memories here. We had to renovate it to ensure there was enough room for the kids."

Dexter's chest flutters with excitement. This was not what he expected.

"You, Dusty, and I will become partners, Dexter," Tilly added. "The restaurant is still under construction, but we will open as soon as you are ready. Dusty will supply the wine from his vineyard in Italy. This will be a wonderful collaboration. Wouldn't you say so?"

Dexter lost control of his emotions and burst into tears of joy. His children sobbed as well. They thanked Tilly and Dusty for saving their lives and giving Dexter a second chance to be a responsible father to his children.

"That's not all, Dexter. Dusty and I want to ensure your children's future," Tilly said, handing him a white envelope.

"What is this?"

"Open it."

Dexter opened the envelope and pulled out a check. His eyes widened when he saw so many zeros written on them.

"A million dollars?" He screamed. "No way!"

When the kids saw the check, they jumped up and down, applauding, yelling, and screaming. They couldn't believe it, either.

"Tilly, I don't know what to say," Dexter cried.

"We're partners, aren't we? Living in New York is pricey. You will need to buy clothes and pay for the children's school tuition. You'll need to buy cookware and other items to start our restaurant."

Dexter wept with joy. He couldn't believe his luck. Dexter hugged Tilly and Dusty and thanked them profusely. It overwhelmed him with emotion. Dexter promised them he would never forget their kindness and generosity. His gratitude for the gift was sincere.

It's funny how a coma and children running away could turn magical. Dexter smiled as he thought of the strange events that led them to this moment. He was forever grateful for the experience and for Tilly and Dusty, who made it possible. Dexter was ready to start the next chapter in his life with his children by his side.

TILLY, DUSTY, DEXTER, and the kids welcomed the guests to Dexter's Bistro's grand opening. They held a ribbon-cutting ceremony to commemorate the event. It was a spectacular affair. Tilly's social circle of friends arrived. Political allies also supported Tilly and Dusty. Journalists and food critics were present.

Dexter prepared the most exquisite meal. Tilly and Dusty helped serve the guests. The children entertained everyone with their singing and dancing talents, followed by soft music. Dexter's culinary skills left a lasting impression on guests, who relished every bite of the mouthwatering meal and the inviting bistro setting. Critics praised it, awarding Dexter's Bistro five stars. Dexter was very pleased with the response and thanked everyone for coming. Their grand opening was a success.

Tilly and Dusty remained outside after the restaurant closed. She looked at the bistro and the apartment above. Tilly never lived in that house, but her mother always brought her there whenever she could. She did not know why her mother kept this property, but now she understands. It was a special place for her parents because magic was in every room. The time had come for her to pass on the enchanting moment her parents once had in the house to a deserving family that loved one another. Tilly and Dusty had full confidence in Dexter's understanding of the lessons he learned from drinking. They knew he had to earn his children's trust and respect again, and they knew he would never fail them.

Jonathan, Jeffrey, Chasity, and Chrystal's story inspired Tilly to restore her parents' empty Brooklyn building into a community center. This provided resources, support, and a safe place for young people. She dedicated the building to her parents and hoped it would serve as a healing and inspirational space for everyone.

Tilly later opened Mrs. M's Haven to help troubled teens and protect runaways and homeless youth from abuse and neglect. It would be a place they could turn to if they needed help, a place where they felt safe. Tilly's commitment paid off as her shelter became a refuge for those in need. Hundreds of people passed through the building, looking for help and solace. Tilly was proud of her work and the impact it had on so many people.

What would Tilly give to have her mother beside her right now, telling her everything she had accomplished? Even though she had done so well, it wasn't enough. She wanted to assist as many people as possible and provide opportunities.

However, the day was still young...

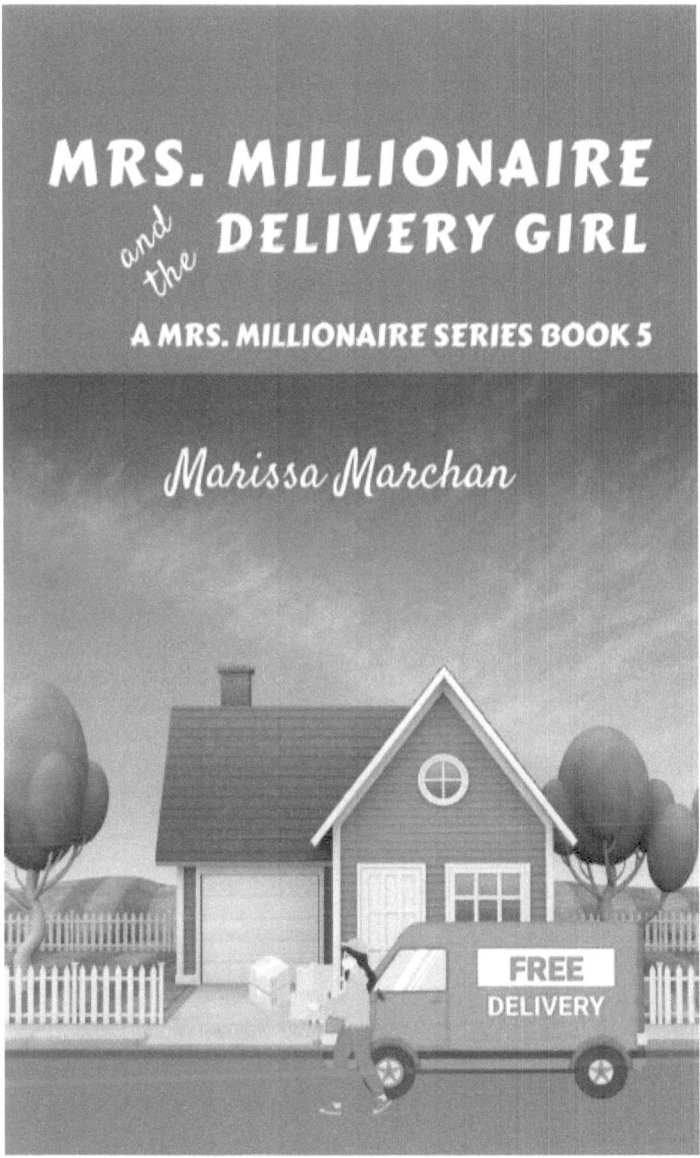

MRS. MILLIONAIRE
and the DELIVERY GIRL

A MRS. MILLIONAIRE SERIES BOOK 5

Marissa Marchan

MRS.
MILLIONAIRE
AND THE
DELIVERY GIRL

CHAPTER ONE

Nancy's pickup truck rumbled a mile away. She drove down the dusty road, and her tires kicked up dust clouds. The sun was setting, and the sky was aglow with vibrant colors. Honking her horn, she waved at protesters holding signs demanding shorter work hours and higher wages outside a factory. Nancy drove past them, keeping her eyes on the road. She honked again to show her support for the demonstrators.

Nancy glanced at her sleeping son in the back seat as she drove down a long, winding road. She felt a rush of emotion as she thought about how small and vulnerable he looked. Nancy took a deep breath and resolved to be a better mother for him, no matter what life threw her way. She was determined to give him all the love and support he needed.

He awoke a few minutes later, crying. Nancy pulled over to the side of the road and took a fresh bottle from the icebox. She inserted the nipple into the baby's mouth and watched as the baby sucked greedily. Nancy's mind wandered between events in her life as she pondered how she had reached this point. She had to admit that falling in love with a bad boy was her biggest mistake. She remembered the promises and dreams they made together. Nancy felt a deep sadness in her heart, knowing her life would never be the same.

Her husband enjoyed chasing women, even after marriage. He had roving eyes, and he loved flirting. Nancy regretted not leaving him earlier. Despite her best efforts, the love she felt for him blinded her. She should have known this would happen. Nancy never intended to become a delivery girl. She had plans, high aspirations, and big dreams. Nancy promised herself a long time ago that when she graduated and got a job, she would drive a red convertible and have her own apartment. Although she worked hard for this goal, it never came true. She may have settled for a minivan, but that hadn't happened either. Instead, she drove a delivery truck. Things did not turn out well for her. She worked hard to achieve them, but life had different plans for her.

Nancy was the most attractive girl in high school, in every sense of the word. Partying and mischief were Nancy's and her friends' favorite pastimes. They voted her homecoming queen, prom queen, and 'Most Likely to Succeed' by her peers.

After receiving a scholarship and admission to college, Nancy transformed her wild ways and pursued a nursing career. She concentrated on her academics, became involved in several social groups, and put off dating until she had a career. Nancy worked hard and excelled at her studies. Her parents were proud of her.

Then she met Julius at a school function, an attractive and charming man with a friendly grin and an easygoing disposition. He was not a student there but gatecrashed. Julius was unlike any other man Nancy had ever met before, and she felt a connection with him. He displayed kindness towards her and showed genuine concern for her well-being. They talked for hours, and at the end of the night, she knew she had found someone special.

Nancy felt a spark of excitement every time he was around. But Julius was also a playboy who dated different women every week. Nancy knew he was the wrong man for her. She avoided people like him. Nancy dated a lot of handsome guys in high school, but none of them had a reputation as a playboy, rumored or otherwise. But Julius never gave up and pursued her, persuading her to love him.

As they say, Julius's persuasion and aggressiveness paid off, and he swept Nancy off her feet. Nancy found herself drawn to him again, and they soon started a romantic relationship. She ignored the signs that Julius was not suitable for her as she had fallen in love with his charismatic manner. Nancy liked his bad-boy character, biker image, and rebellious style. It shattered her ambition for a successful career seconds after she fell victim to his charms. She lost her scholarship when she reverted to her wild habits, partying all night with Julius.

Nancy's parents were shocked to learn about her relationship with Julius. They warned her of the risks and pleaded with her to end it. But Nancy refused, and their relationship continued. Nancy expressed her devotion to Julius. Soon after, Julius and Nancy married at city hall in front of only a few friends, with no regard for the implications of their actions. Nancy's parents were furious. They considered Julius unpleasant, arrogant, and disrespectful to them. Nancy's father was upset when she picked Julius over them. He barred her from returning to their home. It tore Nancy apart, but she couldn't blame them. She broke their hearts.

Nancy realized she had made a grave mistake when she and Julius lived together. Julius, she thought, was wealthy and had his place in New York. Nancy should have detected something unusual when he brought her there when they were dating. She wasn't expecting a feminine touch in his apartment, but she was so in love that she never questioned him about it. She moved into Julius' apartment after they married. He became upset when Nancy suggested changing the apartment's look. It turned out that Julius didn't own the apartment. He house-sat for a friend who was a Peace Corps volunteer in southern Thailand. She had been away for about a year, and Julius had remained at her home all that time. Julius was unemployed too, but he never worried about money because his parents supported him.

Several months later, Julius's friend Shirley returned from Thailand to find Nancy living in her house. It angered Shirley, and she demanded an explanation. Embarrassed, Julius explained that Nancy was his wife and that they were staying there until they could afford a place of their own. Julius didn't tell Shirley this, and it angered her. Her impression was that she and Julius shared a special bond and mutual understanding. She let him stay in her apartment for that reason. Shirley felt tricked. She ended their friendship, feeling betrayed and deceived. Julius tried to apologize for not telling her the truth, but it was too late. Shirley threw them out of the house and threatened to call the police if they didn't leave. Nancy and Julius packed up their belongings and left. They had no choice but to live with Julius' family in Milwaukee, Wisconsin.

JULIUS' FATHER, LEROY, owned a courier company that delivered online orders to consumers' homes and offices. He appeared kind but drank heavily and spent most of his free time in bars. In his view, being a provider for the family was enough. Veronica never questioned or interfered with her husband's business or decisions. She left him alone, and Leroy did the same. Their understanding was mutual.

Julius had a sister, Olivia, who was an excellent example of a girl gone wrong. She was a snob and a troublemaker. Nothing satisfied her. Olivia expected her father to take care of her and provide everything she needed, and Leroy was happy to spoil his only daughter.

In the months they lived in her in-laws' house, they took Nancy for granted and treated her as if she were not part of their family. They expected Nancy to do all the household chores and never recognized her efforts. They criticized her for her cooking and housekeeping skills. Julius never stood up for Nancy or defended her against his parents' criticism. Nancy felt she had no one to turn to for help or support. She wanted to leave but had nowhere else to go. Neither her parents nor relatives would allow her to see them. They told Nancy that she was not welcome at their house. Even if she could, Nancy didn't have enough money to pay for the bus ride home. Julius didn't give her his money. There was no joint account, and he controlled their finances. In the end, Nancy had no choice but to stay and try to make it work.

She was determined to prove to her husband and his parents that she could do better. Her dedication to her marriage was unwavering.

When Nancy informed Julius that she planned to look for work, he objected and advised her to stay home. He told her that her job was to care for him and that she should focus on being his wife, not a career woman. Nancy resented this since she was caring not only for Julius but also for his entire family. In her mind, she was a servant, not a wife. Nancy was caught in this nightmare of a life.

Tragedy struck when Nancy's father-in-law died after a heart attack. His family knew nothing about the business or finances. With Leroy gone, everyone had to cut back on spending, which Veronica despised. She was used to having money for anything she wanted, and now she had to watch her spending habits. Olivia would not cut back on partying, socializing, and shopping. Her alternative was to open many credit cards. It wasn't necessary to change Julius' ways, since he slept all the time and was lazy.

Leroy's attorney was on vacation and didn't know of his passing until he returned. He visited the family to read his will. Of course, Veronica received most of Leroy's estate, including the family business. Olivia and Julius also received substantial amounts of money. Veronica sighed with relief when she realized she didn't have to change her lifestyle after all. Olivia exploited her newfound wealth, returned to partying, and spent money on expensive clothes and cars. As Julius no longer needed his parents' support, he spent time with his biker friends. He bought a state-of-the-art motorcycle and a classic car. While Nancy stayed at home, he enjoyed a luxurious lifestyle. Julius drove his motorcycle with his friends to a variety of cities and towns, exploring the countryside. He lived the good life.

Veronica was satisfied with her life, whereas Julius and Olivia squandered their inheritance. Concerned about their future, she wanted to make sure their money lasted. Veronica announced to her husband's business associates that her son was taking over the business. Julius controlled a company he never wanted to be part of. He refused at first, but his mother insisted. They held a meeting between Julius and several people at an undisclosed location. Prominent people from different backgrounds came. Throughout the meeting, Julius listened and absorbed every detail of the conversation. He didn't realize his father had engaged in unethical practices and had learned of his shady dealings. But the power it gave Julius made him feel invincible, and he ignored the warning signs. He took a risk and proceeded with his mother's plans. He continued his father's practices, despite his reservations.

Money trickled back in, and business boomed. Julius spent long hours away from home, traveling for work, and disappeared for days without telling Nancy where he had been. Nancy spent long days and nights alone at home. There was no one to talk to, and Olivia and her mother-in-law avoided her as if she didn't exist. Having worked so long hours, Julius returned home tired, exhausted, and cranky, wanting to rest and sleep for the rest of the day. This resulted in a strained relationship between them.

One day, Nancy prepared a quiet dinner for two in their bedroom. This was their first anniversary, and Nancy had prepared something special, something romantic, for Julius. Soft music played in the background. Nancy waited all night for Julius but gave up and fell asleep, only to be startled when the phone rang. Julius called to say he had some last-minute work to do and wouldn't come home. Nancy felt deep sadness and spent the entire night in tears, unable to comprehend why Julius prioritized his job over their relationship.

Nancy could no longer make special plans for them after that. She spent the holidays alone and couldn't recall the last time they traveled on vacation. Nancy felt a wave of sadness as she remembered all the memories they created together, good and bad, before moving to Wisconsin. The laughter and joy they shared, as well as their connection, were still fresh in her mind. That's all gone now. Nancy knew something was amiss with their marriage. She referred to her husband as her weekend lover because he was rarely present. Nancy wanted to end their relationship but couldn't. She believed that if they could only spend some time alone and restore romance to their lives, everything would be okay.

NANCY BECAME PREGNANT and gave birth to a handsome boy named Mark. Neither Julius' mother nor sister seemed happy about it. Veronica was cold towards Nancy and Mark, whereas his sister was hostile. Nancy could not understand Julius' behavior. Although he appeared supportive and happy, she felt something was missing. She confronted him about it, but Julius denied anything was wrong. Nancy told Julius not to work too much and to delegate work to his employees. The business was prosperous, and they needed quality time together. Nancy hoped Julius would appreciate their baby and enjoy family life. She was determined to ensure a healthy relationship. Julius promised to work less.

While a live-in babysitter cared for Mark, Nancy got involved in the company to show her husband she supported him, too. She handled paperwork, returned calls, and kept the office clean and organized. Nancy and Julius' relationship improved, and they spent more time together. Nancy was content with the way things were going until one night. Julius' cell phone rang while they were asleep, causing Nancy anxiety. She picked it up.

"Who is this?"

Nancy slammed the phone down when no one answered. The phone rang again. Julius told her to ignore it, but the phone calls continued. Nancy silenced the phone and returned to bed, irritated that someone had interfered with her life in that way.

Nancy awoke late the next morning. Her husband had already gotten out of bed. She looked throughout the house but couldn't find him. Nancy called his name but received no answer. She dialed his cell phone number, but it transferred the call to voicemail. Nancy found him in the garage, talking to someone on the phone, whispering, as if he didn't want anyone to hear what he was saying. She walked over and interrupted his conversation, asking who he was speaking to. Julius hung up the phone and acted surprised. Nancy wasn't buying his claim that it was a wrong number.

After that incident, Nancy noticed her husband receiving strange calls on his cell phone all day and night. She would pick it up, and her husband would pull it from her hand and say he got it. He would then leave the room and go outside to answer the phone.

With no explanation, Julius returned to working long hours, delivering packages to out-of-state addresses, and didn't return home for several days. Nancy noticed he had acted differently. On the days he was home, Julius was no longer intimate with her. His behavior confused Nancy, and she worried something was wrong. She confronted Julius, but he denied any issues. Nancy believed her husband kept something from her.

One day, Nancy arrived at the office to find everyone panicking. One of their drivers got into an accident, and they took him to the hospital. There was no driver available to take his position. If the company didn't transport the shipments that day, it would jeopardize its reputation. Nancy tried calling Veronica, but she did not answer her call. She contacted Olivia, but she never called back. Julius was out of state on business. Nancy reached out to him several times, but he didn't answer his phone.

With no other choice, Nancy took action, donning a company T-shirt and delivering the packages herself. Nancy was exhausted but satisfied, knowing she had completed the deliveries. She saved the company's reputation and kept her customers happy.

It was not long before her involvement as a delivery girl became a regular job. This was when Julius began sending his drivers to distribute packages outside the state. Local delivery was Nancy's responsibility. She wasn't happy about it, but Julius assured her it was temporary until they hired more people.

A few weeks passed. Nancy was at the grocery store, buying formula for her baby, when she noticed Ernie, one of the company's drivers, in the produce section. She was close friends with Yolanda, his wife. She walked over to say hello to Ernie, but he was on the phone. As she was about to leave, Ernie mentioned Julius' name, and Nancy wanted to eavesdrop. Ernie mentioned Julius' girlfriend living in Madison, an hour and a half from Milwaukee.

Nancy was outraged, but it made complete sense. She had thought her husband had been cheating on her for some time, but she had no actual proof, only suspicions and inconsistencies. Nancy caught Julius on a private phone call several times and asked him who he was talking to. He would always say, "Nobody in particular." It would end up in a big fight if she pressed Julius on the subject.

Nancy returned home and checked Julius' credit card statements and phone records online, but she could not access them. She searched his pockets and checked his shirt in the laundry for lipstick or evidence but found none. Despite her thorough search of the house, garage, and cars, she found no unusual items.

Nancy drove to the office and checked Julius' delivery records. All she found was during the first month after he took over his father's business. No one recorded his deliveries after that. He had been away for weeks with nothing to show for it. Where did he disappear? Nancy knew Julius was cheating on her. Now more than ever.

Nancy checked all the drivers' work order receipts and discovered that there were no records of deliveries outside of Wisconsin, which surprised her. Where did their drivers go on their trip out of state? What happened to Julius' trips to Detroit, New York, and other cities? Where did her husband go during the days, if not weeks, when he was unavailable? What did she not know? Was Julius' family running a shady business? Was the courier business a front for something else? It looked suspicious that the courier business was so profitable. It could have been used to launder money or smuggle goods. Nancy's suspicions intensified. There was no evidence that the company delivered outside of their local area. Nancy became convinced that the courier company was engaged in illegal activity.

Nancy became so agitated and enraged that she dialed Julius' number to get a straight answer, but he did not pick it up. She checked her husband's business cell phone records in the filing cabinet. Her heart raced as she looked through them. Nancy noticed many numbers she didn't recognize. She understood they could be clients but suspected something else was going on. Nancy thought they could be his other woman's number, too. Her jealousy and panic rose as she tried to reach her husband again, but he didn't respond. When he called her back, he made excuses for not responding, claiming he wasn't in the coverage zone or couldn't hear. That was the last straw. Nancy couldn't stand it anymore. She told Julius that she had discovered his affairs and wanted a divorce. She then hung up before her husband could say anything.

Nancy returned home, packed her suitcase, and told the babysitter her service was no longer needed. She asked her to collect her check from her husband. It surprised the sitter when Nancy ended her employment, but she acknowledged the rationale behind the decision. There was a noticeable tension between the family as if they were engaged in a battle.

Julius arrived shortly, surprising Nancy. He claimed to have stayed in a motel in Texas. How did he return so quickly? A heated argument led Julius to admit he had a girlfriend living a few miles away. He arrived a couple of nights ago, but instead of returning home, he stayed with his girlfriend.

Enough was enough, and no matter how much Julius claimed his affair was not serious and begged her to stay, Nancy refused to believe him. If she stayed, she would only get hurt. She knew their relationship was over and had to move on. It was a tough decision, but it was the right one. Yolanda, Ernie's wife, arrived to pick her up. Nancy left her husband and never looked back.

Veronica heard their arguments, and, judging by her expression, she was happy. After all this time, she still disliked Nancy as her son's wife. Veronica peered out the window as Nancy got into the car. She nodded. She felt like she had won this battle. As the car drove away, Veronica felt a sense of peace wash over her as she watched Nancy leave. Veronica had a wicked grin on her face. It was her duty to protect her son at all costs. She hoped this would be the last time her family saw Nancy.

CHAPTER TWO

D ays turned into weeks, and weeks turned into months. It had been three months since she left, and Nancy never saw her husband again. Julius knew where they were staying, but he didn't follow up or phone her. Julius showed no concern for her or their son. Ernie and Yolanda displayed kindness towards her, going as far as purchasing formula and diapers for the baby. Although they became close friends, she felt she had extended her stay. Nancy yearned to return home to the haven of a forgiving mother, to hold her and tell her everything would be okay.

Nancy swallowed her pride and got up, picking up the phone with all the strength she could muster. She dialed her parents' number and waited for an answer.

"Mama, it's Nancy," she began.

"What do you want?" her mother asked.

"I'm sorry, Mama, I let you down. I'm leaving him."

"You called me to say you're coming home after what you did?"

Her mother spits angrily. Nancy expected this. She begged her mother to forgive her.

"You disappointed us, Nancy. We thought you were studying hard to get your degree. You lied to us."

"I'm sorry I hurt you, Mama."

There was an awkward pause between them.

"Mama, you have a grandson. He's over a year old, and his name is Mark."

"Am I supposed to care that you have a child with your arrogant husband? If that's what you believe, you're wrong."

"I just thought you'd like to know."

"You were mistaken in your thinking. You might call me bitter and hateful, but you are no longer welcome here. Nancy, you hurt us. You're the only chance we have to escape poverty, and you promised to support us in our old age. We warned you of the risks and pleaded with you to end your relationship with that man. Your father and I were both upset that you married without informing us. What hurt the most was that we came to your school to surprise you. Instead, we got the shock of a lifetime. They informed us that you had dropped out and married that arrogant, disrespectful man. You deceived us! And to hear it from a stranger made your father and I humiliated and angry."

Nancy's mother felt emotional and slammed her phone down instead of finishing her sentence. Nancy sobbed. She knew her parents were upset with her, but she couldn't believe her mother wouldn't see her even after she told her about Mark. Nancy thought her mother and father would forgive her and love her. It didn't seem to matter that she needed their support. What a mess she made of her life! She admitted she had no right to blame them. She betrayed their trust. It was her fault.

There was a knock on the door a few moments later. Yolanda opened it to find a police officer looking for Nancy.

"I'm Nancy. What can I do for you, officer?" she asked. Her heart dropped when she saw his expression. Nancy feared that something terrible had happened. "What is it? Please tell me."

"I'm sorry to inform you that your husband was killed in an automobile accident this morning. We'd like you to accompany us to identify his body."

Nancy didn't hear the rest of the officer's words. She passed out and fell to the floor.

NANCY ATTENDED HER husband's memorial service. She struggled to hold back her tears as she listened to his eulogy. Nancy recalled all the special moments they shared and experienced happiness, laughter, sadness, and grief. She vowed to honor his memory and keep him alive in her heart for their son. Nancy placed two roses on the casket as a silent farewell. One was from her, and the other was from their son. Nancy held her composure until the end of the service.

Veronica was also present. She intended to embarrass Nancy, and she told everyone about it. She blamed Nancy for everything that happened to her son. Veronica claimed that if Nancy hadn't walked out on him, Julius would still be alive. Nancy believed everything Veronica had said and left the scene, her heart still heavy with regret. Veronica screamed and cursed at Nancy in the background, and Nancy heard everything she said. She cried while sitting on the bench. Nancy felt guilt and shame, knowing she was partly responsible for Julius' death. She dashed away, crying.

Nancy knew she could never make up for what she had done to Julius. It filled her with remorse and regret.

Attorney Salas, Julius's lawyer, visited Nancy one day.

"What can I do for you?" she asked.

"I would like to speak with you about your husband's will. May I come in?"

"Of course," Nancy answered as she led him to the living room. Then she walked into the kitchen and prepared some refreshments.

"Your husband provided a substantial trust fund for your son until his 21st birthday. Julius left you with his assets in his original will but changed them before the accident. Unfortunately, he left you with nothing," he added.

Nancy sighed. She expected it.

"For what it's worth, it wasn't Julius' idea. His mother pressured him into changing it."

"What about the business?" she asked.

"Julius ran it. Veronica owns the company."

"Is that it?" Nancy asked.

"There's another thing," the lawyer added. He took something from his coat pocket. He gave Nancy the key and title to her husband's custom-built truck.

"What is this?" Nancy asked.

"Julius bought the truck in Texas a week before he died. He paid cash for it. It will arrive at the dock on Friday. Since you are his surviving spouse and the co-owner listed on the title, it is yours," Attorney Salas explained.

Nancy couldn't understand why Julius added her name to the truck's title, considering they had been separated for months and hadn't communicated. She thought he didn't care about her. Why would he do that?

"As far as I know, there is no insurance on the truck yet, so you should get one before driving it."

Nancy couldn't stop crying.

"Are you okay?" Attorney Salas asked, concerned.

"I'm sorry. I felt responsible for my husband's death. He may still be alive if I hadn't walked out on him."

The lawyer scowled, perplexed. "Pardon me, but do you know how Julius died?"

"Yes, he died in a car accident." Nancy retorted.

"And what caused the crash?"

"My mother-in-law stated that my husband was unhappy after I left him and was not paying attention to his driving because of me. She blamed me for his death."

"Your mother-in-law said that? It's no surprise you're despondent. I'm sorry to break the news to you, Nancy. It's true. Julius was in an automobile accident. He lost control of his car, skidded off the road, and collided with a tree. He was with another woman at the time of the crash. The police found him unconscious, and the woman fled the scene. They found her a block away. They took your husband to a hospital, and the doctors pronounced him dead shortly after. According to the woman's statement, they were arguing at the time of the accident. Her comment about you enraged Julius, who drove faster and got angry. The woman tried to leave, but Julius lost control of the vehicle, swerved off the road, and crashed into a tree."

Her husband's affair with another woman hit Nancy like a ton of bricks. Even worse, Veronica made her feel guilty for Julius' death despite knowing her son had cheated on her and caused his death. Nancy had no memory of hating anyone, but that day, she wanted to tell Veronica what she thought of her—a vindictive and manipulative witch. It was at that moment that she recognized Veronica was not deserving of her time and energy. Nancy knew the truth, and it didn't matter what anyone said. She wasn't responsible for Julius' death. Nancy refused to feel guilty anymore about something that wasn't her fault. Her most effective revenge was to stay away from Veronica's family, earn her own money, and provide her son with a good life.

Attorney Salas was long gone when Ernie arrived home. He took off his shoes, flopped on the couch, and exhaled. It surprised his wife to see him so soon after he left for work two hours ago.

"What's the matter, Ernie? Why are you at home? Are you sick?"

Ernie gazed out the window. "We need to call Nancy. She needs to hear this."

Yolanda frowned, her eyes tense. She stood up and knocked on Nancy's bedroom door.

"Nancy, are you decent?"

Nancy opened the door. "Yes, Yolanda, what is it?"

"Ernie has returned home, and I believe he has some unpleasant news to share with you. He looks troublesome to me."

Nancy and Yolanda entered the living area to see Ernie clutching a beer.

"Did you want to see me, Ernie?" Nancy asked, puzzled and concerned.

"Yes, Nancy. Please sit down."

Silence reigned between them.

"For the love of God, Ernie, don't keep us in suspense anymore. Tell us what's wrong already."

"When I came to work this morning, Veronica was waiting for me," Ernie stated, taking a deep breath in between statements. "She called me to the office and said if I wanted to keep my job, I had to kick you out of my house."

"That is absurd," Yolanda stated.

"She handed me my termination notice and my last paycheck. That's how serious she was."

Nancy sighed. "I knew it would happen, but I didn't expect it to be this sudden." She bit her lip and looked away. Nancy knew she had to face whatever was coming, but she wasn't ready. "I guess I should have known better. Veronica and I never got along. As you already know, she despised me."

"But where would you go?" Yolanda asked. "Your parents want nothing to do with you."

"The last thing I want is for Ernie to lose his job because of me. Besides that, you can't keep supporting us. You have children to worry about."

"Nancy, there is something else you should know," Ernie said.

"What is it?"

"Julius gave me the money to cover your expenses when you and your son moved in with us. He told me to keep it quiet. He didn't want his mother to know."

Nancy stared at Ernie in surprise. She tried to speak, but nothing came out of her mouth.

"There's more," Ernie added. "The lady you mistook for his girlfriend in Madison was just a business deal. Nothing more. However, he was with his girlfriend when he crashed. Veronica arranged their relationship. She intended to end your marriage so Julius could marry that woman. The girl was Julius' childhood sweetheart. They broke up when Julius moved to New York. He told me he didn't love her. Julius made a mistake by letting his mother control his life. He planned to end the relationship with the woman and win you back. I guess that's why they fought in the car and caused the accident. Julius intended to do the right thing with you. Sadly, he never followed through with his plan. He died before he could make amends."

"I don't see how that information could benefit us now," Nancy said.

"I thought I should share what he told me," Ernie explained. "Julius was a lot of things, but I don't want you to think he didn't care about you or your son. He wanted his family back together."

"Why don't you sell the truck?" Yolanda said.

"The truck?" Nancy asked.

"Sure. You heard what the lawyer said. It's yours. What did Julius give you? A trust fund for your son that you won't see until he is 21. Fortunately, he bought the truck before he passed away. At least he left you with something."

"That's true. The truck is mine."

"Listen," Ernie said. "You need to hurry. It's only a matter of time before Veronica finds out, and I'm sure she'll do everything in her power to take it away from you. We both know this isn't about that truck. Veronica wishes to control and manipulate you. Her boyfriend will want the truck too since he drives Julius' motorcycle now."

"Veronica has a boyfriend?"

"Yeah, you didn't know? She's been seeing this guy for six months," Ernie said.

Nancy paused.

"Ernie, I'm giving you this advice because you are my friend. I know Leroy runs a shady business. There were some inconsistencies with their records, and I don't know what they were, but I understand it's illegal. Leroy passed it down to Julius, and now that he was gone, Veronica and Olivia would run the company. If I were you, I would get out now. You need to quit and find another job before the police catch up with them. Do this for your children before it's too late."

"Thank you, Nancy. I know about their business and have chosen not to speak out. You are right. I don't need to return to work. It's time to find another job."

"Good for you, Ernie," Nancy said.

Nancy called Attorney Salas and confirmed the truck's arrival at the dock. She said she planned to pick it up.

"According to the bill of lading, it should arrive at the pier tomorrow morning at noon. I rarely do this, but I'll make an exception. It's the least I can do for you. Julius was a dear friend. Come to my office at eleven o'clock, and I'll help you pick it up," the lawyer said.

"Thank you, Attorney Salas. I appreciate everything you've done for me. I'll see you tomorrow."

Nancy told Ernie and Yolanda what she had discussed with the lawyer. Yolanda and Ernie were relieved to hear the news.

"I'll drive you there, Nancy. Don't worry."

"Thank you, Yolanda."

"When you get the truck, what will you do?"

"My son and I will let the truck decide where we should go."

"I'll miss you, Nancy."

"Me too, Yolanda. I'll never forget you and Ernie."

"One more thing, Nancy," Ernie said. "I mentioned earlier that Julius gave me some expense money for you and Mark."

"Yes."

"There is still some money left, and I should return it to you. It will give you a fresh start."

"How much are we talking about?"

"Julius gave me $10,000, of which we already spent $2,000. There is still $8,000 left." Ernie walked into the bedroom and emerged holding the cash. Counting the money, he handed it to Nancy.

"Ernie, I think we should divide it up. Both of us need money. It will help me get to my destination, and it will support your family while you look for work."

"Thank you, Nancy," Ernie said.

The friends cried. They shared a warm hug and promised to stay in touch. As they parted, they felt sadness. But they knew that one day they would reunite.

Nancy drove across the country on I-64, her destination unclear. Her son sat in the back seat. She was overwhelmed with uncertainty and fear. As she traveled on her journey, Nancy did not know where she was heading or why she was taking this route. All she knew was that she needed to leave

Wisconsin. It didn't matter where she ended up; she knew she had to escape the Winslow family.

Julius's custom truck made Nancy's drive smoother. She got lost a few times, but got back on track with her GPS. Nancy found a motel sign and stopped there. She checked in and collapsed on the bed, exhausted from the long drive. Nancy imagined how pleasant it would be to have a proper house to come home to. She would settle in a small town and live a normal life with her son.

"Someday," she told herself.

CHAPTER
THREE

Tilly and her husband, Dusty, a globe-trotting multi-millionaire power couple, led a glamorous lifestyle, but they were also serious philanthropists. When they were not busy running their businesses, they volunteered for their charitable foundations. Tilly and Dusty worked non-stop and wanted some alone time. The two took a break from their daily routines and went somewhere far away from home. They packed their bags and headed to the mountains. Little did they know they were about to embark on a trip and discover something more valuable than riches and fame—something more precious than all the world's comforts.

Tilly and Dusty traveled to Tennessee for leisure and recreation in the Great Smoky Mountains. Dusty wanted to enjoy fishing and camping, while Tilly planned to go on nature walks and cozy up with her favorite book. They owned a cabin there and decided it was a good time to visit. It was a spur-of-the-moment decision to spend a week there. They drove instead of flying to see the breathtaking scenery along the way.

It was a smooth drive to Pennsylvania and Maryland, traveling through the picturesque Virginia countryside. When they spotted a warning sign showing traffic on I-81, they took a detour. They pulled over to check the map. They ended up taking a route that was much slower, but the scenery was much more beautiful. The drive was peaceful and scenic. The last town they passed was miles away when they ran out of gas in a remote location. Dusty turned on his right blinker and pulled over to the side of the road.

"I'm sorry, sweetheart. I neglected to check the gas gauge," Dusty said.

"What are we going to do?" Tilly asked as she peered around. There was nothing but cacti and sand.

"We'll just have to wait for someone to come," Dusty said. "Hopefully, it won't be too long."

Despite Tilly's nodding, her eyes showed worry. Dusty called the auto club but couldn't connect. They had no signal where they were.

"I'm sure someone will come along soon," Dusty said. He appeared optimistic but concerned. There was no house or building in sight. Dusty exhaled and knew they were in trouble. They needed a miracle to get them out of this bind.

Two hours had passed since they saw a car pass them. Their anxiety grew as the sun set, and the temperature dropped. It was getting dark, and they could hear coyotes howling. Tilly grew terrified and returned to the car. Dusty retrieved the emergency flares and bright red warning triangles from the trunk and positioned them on the road behind their disabled vehicle. Tilly huddled in the back seat, her eyes wide open in fear. Dusty stayed outside, waiting for help. Finally, he saw a distant car approaching, and Dusty waved frantically. Tilly got out of the car and ran towards it.

Meanwhile, Nancy was driving down the road when she noticed a Mercedes-Benz parked on the side. A man and woman flagged her down as she slowed down. She rolled down the window and poked her head out.

"Are you okay?" she asked.

"Thanks for stopping by," Dusty said. "We've run out of gas. Could you give us a ride to town?"

Nancy tried to read Dusty and Tilly. She hesitated. Nancy maintained a cautious attitude towards strangers while also feeling sympathy for them. She knew they needed help. Nancy didn't have to think twice about it.

"No problem. I'll give you a ride."

Nancy unlocked the door, and Dusty placed their luggage inside. He locked the car before helping Tilly get into the truck. It surprised them to see a baby in the rear seat.

"Your baby?" Tilly asked.

"Yes."

"How old is he?"

"He's more than a year old."

"My name is Tilly, and this is my husband, Dusty."

"Nice to meet you both. My name is Nancy, and this is my son, Mark."

Tilly calmed down as her stomach growled. Nancy grinned when she heard it.

"There are sandwiches in the bag and ginger ale in the cooler."

"Oh, thank you. We haven't eaten since this morning," Tilly said, taking a ham sandwich and sharing it with her husband.

"Do you mind if I ask you a question?" Tilly asked.

"Of course not. I don't mind," she said, her gaze locked on the road.

"Where are you and your baby heading?"

Nancy sighed. "To be honest, I'm not sure," she said.

"What do you mean?"

"It's a long story."

"It's a long drive," Tilly said. "If you want to share it with us, we'd love to hear it. We are terrific listeners."

Nancy glanced over at her sleeping son in the car seat. She believed it was a sensitive matter. She wasn't ready to share her life story with strangers. Tilly could see she was apprehensive.

"You don't have to tell us anything, Nancy. I was just trying to start a conversation."

"It's all right. I'll have to talk to someone, eventually. It might as well be you," Nancy joked.

Nancy told them everything from beginning to end. The words she spoke shocked Dusty and Tilly. Nancy was relieved to get the weight off her chest. She may have wanted to end this chapter of her life and begin the next one.

"I'm sorry to hear that," Tilly replied after Nancy ended her story. "Your parents' decision to abandon you is beyond belief."

"I tried calling my parents several times, but every time they recognized my voice, they hung up. Their phone was out of service the last time I called," Nancy explained. "I guess they no longer want to hear from me. I caused this to happen. It was my fault. Oh, what would I give to have my family back again? I just feel alone now." Nancy wiped away her tears.

"And what about your husband? You didn't know he cheated on you?"

"When I met my husband, I knew he was a womanizer, but I fell in love with him, anyway. He wasn't a bad guy. We were just stuck in a terrible place. My mother-in-law coerced my husband into seeing someone she thought would be a suitable match for her son. She wanted me out of the picture so Julius could marry someone she approved of. My husband's life was under her control, and he allowed it."

"Oh my God!" Tilly exclaimed. She felt sorry for Nancy.

Nancy shook her head and said, "It's not my husband's fault. He didn't know better. Julius trusted her mother and believed what she said. He was so blinded by her influence he couldn't see what was happening."

Tilly felt even more sorry for Nancy. She wished there was something she could do to help her.

After driving for a while, they arrived in a small town in Bristol, Virginia. They got out of the truck and looked around. It was a quiet little town with quaint shops and restaurants. They stopped at a coffee shop to eat. The server gave Dusty directions to the nearest gas station after he asked for them. Dusty glanced at his watch. It was eight o'clock. It was already late. They needed to rest. He decided to stay overnight and pick up the car in the morning.

"Is there a place to sleep around here?" he asked.

The server said there was a motel around the corner.

"Nancy, how about staying for the night?" Tilly asked. "I'm sure you'll appreciate sleeping in a comfy, warm bed, especially Mark. It would give you a chance to rest and recharge for tomorrow."

"You are right. It would be nice to take a shower and sleep in an actual bed for a change."

"Okay, it's settled," Dusty said. "Let's start with some food. Order whatever you want, Nancy. It's our treat."

"If you insist," Nancy chuckled as she took the menu from the table.

SOMEONE KNOCKED ON the door early in the morning. Nancy opened it, thinking it was Tilly and Dusty. It surprised her to see a man in his late fifties wearing a cowboy hat standing at the front door.

"Who are you?" Nancy asked.

"I'm a process server. You have been summoned to appear in court in Wisconsin."

"Wisconsin? How did you find me?"

"We tracked you down using the GPS tracking device on your truck," the man said. "I've been following you for a while."

Nancy shook her head in disbelief. She knew it was Veronica. It confused her how she learned about Julius' truck so fast.

"What is this summons for?" Nancy asked.

Tilly and Dusty, who were staying in the adjoining room, heard the commotion outside and hurried to check on Nancy.

"Is everything okay?" asked Tilly.

"This man gave me this paper."

Dusty took it from her hand and read it. "Who is Veronica Winslow?"

"That's my mother-in-law," Nancy said.

"Just make sure you show up to court. The hearing is in two days," the man said before leaving.

Nancy was lost for words. Panic set in.

"Your mother-in-law must have some kind of connection for her to get this out-of-state summons issued and serve you so quickly," Dusty said.

"Tilly, do you think Veronica wants custody of my son? I believe she wants the court to deem me an unfit mother. Veronica knows how to play the system. I can't lose my son. He is everything to me."

"Courts rarely take children away from their mothers unless they cannot care for them," Tilly said.

"I can't fight someone like Veronica," Nancy said. "I have nothing to show for myself compared to her. She is powerful and influential."

"Don't worry, Nancy. Everything will be fine. My husband and I will accompany you. We won't leave you alone until we know you and Mark are safe. We'll be here for you."

Nancy was relieved to hear this. The words Tilly spoke gave her strength and reassured her that everything would be okay. She cried.

"Why are you so kind to me, Tilly? You don't even know me."

"We were strangers to you, but you still stopped to help us. You took a risk with us. We are doing the same for you.

It's the least we could do to show our gratitude. We know you are in trouble, and we are here to help you. Just get ready. It's a long drive to Wisconsin, and we're running out of time," Tilly stated.

"I don't know what to say except thank you," Nancy added. "It means a lot to me. Veronica is vicious and powerful. I need someone to stand by my side."

"Well, you have us now," Tilly said with a smile.

"What about your car? Your road trip to the cabin? I don't want to derail your plans. This is my problem, not yours."

"Don't worry about it," Dusty said. "We'll send someone to tow the car. The cabin can wait. We need to get you back to Wisconsin so we can figure out what's going on."

Nancy thanked Tilly and Dusty before returning to her room to prepare for the long drive.

THERE WAS SUCH AN UPROAR in the courtroom, especially among Veronica's friends. The judge had to pound his gavel a few times before everyone quieted down. Veronica did not seek custody of her grandson, as Nancy believed. She wanted Nancy to return Julius' truck to her. Veronica discovered in a letter addressed to Julius that her son had bought a truck in Texas. It enraged her when Nancy beat her to the dock.

Veronica used every resource she had to find Nancy and retrieve the truck, no matter what it took. She was confident of winning the case. But the court's decision to allow Nancy to keep the truck surprised her. The judge ruled in Nancy's favor, and she got the truck. It listed her as a co-owner with Julius. Nancy thanked Attorney Salas for giving her the original documents.

Veronica refused to believe it. Even with the documents presented, Veronica still couldn't understand why the judge ruled in Nancy's favor. Her anger was clear, and she vowed to reclaim the truck another way.

"You witch!" Veronica yelled. She followed Nancy out of the courtroom. "My son worked hard to buy that truck, and now he's gone. You have no right to take that away from me."

Nancy stared at her, feeling no remorse.

"That's where you're mistaken, Veronica," she pointed out. "I have the legal right to take my husband's truck. I was his wife."

Veronica never expected Nancy to blow up like that. Her response shocked her, and she couldn't believe her ears. Nancy was different. Her confidence had grown, and she was now a strong, self-assured woman. She brushed it aside. Nancy did not affect her.

"Don't believe this is over, Nancy. I will get the truck if it's the last thing I do!"

Nancy stopped walking and turned to her.

"You and I both know this isn't about the truck, Veronica," Nancy stated. "If this is your way of making my life miserable, you're doing a great job, but it's over. Please leave me alone!" Nancy stared at her for a moment, then turned and walked away.

"Come back here; we're not done talking yet," Veronica yelled at the top of her lungs. It didn't matter to her that others were watching.

Nancy ignored her and continued walking.

"What are you planning to do now, Nancy?" Tilly asked. They were in front of the courthouse.

"Now that it's over, I suppose we're heading to Las Vegas after I take the GPS tracker off the truck," Nancy said. "It's far enough away that Veronica won't cause us problems. Of course, we'll have to keep a low profile, and I'm sure I'll find employment soon. I'm confident we'll be fine."

"Let us celebrate your win with a feast," Dusty said.

"Great! I'm starving," Nancy said.

They ate lunch at a nearby restaurant. Tilly wanted to stay longer to get to know Nancy more, but Dusty received a call from his office. They had to fly back to New York for an urgent meeting with one of their foundations. Tilly gave Nancy her business card and told her to call her when they arrived in Las Vegas. She wanted to make sure they were safe.

"Yes, Tilly. I promise I'll call you," Nancy replied as they hugged.

Dusty took their luggage out of the truck while Tilly played with Mark. Moments later, a taxi pulled up in front of the restaurant to take Tilly and Dusty to the airport. Nancy waved goodbye as the taxi drove away. She walked to her vehicle while carrying her son in a baby carrier. Two women waited for her. Nancy felt fear as they approached.

"Nancy?" one of them asked.

"Yes?"

"Come with us," they said, grabbing her tight.

"Where are you taking me? Let me go."

They dragged Nancy into a back alley. Nancy tried to scream for help, but the women were too strong. They pushed Nancy to the ground and covered her mouth. It was the last thing she remembered. A restaurant server was taking a coffee break when he found Nancy unconscious. Her son, Mark, cried beside her as she lay on the ground.

CHAPTER FOUR

Nancy opened her eyes to find herself in a hospital bed. She had a bandage around her head, her arm in a cast, and her leg in a cast elevated in traction.

"Nancy, how could this have happened?" Tilly wept. She couldn't stand seeing her new friend in such a state.

"Tilly, what are you doing here? Where is Mark? Who looks after him?" Nancy asked in a low tone.

"Don't worry, a nurse watches him."

"How did you know I was here?"

Tilly explained, "We were at the airport when the police called. They found my business card in your purse. They said someone attacked you in the restaurant's parking lot. Maybe if we had stayed longer, this would not have happened."

"I remember now," Nancy said. "Two women ganged up on me as I got into the truck. They dragged me into the alley, and that was the last thing I remember."

"Oh my God!"

"I have a pretty good idea who did this to me," Nancy stated.

"Who?"

"Who else? My mother-in-law?"

"Are you sure?" Tilly asked.

"Who else would do this to me? Veronica is vindictive. The judge awarded me the truck, and she couldn't handle it. So, she enlisted her friends help to teach me a lesson."

"Do you believe she'd do this to you for a truck?"

"It's not about the truck, Tilly," Nancy clarified. "Veronica is the owner of a courier service and has a large fleet of vehicles. She never liked me from the start and would resort to any lengths to ruin me. She wanted to watch me suffer."

"Tell the police what you know, Nancy. It will help them investigate."

Nancy nodded.

"What do you intend to do after the doctor releases you?"

"All I have left is that truck. It is now mine. I think it's wise to sell it and use the money to move out of here as quickly as possible. I'll get an apartment, go back to school, and get my degree, so I can provide for my son and—"

Dusty entered the room and interrupted their conversation.

"I am sorry to tell you this, Nancy, but the police said whoever did this also trashed your truck. They destroyed the interior, ruptured the tires, and damaged the body. The truck has suffered irreparable damage."

Nancy's heart broke. She could not hold back her tears as she heard the news. She felt helpless and overwhelmed. Nancy cried. What would she do now? Attorney Salas advised her to insure the truck, but she failed to do so. Her entire world crumbled in front of her eyes.

"Forget about the truck, Nancy," Tilly said. "The first thing you need to do is get well. Those people did a number on you."

"I want them to pay for what they did to me."

"Don't worry, Nancy," Dusty added. "Police are reviewing CCTV footage from the restaurant and nearby establishments. They are doing everything to identify those responsible. It won't be long before an arrest takes place."

THE SUN SHONE WHEN the nurse wheeled Nancy out of her room and to the front of the building. The attendant was carrying her baby. Nancy wanted to call Tilly to thank her for paying her hospital bills. However, the police failed to return her business card, and she didn't know how to contact Tilly or Dusty.

The attendant called a taxi for them. Nancy told him they would wait in the parking area and assured him they were fine. Nancy waited for the taxi after the attendant left, but it did not arrive. Frustrated, Nancy opted for a walk.

"Alright, Mark, should we go left or right? We no longer have the truck, so we have to take the long way. I hope this isn't a problem for you."

Mark gave her the cutest smile.

The walk was a challenge for Nancy since she hadn't recovered yet. Nancy expressed gratitude for the stroller that the nurse found in Lost and Found for Mark. It made their journey easier. Nancy pushed the stroller and supported herself with the handles. Nancy was exhausted but determined to continue. They made their way down the sidewalk when she noticed a black limousine behind them. Nancy froze. It could be Veronica or some thugs she hired to trouble her again.

Nancy tried to hurry away, but the limo sped up and followed them. She felt her heart racing, and panic set in. As the car stopped, a man stepped out and called out to her.

"Nancy?" he called.

"Yes?"

"I'm here to pick you up."

"Who are you?"

"Tilly and Dusty sent me to get you. They apologized for not being here. A meeting held them up. They asked me to fill in for them. My name is Garrett. I'm here to take care of you and ensure you feel safe and comfortable. A private plane is waiting for us to take us to New York."

Garrett dialed Tilly's number on his phone. He handed it to Nancy, and they talked. Nancy ended the call a few minutes later. She handed the phone back to Garrett with a smile on her face.

"Well, Mark," Nancy murmured to the baby. "What do you think? We have nothing to lose, so why not do it? Besides, we never thanked Tilly and Dusty for covering my hospital expenses. I believe it is only right to see them in New York and thank them."

When Nancy noticed Garrett looked at her funny, she apologized.

"I always talk to the baby like he understands me," Nancy said.

Garrett smiled. "Don't mind me. I just look at people that way. It means nothing."

Nancy jumped in with her son when Garrett opened the door for them. Once everyone settled in, the driver drove off. They arrived at the airport moments later and boarded a private plane.

The first-class treatment piqued her interest. The plane's luxurious amenities left Nancy in awe of its spacious seats, wide aisles, and intricate entertainment system. A delicious meal prepared by the flight attendant made her feel like royalty. Steak and lobster with caviar and red wine were served. Nancy knew Tilly and Dusty were rich but didn't know how wealthy they were. Nancy considered herself privileged to be a guest of Tilly and Dusty. After eating, Garrett joined her to watch a movie together.

They arrived in New York to find a limousine waiting for them. The driver was dressed in a black suit and greeted them with a smile. He opened the door and led Nancy, Mark, and Garrett inside the car. Nancy enjoyed the ride as she watched the city lights pass by. Seeing New York again was surreal for her. She missed it so much.

The limousine pulled up in front of the Cosmo Hotel. The bellman opened their car door, and the hotel manager greeted Nancy with a smile. He led them into their suite. The special treatment made Nancy feel like a movie star.

"Enjoy your stay, Nancy," Garrett said.

Nancy asked, "You're not coming in?"

"I need to get moving. I have a lot of work to do."

"Thank you, Garrett, for everything."

He nodded and wished her luck.

Nancy entered the room to find baskets of flowers and fruits on a silver platter. Mark also had milk and baby food.

"Wow! Look at that. Isn't this lovely?" Nancy asked her son.

Mark flashed her an endearing smile.

"How was the flight?"

Nancy heard a familiar voice behind her. As she suspected, Tilly and Dusty were standing at the door, smiling at her.

"Tilly, what have you done? I expected nothing like it," Nancy responded, hugging them both. "After being released from the hospital, I wanted to call you, but I couldn't find your card."

"Nancy, I'm sorry we weren't there to meet you," Tilly said. "That's why we sent Garrett to get you. I hope the flight was fine."

"You have done so much for me, Tilly. You too, Dusty. I don't know what to say."

"You still need time to recover from your injury, Nancy," Tilly remarked.

Garrett entered the room a few moments later. It surprised Nancy to see him back.

"Did you forget something?" she asked.

"Nancy, this is Garrett, our private investigator," Dusty said. "He will update us on your case."

"Your private investigator?" Nancy asked, confused.

"My apologies, Nancy. It was my fault that I did not introduce myself properly. Although I work as Dusty's private investigator, lately I'm doing more work for Tilly." Winking at Dusty, Garrett said, "She's quite a handful."

Nancy chuckled. "It's a pleasure to meet you, Garrett."

"I visited your mother-in-law a few days ago. That woman is something else. As soon as I mentioned your name, she threw things at me."

"That's Veronica for you," Nancy said. "I wish I knew why she hates me so much."

"Seriously, that woman has no shame," Garrett said. "Anyway, I found out Veronica paid someone to take care of the two women who ganged up on you."

"Wait, what? Why?" Nancy asked, shocked.

"Vandalizing the truck was not part of their agreement. Veronica planned to teach you a lesson and return Julius' truck to her with no dents or scratches," Garrett explained. "The women, Velma and Lois, did the opposite. According to their statement, they misunderstood Veronica's directives and damaged Julius' truck instead. Veronica was furious. She and her friends ambushed the two on their way home one night, knocking them unconscious. The women reported the incident to the police when they recovered. They admitted Veronica hired them to hurt you. The women will testify against her. They also sued Veronica for assault and asked for damages."

Garrett's words shocked Nancy. "What happened to Veronica?"

"She claimed the two women had set her up, and she was innocent. What she didn't know was that Velma and Lois' next-door neighbor had videotaped the attack. The police identified Veronica as one of the attackers."

"That's a shame," Nancy added. "Even though we don't like each other, I don't want terrible things to happen to her."

"There's more," Garrett added.

"What do you mean?" Nancy asked.

"Leroy's business was under surveillance for some time, but they couldn't gather solid evidence. He was smart. His work was clean. The police thought they would get a break when Julius took over the business. They set up the sting operation, but Julius died before executing the plan. Then Veronica and Olivia took over. The police assumed the mother and daughter's lack of experience made them easy prey, but they were wrong. They believed Veronica to be the mastermind of the entire operation. Despite their best efforts, she outsmarted them at every turn. The police had nothing to show for their investigation."

Nancy shook her head in disbelief.

"Then they got a break on the case. An informant alerted the police to Veronica's criminal activities. He not only provided videos but also recordings of conversations, and documents pertaining to the Winslows operation. This time, undercover cops were involved. Based on snitch's information, Veronica concealed their illegal operation using their courier service. However, they actually transferred stolen goods to other states using their delivery trucks. An undercover police operation caught the Winslows and their accomplices in the act, shutting down their operation. It was one of the biggest arrests they ever made."

"Oh, my God!" Nancy exclaimed. She couldn't believe it. Nancy suspected Julius' family was involved in shady business, but this was a big deal. That's why her husband traveled so much. It was he who transported the stolen goods to other states.

"You don't have to worry about your mother-in-law anymore, Nancy," Garrett added. "She is currently in jail. Veronica has enlisted the expertise of a reputable criminal defense lawyer. However, there is ample evidence to warrant indicting both her and her daughter. I'm confident they'll be in jail for a long time."

In a telephone call from Yolanda, Nancy learned that Ernie was the informant. He provided the police with evidence implicating Veronica and her shady business practices. Nancy could not thank Ernie and Yolanda enough for doing the right thing. They were finally free from the Winslow family. Yolanda said they would be away for a while. The police took them into protective custody until the trial began. Nancy and Yolanda cried and said they would see each other soon. They had a lot of catching up to do.

It's a brand new day. Nancy slept like a baby, and her son slept soundly. She woke up the next day feeling refreshed and energetic. She got up and started her day smiling. Nancy was getting ready to meet Tilly downstairs for breakfast when the doorbell rang. A woman in her early forties entered the room when she opened it.

"Yes?" Nancy asked.

"Hello, my name is Stella. I'm the baby's nanny."

"Nanny? For whom?"

"For your son. Where is that handsome boy?"

"Excuse me, but this is a mistake. I didn't hire a nanny."

"Mrs. Bonaventura did. I started today."

"Mrs. who?"

"Didn't I tell you my last name, Nancy?" Tilly laughed.

Nancy spun around when she heard Tilly's voice behind her. It surprised her to see Tilly as she thought they would meet downstairs.

"This is Stella, Mark's nanny," Tilly explained.

"I don't need a nanny, Tilly. I can't afford her," Nancy explained. "We don't even have a place to live."

"You're going to need a babysitter while at school."

"School? I don't understand."

"Lucy will take you tomorrow. She'll drive you to school and help you enroll."

"Who is Lucy?"

"Like you, her stepmother abused her. In your situation, it was your mother-in-law. She worked as a waitress in California. We rescued her from that situation, and she is now in college and will graduate soon with honors. Dusty and I will do the same for you. We want to give you the chance to make a better life for yourself and your son. I checked your records, and you're only a few credits away from your nursing degree. Dusty and I are giving you the opportunity of a lifetime. Wouldn't you like to finish school?"

"Of course, Tilly. I would love to finish and graduate now, more than ever, for my baby. Are you sure about this? The nanny, school, a place to live, and other necessities—they're not cheap."

"The moment has come for you to shine, Nancy. Your parents will be proud of you when you graduate and become a registered nurse. I think that is what they wanted. Your family will become whole again."

"I hope so, Tilly."

"In the meantime, I found you an apartment on the first floor near the university. Stella will look after Mark while you're at school."

"How do I pay for it, Tilly? I'm broke."

"Nancy, you don't have to worry about anything. All you need to do is complete this lease agreement for the apartment, so you can move in right away," Tilly said, handing her the application. Nancy signed it and handed it back to Tilly.

"Tilly, you have done so much for me. There are no words to express my gratitude."

"Nancy, this isn't just about you. It's about your child, too. So come on, let's have lunch, and then I'll take you and Mark shopping and show you your apartment."

"You don't have to ask me twice. I love shopping! That would be fantastic." Nancy giggled.

CHAPTER FIVE

Nancy was ready for her first day at university. She packed her bags and books, double-checked her schedule, and made sure she had all her necessary supplies. Nancy was nervous but excited to start the next chapter in her life. She was determined to work hard and make lasting connections. Nancy was excited to meet new friends and challenge herself. She was ready to face the world.

Stella was running late, so Nancy fed and changed Mark, then put him back in the crib to sleep. She checked to make sure he was comfortable and kissed him when she heard an outside car honking.

She yelled out the window, "Keep it down, will you? You're waking up the baby."

The car stopped, and a young man got out.

"I'm sorry, Miss," the driver said. "I'm lost, and I forgot my phone at work. They expected me to deliver this car to a customer this morning. I have the correct location, but they neglected to provide the apartment number. I hope the customer isn't too angry."

"Sorry, but I can't help you," Nancy said. "I've just moved in and don't know the tenants. It might be a smart idea to ask the superintendent. Just press the buzzer."

"I did. Nobody answered. That's why I honked."

"Just keep trying," Nancy said. "Maybe someone will answer soon. Please don't honk. It's rude and annoying."

"Sorry about that, Miss. I promise I won't do it anymore."

"My name is Nancy. Do you need a phone to call your boss?"

"Nancy? Nancy Winslow?" the driver asked.

"Yes, that is me."

"How do you like that? You are the one I'm looking for."

"What do you mean?"

"I'm from the dealership. All I know is that I'm bringing this brand new red convertible to Nancy Winslow."

"That's me, but I didn't buy a car."

"Yes, you did. The paperwork is all in order, and I just need to deliver the car to you."

"I didn't order, buy, or do anything like that."

"Yes, you did. It said so on the paper," the driver said, showing the order form he was holding.

"I don't know what you're talking about. I'm not the one who bought the car. It must be someone else."

The driver and Nancy continued to argue when Tilly and Dusty arrived. They intervened and calmed the situation down.

"What's going on here?" Tilly asked.

"I told this man to take this car back, and he insists it is for me."

Tilly and Dusty laughed.

"What's so amusing about it?" Nancy asked.

Tilly and Dusty exchanged glances, then Dusty stepped forward. "We bought the car," he said.

"Nancy, there is no mistake. This is your car," Tilly explained. "This is how you get around."

Nancy shook her head in disbelief.

"Do you think we will let you commute to school without transportation?" Tilly asked. "We want you to be safe and get home to your baby after school."

"A babysitter, an apartment, school, and now a car? It's too much, Tilly. I can't accept it. You didn't have to spend that much money on me."

"It's not too much, Nancy. We invest in you," Tilly said. "You and your child deserve the best, so we're giving you the tools you need to succeed and take care of your family. This is our way of showing you how much we care. Nancy, you need a car to get to school. Do I need to say more?" Tilly laughed. "This is our gift to you."

"But—"

Tilly and Dusty dashed to the apartment to see baby Mark before Nancy could say anything. Nancy followed them while the driver scratched his head in perplexity.

"How about the car? Who will sign for it?" he asked.

Nancy stopped in her tracks and turned around to face the driver. "Don't worry about the car. I'll sign it."

Nancy signed the form and gave it back to the driver, who gave her the car key. As she rushed back to the apartment, she saw Tilly holding her baby. Emotion overcame her as she watched Tilly cradle Mark in her arms. Tears streamed down her face. Nancy ran up to them and embraced them both in a heartfelt hug.

"We'll watch him until Stella arrives," Tilly said. "Go to school, Nancy. You don't want to be late on your first day."

Nancy shook her head and stepped out the door, laughing. She turned around and thanked Tilly and Dusty again.

"You're welcome," Tilly said. "By the way, Nancy, I hope you don't mind. I took some of your personal information from the lease application you filled out and opened a bank account for you at Symphorialto Bank down the street. You still need to visit the bank and speak with Mrs. Duff. She's waiting for you to complete the process and get your ATM card to use. They must verify your identity before funds can be released."

Tilly handed Nancy an envelope with her bank transactions. "You'll need to show this to Mrs. Duff when you go in. She'll take care of everything."

Nancy thanked Tilly for her help and hugged her before leaving. She walked to her car and saw the driver still sitting on the curb.

"Do you need a ride? A phone?" Nancy asked the dealership guy.

"Thank you, but someone should pick me up soon. Enjoy your car."

Nancy waved goodbye. "Thanks," she replied.

Nancy cried as she sat in her red convertible. She never thought she would own one, but here she was, sitting in her dream car. Nancy took a deep breath and wiped away her tears. She adjusted the mirror and smelled the leather seat. Nancy couldn't wait to drive it. She imagined the thrill of feeling the wind in her hair as she drove down the highway.

Nancy took a deep breath and counted to 10. She put the car in gear and pulled away from the curb.

Nancy drove to the bank to handle her account before class started. She parked her car and walked inside. Mrs. Duff, the bank manager, greeted her. Nancy gave her the envelope Tilly had given her and showed it to Mrs. Duff. Mrs. Duff smiled and took her to her office. Nancy handed over her identification, and Mrs. Duff checked her records and confirmed all was well. Nancy signed the documents, and Mrs. Duff returned her IDs.

Mrs. Duff discussed different investment portfolios, safe high-yield investments, personal banking, and other savings plans. She informed Nancy about the stock market, types of investments, and potential returns. Mrs. Duff advised Nancy to do some research and make an informed decision. Nancy found it confusing that Mrs. Duff discussed investments with her when she had little to invest. Nancy thanked Mrs. Duff for her time but declined the offer, saying she wasn't interested in any. Mrs. Duff told her to take her time and come see her when she was ready.

"Is there anything else I can do for you?" Mrs. Duff asked.

"No, thank you. I'm good."

Mrs. Duff handed Nancy her business card and said, "Don't stand in line next time you come to the bank. Just ask for me."

"Thank you for your offer, Mrs. Duff. I'll keep that in mind."

"The bank will not send you a statement until a later date. Would you like to know your current balance?"

"Yes, of course. Thank you."

Nancy thought she needed to know how much money she had in the bank to budget wisely. It didn't seem right to take advantage of Tilly's and Dusty's generosity. She planned to look for a part-time job as soon as possible. A job would help her save money, so she could pay Tilly and Dusty back. She was determined to support herself and pay for her living expenses without relying on Tilly or Dusty all the time.

Mrs. Duff gave Nancy a receipt with an account balance stamped on it. Nancy took it from Mrs. Duff's hand and thanked her before leaving. She placed the receipt in her purse and walked to the parking lot. Nancy looked at her watch. With thirty minutes to spare, she knew she could get to school on time.

Nancy glanced at the slip as she entered her car, and her eyes widened. One million dollars were available. She knew she had misread the receipt. It showed she had a million-dollar balance on her account. Nancy was sure it was an error. Tilly would never give her that much money, no matter how wealthy she was. Nancy returned to the bank and asked Mrs. Duff to check her balance again because it was wrong.

"I thought I checked it," Mrs. Duff replied. She checked the computer and confirmed Nancy's account balance was correct.

Nancy almost passed out. She couldn't believe her luck. Nancy never imagined that giving Tilly and Dusty a ride when their car broke down would yield such a huge return—a gift of a million dollars. She was living proof that miracles can happen. Nancy felt overwhelmed and could only express her gratitude. She realized that the only way she could repay Tilly and Dusty was to study hard and earn her degree. She would dedicate it to them as an acknowledgment of the second opportunity they gave her to achieve something in her life. Nancy vowed to make them proud and prove their efforts were not in vain.

Nancy was driven to prove to her parents she could turn her life around. She was determined to pay it forward and do something meaningful with her newfound wealth. Nancy would use the money to fund her nieces' and nephews' education and make their dreams come true. She would share this good fortune with her parents, and she couldn't wait to tell them the good news. Nancy did not doubt that her family would forgive and accept her back. This was a huge milestone in their lives. She couldn't wait to see them and become one happy family again.

DUSTY WATCHED TILLY laugh and giggle as she played with Mark. Her laughter echoed in the room. Dusty felt his heart warm as he watched the two interact. He knew Tilly had found something special in Mark. The baby clung to Tilly when she put him in the crib. He looked up at her with his big brown eyes and smiled. Tilly liked how it felt. Her heart melted. She realized the greatest treasure was not fame or wealth, but your child.

"Don't worry, honey," Dusty said. "Someday, we'll have our bundle of joy."

Dusty wrapped his arm around his wife's shoulders. He smiled and kissed her forehead, reassuring her that everything would be alright. She returned the hug, embracing him. They stood there, watching Mark fall asleep. Tilly kissed Mark goodbye and left the room. Stella waved at them before closing the door.

Tilly and Dusty walked hand in hand to their car after another job well done. They made a difference in Nancy's life. Dusty knew Nancy would be fine. He was proud of his wife for helping another person in need. Together, they were a team that always supported each other. They believed Nancy's commitment to improving her life for her son and desire to reunite with her family made her an excellent candidate for success. Whatever happened, they would always be there for her.

ABOUT THE AUTHOR

M arissa Marchan writes young adult, new adult, and middle-grade fiction. Her grandson, Ray Angelo, was the inspiration for A Magical Storybook series: A Ray of Sunshine and Ray and Haley in the Kingdom of the Gobtrolls. It tells the incredible story of a young boy full of love, faith, hope, and courage. It contains heartwarming stories that will uplift your spirits and warm your hearts.

We all express grief and loss. When Marissa's father died many years ago, she discovered she had the remarkable ability to create the most wonderful world of pure imagination. She spent endless hours fantasizing and making up stories. This was her way of dealing with grief.

Another tragedy struck Marissa's family shortly thereafter, with the death of her sister, Mirla. Marissa struggled with grief and loss for a long time. Ray gave her the strength to move forward. He was a source of love and inspiration for her. Ray instilled in her the courage and ability to persevere in the face of adversity and fear.

Marissa started writing and could finally put her thoughts into words. Since then, Marissa has pursued a writing career, and she is the author of the *Spoiled Brats series*: Forbidden Love and Runaway Romance. Four more novels are in the works. It was a dream she had about her mother that inspired the *Mrs. Millionaire series.*

Read more at https://marissamarchan.com[1]

---

1.   https://marissamarchan.com/

CONNECT WITH THE AUTHOR

WEBSITE:
Marissamarchan.com[1]
EMAIL:
marissa.marchan@yahoo.com
TWITTER:
@marissamarchan[2]
FACEBOOK:
booksbymarissamarchan[3]
LINKEDIN:
linkedin.com/in/marissa-marchan-41474854[4]
INSTAGRAM:
instagram.com/marissamarchan[5]

---

1. http://www.marissamarchan.com/

2. https://twitter.com/marissamarchan

3. https://www.facebook.com/Booksbymarissamarchan/

4. https://www.linkedin.com/in/marissa-marchan-41474854

5. https://www.instagram.com/marissamarchan

A MRS. MILLIONAIRE SERIES

Mrs. Millionaire is a series of fictional stories with heartwarming endings. Each story revolves around an unfortunate individual or family who crosses paths with Tilly. She helps them out of financial problems or situations and gives them a new lease on life. Mrs. Millionaire is a symbol of hope, generosity, and kindness. This book emphasizes the notion that everyone deserves a second chance.

Matilde "Tilly" Jane Parker is famous for her rebellious streak, wild antics, and party-loving attitude. She comes from an affluent family and lives in luxury. Tilly's life took a different turn after a personal tragedy. This experience has changed her life. She has become more resilient and stronger in the face of adversity. Rather than living as a victim, she uses her wealth and power to assist those who cannot defend themselves. Tilly often finds herself embroiled in different situations and sometimes assumes the role of an amateur detective to help the people she is involved with. Tilly relies on her intuition and gut feelings to find clues. She is determined to make a difference and is not afraid to take risks. Tilly inspires many, and her story reminds us that even the darkest moments can lead to positive change.

A MRS. MILLIONAIRE SERIES
VOLUME 1

Mrs. Millionaire and the Homeless Woman Book 1

∞

MATILDE, OR TILLY TO her family and friends, has gained a reputation for her rebellious streak and party girl image. She comes from a wealthy family but pushes the boundaries of acceptable behavior and is often the center of attention. Tilly is determined to live life to the fullest and refuses to let anyone tell her what to do.

After Tilly meets Dusty, the man of her dreams, she learns that love is about compromise and acceptance. It also means giving in and knowing when to walk away from a relationship.

Events, even those that are uncontrollable and tragic, can bend our views, shape our lives forever, and teach us lessons no one can forget. Someone attacked Tilly in a parking lot, but a homeless person saved her. Tilly learned the importance of kindness and empathy from the incident. She has since dedicated her life to helping others in need. Her experience changed her outlook on life and made her a better person.

Mrs. Millionaire and the Bad Father Book 2

∞

Matt Calderon is a caring husband and father of two children. His wife, Maria, suffers from a condition that limits her ability to perform manual work, forcing Matt to work two jobs. Despite the long hours, Matt always finds time for his family, ensuring Maria and the kids get the support they need. He tries to give them the best life possible.

But sometimes life throws a curveball. Matt's boss accuses him of stealing money from him. Matt is innocent and shocked by the accusation. His boss refuses to listen to his explanation and calls the police. Matt's greatest fear is being charged with a crime he did not commit. He leaves town with his family, taking only a few items with them. Matt is determined to protect his family and will do everything in his power to ensure they stay safe.

Just when things couldn't get any worse, Matt becomes embroiled in a gas station robbery. Despite his best efforts to evade, Matt's situation escalates into a dangerous and chaotic one as the police surround the place. To protect his family, Matt must decide whether to take a risk and escape or stay and hope the situation resolves itself.

Can they make the most of their current circumstances to create a better tomorrow? Is there hope for the family?

Mrs. Millionaire and the Waitress Book 3

∞

Lucy was only two years old when her mother died. Her father remarried a widow with two children. Her stepmother is cold and unsympathetic. She treats Lucy like an inconvenience. Lucy feels left out and misunderstood. She learns to be independent and rely on herself. Lucy's father is loving and supportive. He is her source of comfort and love.

Lucy grew up without knowing the truth, so she believes her stepmother is her real mother. Her father dies several months before graduating from high school, leaving Lucy with the only family she knew, and they reveal their true colors. Lucy's stepmother transfers her inheritance to herself and tells Lucy that her father left them penniless. Lucy leaves school to work as a waitress to support her family. Her stepbrother steals money and valuables from Lucy's work. The owner accuses Lucy, and the police arrest her. Will Lucy ever discover the truth about her past? Or would she rather not face the truth?

Mrs. Millionaire and the Runaway Kids Book 4

∞

Following his wife's death, Dexter Curtis accepts a position at a textile company. He moves to Connecticut, determined to provide a better life for his four children. The family settled into their new surroundings and made friends with their neighbors.

However, a colleague at Dexter's job is cruel and jealous of him. His badmouthing of Dexter behind his back and questioning his authority and decision-making made Dexter look unprofessional in front of his co-workers.

Dexter's reputation was further damaged when a job order mysteriously disappeared from his computer, resulting in his termination. He becomes depressed when he cannot find work and turns to alcohol for relief. A tragic accident left him unconscious, and he fell into a coma. Child Protective Services placed his children in a temporary shelter until they could make other arrangements for them. Upon learning about their impending separation, the children stow away in a van and run away to stay together.

This emotionally charged story centers on Dexter and his children facing a dilemma: do they have a chance at reconciliation and reunification? Will the siblings stay together?

Mrs. Millionaire and the Delivery Girl Book 5

∞

The last thing Nancy wants to do is become a delivery girl. She has big aspirations. Nancy dreams of owning a successful business. She is determined to make it come true and won't let anything stand in her way. After holding off on dating until she gets a job, Nancy makes it a priority to stay in school and take part in as many activities as possible. Her perception of bad boys and bikers changes when she meets Julius. Nancy sees him in a different light, and they hang out together. Despite his unflattering reputation, she falls in love with him. Nancy's career ambitions get crushed. They married at City Hall with just a few friends present. Nancy's parents disown her and refuse to speak to her.

When Nancy moves in with Julius's parents in Wisconsin, things turn disastrous. His mother is vengeful and strict. She keeps track of every detail of her stay, which irritates Nancy even more. This has caused friction in her marriage. Nancy discovers her husband cheats on her and threatens to leave him. Julius begs her to stay and promises to change. Nancy is not sure she can trust him. Will Nancy forgive her husband for betraying her trust and give him another chance? Or will she walk away?

A MRS. MILLIONAIRE SERIES
VOLUME 2

Mrs. Millionaire and the Thief Book 6

∞

HAVE YOU EVER EXPERIENCED a moment that blindsided you and left you wondering what happened? The feeling is unpleasant. It can be disorienting and overwhelming.

Advertising account executive Dan Collins works hard to get the coveted promotion so he can propose marriage to his girlfriend. However, a colleague threatens his hopes for a happily ever after. Diego is also aiming for the same promotion and will do whatever it takes to get it.

Upon receiving news from a reliable source that Dan has landed the job, Diego turns to unethical tactics. Dan soon finds himself in a difficult situation. A client accuses Dan of stealing a diamond necklace from her. Dan denies it and insists he did not take it. Following the discovery of the necklace in his office, Dan's boss dismisses him from his position, and the police take him into custody.

Will Dan prove his innocence? Is marriage still possible for him?

Mrs. Millionaire and the Housekeeper Book 7

∞

Lesley is the single mother of five-year-old Haley. Her boyfriend, Stanley, disappeared from her life after her baby was born. They evict her from their apartment after she returns from the hospital. Lesley makes amends with her mother and returns home. She gets a job at a local gas station. Lesley works hard to provide for her daughter and to make ends meet.

Her life seems to have improved, and she feels hopeful. When Lesley's mother marries Jacob, a man ten years younger, it causes her life to crumble. Her relationship with him is strained, and they fight constantly at home. After Lesley's mother chose her husband over them, she and her daughter moved out.

Will Lesley and her mother mend their relationship and live together again? Or will Lesley's mother remain distant and unwilling to reconcile?

Mrs. Millionaire and the Reluctant Hero Book 8

∞

Ray Griffin has a remarkable talent for guitar playing but has suffered unfortunate circumstances. His wife divorced him and took their 8-year-old daughter after he lost his job as a supervisor at a home improvement store. Unable to find work, he lost his apartment and became homeless. Ray uses his musical talents to make ends meet. He moves from place to place, looking for work, but bad luck always follows him. As Ray's life spirals out of control, his talent remains his only hope. He is determined to get his life back on track and regain custody of his daughter, but will he succeed? Will Ray get a second chance at fatherhood, overcome all obstacles, and reunite with his daughter, or will they remain forever apart?

Mrs. Millionaire and the Elevator Man Book 9

∞

Carlos Angelo, a sixty-two-year-old Italian man, works as an elevator operator in the Lower Manhattan neighborhood of New York City. He lives in an apartment a few blocks away from his workplace. It was his first and only job in America, after four decades in the country.

Carlos has been a loyal employee for many years and always arrives at work early. He enjoys his job and has made many friends in the building. Carlos has received several "Employee of the Month" awards throughout the company for his dedication, loyalty, and friendliness. Carlos is relieved of his duties without notice after building management installs an automated elevator. He feels betrayed and devastated. His age and lack of experience make it difficult for him to find another job. He faces an uncertain future and does not know how to move forward. Without other skills, how would he support himself? Will he find another job that recognizes his hard work and loyalty? Or will he have to start over?

Mrs. Millionaire and the Taxi Driver Book 10

∞

Regie Adams has spent most of his life working on a dairy farm. After several years of feeding, cleaning, and milking cows every day, he's had enough. As he approaches forty, he leaves his farmer's life behind to find work in the city. He wants to try his luck elsewhere, despite his mother's protests. He is determined to make a new life for himself and prove to himself that he can do more than just milk cows. Regie finds himself in a series of unfortunate circumstances after boarding a bus.

However, his determination to achieve a better life remains unshaken, even with this setback. Regardless of the sacrifices involved, he remains dedicated to pursuing his dreams and discovering his true calling. Regie is determined to make something of his life, no matter the cost. He will not return home, regardless of what happens.

Can Regie triumph over his family's centuries-old dairy farming tradition? Will he find a way to a better future?

SPOILED BRATS
SERIES

In the affluent city of Beverly Hills, this new adult novel series revolves around six teenage friends. They lead a privileged and wealthy life, surrounded by luxury items and parties. The story also emphasizes the challenges the characters face as they navigate their young adult lives. They must learn how to find their own paths and make decisions that will shape their future. These books feature romance, personal discovery, and love encounters in unexpected places.

FORBIDDEN LOVE
Spoiled Brats Series Book One

VANESSA FLORENCE GRANDEVILLE, a Beverly Hills socialite and infamous spoiled brat, celebrates her 21st birthday in Honolulu with her wealthy friends. A fisherman from a nearby island meets her by chance on the same day. Vanessa's beauty captures Michael's attention. She humiliates him, but Michael is smitten from the outset. They are unaware that their paths will converge in the future.

Vanessa rents a yacht with her friends for a weekend cruise when complications arise. A fierce storm capsized their boat, sweeping them overboard. The Coast Guard rescued everyone except Vanessa, who drifted away. Michael found her at sea, suffering from a head injury and amnesia.

Unexpected and remarkable events brought their lives together. Is life playing a joke on them? Or was it fate that brought them together, destined to be in love despite the odds? As they face their uncertain future, will they realize that life isn't just about coincidences? Will they find the strength to follow their hearts and take a leap of faith?

RUNAWAY ROMANCE
Spoiled Brats Series Book Two

SAMANTHA ISABELLA ST. James, a 22-year-old Beverly Hills socialite, becomes devastated when she learns her father intends to force her into marriage to a wealthy business executive's son to settle a debt. On her wedding day, she flees without knowing the consequences.

Samantha embarks on a journey of self-discovery, finding inner strength and courage to face her father. After losing her wallet and being left penniless, she takes refuge in a quaint town and reluctantly works as a nanny. She meets Benjamin McClain, the charming and handsome father of the child she will care for. There is a clear and immediate attraction between them. She realizes Benjamin is the one for her as they develop a deep connection. Samantha and Benjamin soon begin a passionate love affair, but Samantha hesitates to escalate it. She fears Benjamin will not forgive her for lying about her true identity. Will Samantha's life become complicated if she has to choose between saving her father and following her heart?

A MAGICAL
STORYBOOK
SERIES

A Magical Storybook Series tells the story of a young boy who embarks on an adventure filled with magic, love, faith, hope, courage, and faith.

Dive into a mesmerizing experience packed with heartwarming tales that will uplift and warm your heart. Let these stories take you on a journey of discovery, inspiring and motivating you to reach for the stars. It will transport you to a world of wonder and imagination. They will make you laugh and cry and take you on a ride of fun and excitement. It will inspire you to dream beyond your limits and believe in the impossible. Featuring magical creatures and lands, these stories will charm and engage readers of all ages.

A RAY OF SUNSHINE
A Magical Storybook Series Book One

MARY AND THEO, A DEFORMED couple living in a small town, face constant mockery. They have driven away from the place they called home. With only a few possessions, Theo and Mary travel to the forest, where they discover a world of beauty and happiness. They soon had a child. A handsome little boy named Ray was born to them. They dedicate their lives to him and love him dearly. To Theo and Mary's surprise, he has healing abilities and a connection to the elements. This allows him to heal, talk to animals, and control the weather. Theo and Mary are unsure how he can perform such feats since they have never heard of these abilities before.

Will Ray's magical abilities teach the town the true meaning of unconditional love? Can people finally accept Theo and Mary despite their unappealing appearances? Find out in this charming tale of a family with special abilities.

RAY AND HALEY
In the Kingdom of the Gobtrolls
A Magical Storybook Series Book Two

THEO AND MARY LIVE in a forest far from civilization with their son Ray and daughter Haley. They lead a simple life and enjoy the beauty of their surroundings. The family lives in harmony with the forest and its creatures. Ray and Haley love exploring the jungle and discovering its secrets. They become close to many animals, and they often share their adventures with them. In this place, Theo and Mary discover that their children have unusual abilities. Ray possesses extraordinary abilities, including the power to communicate with animals and the elements, while Haley can communicate with plants and animals.

After learning that the people who drove them away many years ago wrongly accused them of destroying their former town, Theo seeks to prove their innocence. Ray relies on his cleverness and abilities to locate Theo and Haley after they disappear into the most polluted and foul-smelling place on earth.

Thank you for reading!

Thank you for reading *Mrs. Millionaire Short Story Book Series Volume 1*. If you enjoyed it, please tell your friends or post a review. Word of mouth is an author's best friend, and it is much appreciated.

Please check out the rest of *A Mrs. Millionaire Series, Spoiled Brats Series,* and *A Magical Storybook Series* through various online book retailers and distribution channels. These books are available as eBooks and in print. Happy reading!

Marissa Marchan

About the Publisher

3 Ways Publishing is an independent publisher established in January 2020 to gain recognition and traction in the publishing world.

Do you ever wonder where your book idea came from? Did it come from a dream? Perhaps a personal experience or story told by your mother or grandmother? Whatever it is, one important thing is that you have to feel passionate about what you write, which leads to a satisfying ending.

3 Ways Publishing publishes books they are passionate about—books of fictional and entertaining stories with heartwarming endings. They also publish fantasy, romance, and fiction for a variety of age groups with a strong female protagonist.

Read more at https://3wayspublishing.wordpress.com/.